OTHER BOOKS by KASSANDRA LAMB

The Kate Huntington Mysteries

Psychotherapist Kate Huntington helps others cope with trauma, but she has led a charmed life...until a killer rips it apart. (10 novels)

The Kate on Vacation Mysteries

Even on vacation, Kate Huntington can't stay out of trouble. (4 novellas)

The Marcia Banks and Buddy Cozy Mysteries

Marcia Banks trains service dogs for veterans, and solves crimes on the side, with the help of her Black Lab, Buddy. (12 novels/novellas–1 more to come)

The C.o.P. on the Scene Mysteries

Eight days into her new job as Chief of Police in a small Florida city, Judith Anderson finds herself one step behind a serial killer. (spinoff from the Kate Huntington series; 1 novel– more to come)

Romantic Suspense

written under the pen name of Jessica Dale

TO BARK OR NOT TO BARK

A Marcia Banks and Buddy Mystery

Kassandra Lamb

author of the Kate Huntington Mysteries

a *misterio press* publication

Published by *misterio press LLC*

Cover art by Melinda VanLone, Book Cover Corner
Photo credits: silhouette of woman and dog © Majivecka (right to use purchased through dreamstime.com)

To Bark or Not To Bark is a work of fiction. All names, characters, events and most places are products of the author's imagination. Any resemblance to actual events or people, living or dead, is entirely coincidental. Some real places may be used fictitiously. Crystal County and the town of Mayfair, Florida are fictitious.

The publisher does not have control over and does not assume any responsibility for author or third-party websites and their content.

ISBN: 978-1-947287-34-1

CHAPTER ONE

For the first time in my adult life, I wanted to call a human being by the word I usually reserve for female dogs.

Which surprised me. I normally dislike swearing, a residual of having grown up as a preacher's kid. But the hormones of pregnancy had loosened the reins on my emotions—and had reduced my patience as well, apparently.

I'd already felt self-conscious standing on my client's front porch, my dogs on either side of me. Sweat trickling along my spine in the July heat, I yanked my oversized tee shirt farther down over the stretch capris covering my expanding hips.

Granted, my hips had always been expansive, but they were more so now. *I'm pregnant. There's a legitimate reason for my weight gain.* But I wished I were farther along, with a more obvious baby bump, so people would get why I was expanding.

A woman answered my knock on the client's door, bringing me up short.

She was borderline anorexic, and "dressed to the nines," as my mother would say. Tailored coral pantsuit, pearl choker necklace, carefully coifed blonde hair. Smooth cheeks, but the crow's feet around her eyes said she was at least forty-something.

My client's older sister? He was thirty-five, according to his file.

The woman looked me up and down, her face pinched into a sour expression.

I don't like her, Ms. Snark said inside my head.

I mentally hushed her, although I didn't disagree. "Hi," I said, with false cheerfulness, "I'm here to see Herb Wilson."

She sniffed and opened the door wider. "Herbert, the dog woman is here."

I entered the house with my mentor dog, Buddy and Herb's soon-to-be service dog, Dolly trailing behind.

Part of my anxiety came from doing things out of order. Normally, I'd take a dog to meet its eventual owner *before* I trained the animal. But because of Covid-19—how I've grown to hate that phrase—Herb and Dolly had originally met via Zoom. Not an ideal bonding experience.

Herb crouched down to the Border Collie mix's level. "Marcia, she's even more adorable in person."

I breathed out a quiet sigh of relief.

Marine Sergeant Herbert R. Wilson wasn't a particularly big man, maybe three inches taller than my five-seven, and slender— *wiry* my mother would call him—with short, medium-brown hair. He held out a hand, palm down, for Dolly to check him out with her nose.

The woman sniffed again. "She's rather gangly."

I bristled—even though her statement was not inaccurate. Dolly probably had some larger breed in her. Her legs were longer than most Border Collies, making her almost as tall as Buddy, a Black Lab-Rottie mix. But I thought she looked elegant, not *gangly.*

"And you are?" I asked the woman, a little of Ms. Snark creeping into my tone.

"Charlotte Mathers, Herbert's ex-wife." She held out a thin hand. "Pleased to meet you, Marsha. Call me Char."

Seriously. She'd mispronounced my name! Granted it wasn't the more common pronunciation, but Herb had said it correctly less than twenty seconds ago—three syllables, *Mar-see-a*.

Internally, Ms. Snark uttered the female-dog name.

I struggled not to snicker. I shouldn't be giving my snarky alter ego any encouragement.

I recalled Herb mentioning his ex, that she was a successful real-estate agent, the broker of an agency she co-owned with her fiancé. He'd commented that they were on good terms and she dropped by periodically.

But I hadn't expected her to be there today. I tried to ignore her while I explained to Herb that my assistant, Carla Cummings and I had already tailored the dog to his needs. Now it was just a matter of training him to work with her effectively. *And to not undo what we've taught her*, which I did not say out loud.

I had planned to do some introductory training today, but not with the ex hanging around. So I gave Herb some time to play with Dolly, to get to know her some. Then I outlined what we would be doing, starting tomorrow, and said my goodbyes.

But the ex wasn't done with me. She followed us down the front sidewalk. "I hope you realize that Herbert has special needs." She made her ex-husband, a grown man, sound like a kid with ADHD—despite the fact that he'd received a half-dozen commendations and medals, including a purple heart.

And he had come by his PTSD and agoraphobia honestly in combat.

Literally meaning "fear of the marketplace," agoraphobia's overpowering anxiety keeps people from being able to leave their homes for fear of having a panic attack. But panic disorder was not Herb's issue, and he was restricted to more than his house. He hadn't been able to go beyond his living room and adjoining kitchen, separated only by a breakfast bar, for months.

His anxiety came from being ambushed while clearing a bombed-out building in Syria—which should've been empty. An ISIS fighter, hidden in the rubble, had jumped him as he'd stepped through a doorway. A knife was against his throat when another Marine knocked the guy out.

Herb had come home physically intact but with a crippling

fear of doorways.

"That's why I've trained Dolly to help him," I said to his ex-wife, in a carefully neutral tone.

She gave me a smile that didn't reach her eyes and waved a hand in the air. "I'm not talking about his phobia."

I stared at her, waiting for her to tell me what the heck she *was* talking about.

"He's always been a sensitive soul," she said, "even before he deployed to Syria."

I struggled not to shake my head in confusion. "Sensitive souls" did not enlist in the Marines. Or maybe they did, but only if they had a fairly thick layer of emotional armor guarding that soul.

"I see," I said, even though I didn't.

"Anyway, I'm really glad he's getting this dog." Char Mathers gave me another fake smile.

I nodded, then hustled Dolly and Buddy into the backseat of my car and got the heck out of there…before I had to interact any further with the ex-wife from bizarro-land.

⬩⎯⎯⟶

A little disconcerted after the interaction with Herb's ex, I opted to take the scenic route home, hoping images of green fields and sleek animals contentedly grazing would soothe and distract me. Those hopes were quickly dashed.

Crystal County, Florida had been mostly rural just a few years ago, when I'd been in this area to train another veteran. That situation had gotten messy, after my client became a suspect in the murder of his landlord at the flea market where he was a vendor.

But the county was much more developed now, and not in a good way. Strip malls, warehouses with metal roofs, and cement-block manufacturing plants lined what had once been a country road.

Today, I was commuting the two-hour drive from Mayfair, since my husband expected to get home early this afternoon,

God willing and the bad guys in Marion County behaved themselves. He's a major crimes detective in the sheriff's department there. Tomorrow and for the next few days, I'd be staying with my mother and Clint Burns in Crystal County, where he had been the sheriff until last year.

I was still getting used to the idea that my widowed mom was part of a couple again.

My stomach felt a little queasy. The reminder of the little being currently residing inside of me immediately cheered me up. I keep saltines with me to tamp down the morning sickness—which in my case seems to strike any time of the day or night. I nibbled on a cracker to settle my stomach.

Finally, the human-produced ugliness gave way to horse country, and I was able to get my mood adjusted to something like normal. I entertained myself for the rest of the journey with color scheme options for the nursery.

Will was already home when the dogs and I walked into the house. He grinned at me, his baby blues sparkling. "We've got our first case."

Excitement bubbled in my chest. We'd just officially opened our new enterprise by registering the name—*Baines Private Investigations, LLC.* Baines—a combination of our last names, Banks and Haines. We'd considered *Hanks*, but our octogenarian friend and neighbor, Edna Mayfair had said that sounded more like an auto body shop than a PI agency.

"I guess it's more of an assignment than a case," Will was saying. "The guy's expanding his business and he wants us to do background checks and initial assessments of potential employees."

The bubbles fizzled. *Crapola.* We were supposed to be PIs, not an employment agency.

Disappointment set my stomach off. I grabbed the box of crackers I kept out on our breakfast bar.

Will hadn't seemed to notice my mood shift. "The guy's kinda weird, paranoid. He doesn't want to meet in person, and he wouldn't tell me the nature of the business. He swore me to secrecy.

I'm not even supposed to tell *you* the name of the company. He said it's a highly competitive field, so the expansion is hush-hush."

I pulled myself together. "What do you need me to do?"

"Not much, most likely. He sent me a list of names, which I forwarded to Elise to run background checks. Depending on what she finds, I'll go talk to some of them."

"Okay." I was secretly relieved that I probably wouldn't be needed. I had enough on my plate right now. And the case sounded boring. "What do you want for dinner?"

He gave me a lopsided grin, which brought out those sexy dimples of his. "You tell me. You're the one dealing with Bumpkin. I hope this kid's not as finicky an eater after he/she is born."

I laid a hand on my small baby bump, and my mood instantly improved.

⋖────➤

"So, what's the deal with your ex?" Ms. Snark blurted out, while I was having Herb practice the nonverbal on-duty signal.

Training was challenging because we couldn't work outside, my normal preference, weather permitting—which it almost always is in central Florida.

We didn't have much space to work in. His posture military erect, Herb walked up and down the length of his living room, dodging the sofa bed that was unfolded, the sheets taut with precision corners. He'd stop periodically and hold his palm out for Dolly to touch her nose to it, the you're-on-duty reminder.

This early stage of the human phase of the training is mind-numbingly boring for me. Which was probably how Ms. Snark slipped past my defenses.

Herb shrugged, his cheeks flushing slightly in his boyish face. "She helps me with things that would be hard otherwise."

I mentally clapped a hand over Ms. Snark's mouth, so she wouldn't push him.

"She picks up my prescriptions and my grocery orders," he added, turning and pacing back the way he'd come.

"Okay, stop but don't give her the signal," I said.

Dolly immediately turned and sat down, facing in the opposite direction.

"This is the *cover* position," I said. "Now watch what happens as I walk up behind you."

His shoulders tensed as I moved slowly across the room. "Why's she twitchy all of a sudden?"

Dolly was wiggling her ears and thumping her tail on the wooden floor.

"That's what she's supposed to do, signal you that someone is approaching. That way, no one can take you by surprise and maybe trigger something."

It was one of the many symptoms of PTSD, especially in combat veterans—they startled easily, and that could set off a flashback and/or anxiety attack.

"That's pretty cool." Herb shot me a quick smile as he turned toward me. Dolly stood up, her tail wagging.

I caught myself, about to say, *Good girl*. She needed to stay focused on Herb. "Give her a treat," I told him.

But he didn't move.

My gaze went from the dog to his face. He was staring past my shoulder, eyes wide, mouth hanging open.

I whirled around. There was nothing behind me but the empty kitchen and dining area. Then I saw it. A faint, flickering light running across the ceiling.

I turned back to Herb.

His face was now flushed. He let out a self-conscious laugh. "Doesn't help my nerves that this house is haunted."

Crapola!

CHAPTER TWO

While we ate lunch at Herb's breakfast bar, I discreetly examined the kitchen ceiling. No twinkle lights or signs of a camera or projector. Only acoustical tiles and a few cobwebs in the corners.

Where did those lights come from? Was his house truly haunted?

After lunch, we started working on the release signal. I emphasized the importance of clearly communicating to the dog when she was on duty and when not.

We were winding down our first session of the afternoon, when the ex and her fiancé "stopped by to check on things." I hid my annoyance while they chatted. Apparently, this was a daily thing, checking in on Herb.

My irritation increased. I didn't particularly want the training process to be dragged out because of constant interruptions.

Herb was maybe one hundred-sixty pounds, on a good day. A photo on top of a bookcase showed a younger and happier version of him, in desert camouflage fatigues, surrounded by grinning buddies. He was closer to one-eighty at that time. My guess was the extra pounds were muscle.

But as he sat on the side of his bed, talking to his ex, he seemed to shrink into himself. There was no anxiety in his voice, however. He seemed relaxed enough.

Char lounged in the only armchair. Frank Hawkins, her tall and lanky fiancé, leaned against the breakfast bar, near where I sat on a stool.

From across the room, I caught Herb's eye and pointed toward the kitchen door, then at the two dogs sitting at my feet. I needed to get out of there before Ms. Snark said something rude.

He gave a slight nod, and I took the dogs outside. They were happily sniffing around the backyard when Frank came out the door.

Buddy looked up and his ears perked. I gave him the signal for *friend*, palm out, fingers spread wide. If I'd made a fist, he would have gone into *protect* mode, barking and growling. He wouldn't do anything else, though, unless I told him to.

It was a system Will had taught him, hoping Buddy would be able to protect me, since I tend to "poke around" in things that get me into trouble—Will's words, not mine. One of the many reasons we'd decided to open the PI agency was to put my poking-around tendencies to constructive use.

"Your dogs are gorgeous," Frank said, by way of a conversation starter.

It was a good one. I smiled.

We made small talk for a few minutes, then I blurted out, "Herb says his house is haunted. Any truth to that?"

"Possibly," he said, with only a slight hesitation. "I researched it when he started hearing noises and seeing strange lights. A young woman committed suicide in one of the bedrooms."

"Whoa." I took a step back. "How long ago was that?"

"Over a decade now. There've been a couple of other owners in between. Char and I haven't noticed anything strange, though."

"So Herb's the only one who's seen or heard these things?"

"Yeah," Frank said.

In the past, I would have poo-pooed the idea of a ghost. But having encountered one up close and personal on a tropical island a few years ago—where said ghost helped disarm a killer—I was a believer.

I took a deep breath and told him I'd seen the lights on the ceiling earlier.

Frank's eyebrows went up. "Herb's not imagining things then."

"Not the lights, at least."

"Hey, don't say anything to Char, okay?" Frank ran a hand through his dark, slightly too long hair. It curled around his ears. "She got really pissed when I told Herb about my research. She doesn't think the ghost is real."

"Sure, okay."

After Char and Frank left, I asked my client to suggest they not stop by unannounced for the next couple of weeks. "It's too distracting for Dolly having training sessions interrupted."

I silently apologized to the dog, sitting at my feet. She did not distract easily. It was Herb's concentration I was concerned about.

And my ability to keep Ms. Snark reined in, if we had to spend much time around Char.

The visit I had scheduled the next morning with my bestie had taken on new significance. Of course, I wanted to see Becky and her kids, my adorable godchildren. But now I was also looking forward to venting about my client's frustrating ex-wife, and his possibly haunted house.

In Becky's backyard in Williston—a town twenty minutes north of Mom and Clint's house—we watched the three-year-old twins splash in a shallow inflatable pool.

Without naming names or giving identifying details, I told Becky about my client's rather strange relationship with his ex, and the weird flickering lights across his kitchen ceiling.

"Got no answers about the lights," Becky said, "but the ex-wife sounds like a control freak."

"On steroids."

At that moment, Winnie ran up to me. "Aunt Marcy, pony."

"Winston, what do we say?" Becky demanded, a mock stern look on her fair-skinned, heart-shaped face.

"Peas," he said, with a big grin.

I ruffled his dark curls, so like his mother's, and lifted him up, began jiggling him on my knee. His wet swimsuit soaked the leg of my denim capris, but I didn't care.

"There's something more there than just control stuff, though," I said to Becky. "It's like she wants to keep Herb helpless. Well, maybe not helpless…" I shook my head. "It's one strange dynamic, that's for sure."

"You know, you probably should've become a counselor. You always have to figure out people's 'dynamics.'" Becky made air quotes. Her voice, as usual, sounded like she was about to laugh at any moment.

Jasmine trotted over, demanding her turn on the "pony." I switched twins on my knee as I thought about Becky's observation. I have a master's degree in counseling psychology, but I'd never done much with it, other than teaching some college psych classes and using my knowledge of behavior modification in my dog training.

"Nah," I finally said. "I'm happier working with dogs. They're easier to understand."

Becky snickered.

⊷━━━⊶

I was holding my breath as I pulled to the curb in front of Herb's house mid-morning. But there were no other cars nearby. *Phew*. Char and her fiancé were not here.

In response to the ringing doorbell, the door opened. But instead of Herb jumping back from the opening, as he had yesterday, he stood just beyond the threshold. "I'm trying to make myself stand closer to the door when I answer it."

"How does that feel?"

Internally, Ms. Snark rolled her eyes.

Yeah, I know, that sounded way too much like a therapist.

"A little anxious," he said with his mouth, but his body language told a different story. His wiry frame was stiff, his hands clenching and unclenching. He wiped his palms on his jeans as he backed away to let us in.

The combination of that exchange and Becky's earlier comment had my brain churning. Maybe I should do more than just train Herb to work with his dog. I could at least get him started toward overcoming his agoraphobia with systematic desensitization, a well-established therapy technique for phobias.

"Today," I told Herb, "the plan is to introduce you to the *clear* task."

Gesturing to Buddy to lie down, I led Dolly over to the opening at the end of the breakfast bar, the closest thing to a doorway between the kitchen and dining area. "Clear." I pointed into the kitchen.

Dolly tilted her head slightly, confused by the lack of an actual doorway. But then she ran into the small kitchen, circled around it, came back to the opening and sat.

"Good girl." I gave her a treat.

I turned to Herb. "If she comes back to the door without stopping anywhere inside, that means the room is empty." I looked down at the dog. "Doors."

Dolly ran to the open doorway of the small pantry, sniffed at the threshold, and ran back to us.

"If there had been someone in the pantry, she would've sat and thumped her tail, if it was someone she knows, or she'd bark for a stranger."

Herb gave me a tentative smile.

"Same thing in a room," I said. "If someone is there, she'll sit down in front of them and either stay silent for a friend or bark if they're a stranger to her."

"But how will I see her if she doesn't bark?"

"You will have to at least stick your head around the doorframe if she doesn't come back to the doorway. But if she hasn't barked, you know whoever is in there is someone she knows, therefore it's someone *you* know. In other words, not an enemy."

I stepped into the kitchen and leaned against the far counter. "Stand near the kitchen opening. Give her the on-duty signal to get her focused on you, then tell her to clear."

He complied, his movements slightly awkward. Dolly ran over and sat down in front of me. Her eyes sparkled. She knew she did good.

"You can peek around the counter," I said, "and see her sitting, right?"

Herb leaned over, nodded at Dolly and gave me another small smile.

"Now call her to you and give her a treat."

We ran through the whole scenario again. Next, I stepped into the pantry and away from that doorway, where neither dog nor man could see me readily. "Tell her to clear."

Herb did so and Dolly ran around the kitchen and back to him, then sat.

Without prompting, Herb said, "Doors."

Dolly ran over and stuck her head inside the pantry, sat and thumped her tail.

Herb stepped up behind her. Now his smile was full-blown. "Cool."

"Give her a treat."

He gave her both a treat and a good ear scratch.

"If there's a closed door," I said, "she'll sniff at the bottom. If there's a human in there, she'll let you know. Again, if she recognizes their scent, she'll sit and thump. If not, she'll bark."

I walked to the living room and into the small powder room off of it.

Herb always left the door open so he could make himself go in there. Since it was such a small space, he could force himself to stick his head in, but he'd said it still made him a little nervous. With his tendency toward understatement, I interpreted that to mean a lot nervous, but manageable.

I turned back toward him. "Have her clear the room, then tell her 'Doors.'" I closed the powder room door.

He gave the two commands. Seconds went by. I visualized Dolly running to the front door and to the door leading to a hallway and the bedrooms beyond.

A shadow moved along the crack at the bottom of the powder room door, as Dolly sniffed there. I gave her a second before cracking the door open. She was sitting on the other side, tail thumping away.

"Good," I said. "Give her another treat."

We repeated my going into the powder room several times, until Herb seemed comfortable with the routine.

Was it too soon to up the anté? I decided to try one more level. "How about one of the bedrooms?"

He shook his head, his face suddenly full of anxiety, then he froze for a second. "The hallway."

He walked over, slid open a slide bolt on a doorway, and moved quickly back from the closed door.

I waited a beat. When he didn't move, I said, "I can teach her to open doors." I was mentally kicking myself for not anticipating that need.

He shook his head slightly, stepped forward. Standing so he'd be behind the door, he opened it. "Clear."

Dolly bolted into the hallway, made a circuit, came back and sat.

"Doors," Herb said.

She ran back, sniffed the four closed doors in the hallway, and came back to him again.

The sound of air whooshing out of his lungs. He'd been holding his breath.

"Good girl." He gave the dog a treat without prompting.

"Can you walk down the hall with Dolly beside you?" I asked.

"I think so."

Slowly they moved down the hall together. He stopped and tested the knob of each room. Apparently, he kept them all locked. Then he tested the same doorknobs on the way back.

Okay, that's a tad obsessive-compulsive. But still, he was making progress.

During a break, I asked him if he knew any relaxation techniques. He did, and his favorite was focusing on and slowing his breathing.

"That's great," I said. "I want you to use that technique as we work, whenever you feel the least bit anxious. Just hold up a finger to signal me and stop to do that, until you feel more relaxed. I'll wait."

He nodded, and I hid a smile. We were now fully implementing the systematic desensitization technique.

An hour later, Herb was able to clear and enter the smallest of his bedrooms, set up as a guest room. But he had to have Dolly clear the hallway again, before he could come out. I reassured him that was fine.

I stood in the hallway while Dolly did her circuit, sniffing at each door without being told.

Dang, she's smart!

The distant sound of a key turning in a lock. My heart rocketed into my throat.

I raced out to the living room to intercept whoever was coming in the front door, afraid they would startle Herb and undo his fragile progress.

It was the ex-wife, of course, with Frank trailing behind her.

CHAPTER THREE

"Hello, Char," I said in a loud voice, anxiety combining with anger to make my chest tight.

Char looked around the living room. "Where's Herbert?" she demanded, as if I'd done something to him.

"Clear." Herb's voice from the hallway, and Dolly darted into the living room.

She stopped and sat in front of me, thumped her tail, then ran to Char and repeated the routine, then Frank.

Herb's head was thrust around the corner of the doorway, and he was grinning.

I gave him a big smile back, even though I was doing a slow burn.

"This really works," Herb said to his ex.

"I'm glad," she said. The words were right, but the tone was still sharp, almost sarcastic.

Herb stepped into the room. He closed the hall door behind him and slid the slide bolt into place, his body relaxed.

I blew out air, the possible setback averted.

To the ex, I said, "We're not finished training yet. Perhaps, you could come back later."

She glared at me as she settled into Herb's sole armchair. "I have a meeting later. I *always* stop by at least once a day, to see if there's anything Herbert needs."

I stared at Herb, willing him to say something. He glanced at his ex—his body language now tense—then back at me. "Thanks for stopping by, Char," he finally said, "but I'm fine. Got everything I need for now."

Char glared at Dolly. "I see."

I'd seen this jealousy of a new service dog from a family member before, in one of my earliest cases, when said family member wanted that client to remain dependent. My stomach clenched. That time, the dog had ended up in danger.

Char sniffed and made no move to get up. "I'm parched. Can I trouble you for some iced tea?" This was aimed at Herb.

He moved toward the kitchen.

Something snapped inside and I stepped into his path, facing Char. Ms. Snark was begging me to let her loose, but I managed to keep her reined in.

I was still trying to figure out what to say, when Frank cleared his throat. "We should go, Char. I'm thirsty too, and hungry. We can stop for a quick bite on the way to the office."

She and I continued our staring contest for another beat, then she slowly stood. "That's a good idea, darling," she said, her voice super sweet now. She strolled to the front door and, without even a glance at Herb, opened it and walked out.

Frank gave us a small wave and ambled after her.

I released pent-up air.

Herb surprised me by chuckling. I'd expected our confrontation to make him nervous. "Char's an acquired taste, I'm afraid," he said.

I took a deep breath. Should we try to do more training today, after that disruption? I checked the time on my phone. I had almost two full hours before I had to leave for my mother's house.

Abruptly, I realized what I was doing. With other veteran

clients I would've *asked* them if they wanted to continue. Why was I trying to make that choice for Herb?

His ex's attitude toward him was subtly rubbing off on me. I clenched my teeth. "Do you feel up to doing any more today?"

"Sure," Herb said. "It's kinda fun."

I drummed up a smile and asked if he'd like to try going outside.

His face brightened. "Out back?"

"Yup."

"I'd love that. I'm not afraid of being outside. It's getting past the doorway that's the problem."

I checked out Herb's backyard first, with the dogs in tow. It was surrounded by a high privacy fence, which made things easier. Dolly would treat the enclosed space like a room.

Telling Buddy to lie down in a shady spot, Dolly and I went back inside.

Again, standing so he would be behind it, Herb opened the kitchen door. "Clear."

Dolly darted out, ran around the yard, then came back to the doorway and sat.

Herb glanced my way. "Here goes." He stepped through the doorway and stopped on the small cement stoop. Taking in a deep breath, he scanned the yard. "I love the outdoor–"

Loud, sharp clapping.

Herb twisted around and dove back into the kitchen. He barely missed me, landing on his side on the floor. "Get down," he yelled.

Dolly raced over and cuddled up against his chest, whining, prompting him to pet her to lower his anxiety. But we hadn't covered that yet. Herb had no idea why she was reacting this way.

Char stepped into the open doorway, still clapping her hands. She stopped, gazed down at her ex-husband, who was trembling on the floor. "I was only applauding your success. I didn't mean to scare you, or the dog."

"The dog is *not* scared," I said through gritted teeth. "She's doing her job. Where were you?"

"Just outside the gate," Char said, trying but failing to look chagrined.

Why? Ms. Snark asked internally.

But for once anger trumped curiosity. And this time I didn't hold back. "Get out, and don't come on this property again if you see my car out front."

Char bristled. "How dare you?"

Herb pushed himself to a stand, still shaking slightly. "Just go, Char."

After a sharp glare at each of us, she left.

I turned to him, and suddenly I wanted to cry. I knew the urge was part hormones, but the tears burning behind my eyes were also from frustration. How could I keep this woman from sabotaging Herb's training?

"Can you take her key away from her?" Although that wouldn't have prevented what happened today.

Herb had relaxed some. "That would be tricky."

"Why?"

He took a deep breath. "She's co-owner of the house."

—◦—

I was still seething as I drove to my mother and Clint's house.

Mom greeted me at the door with a big smile, her petite frame swathed in a pink bib apron. She shoved an errant strand of wavy gray hair out of her eyes. "You're just in time. I made your favorite for dinner."

I tried to fake a cheerful attitude, but I must have failed miserably. Or perhaps my picking at the shrimp Alfredo on my plate gave away that I'd had a crapola day.

Barely into the meal, Mom put down her fork. "Marcia, what's going on?"

I sighed, glanced at Clint.

He kept his gaze on his plate, as if to say, *Don't mind me. I'm just a bump over here. Talk to your mom.*

But his presence was hard to ignore. He's a big man.

I sighed again. "Short version. My client has an ex-wife and she's a female dog."

Clint snorted and choked on a piece of food. Grabbing his water glass, he drank heartily, winking at me over the rim.

I suppressed a grin. My mother loathed swearing. But Clint was retired law enforcement, and they cuss, a lot.

Without giving away anything that might identify Herb, I told them the gist of the afternoon's events.

My mother gasped when I got to the part about Char clapping and setting off a flashback. "I see what you mean," she said, her brown eyes warm with sympathy.

"I told the ex to stay away if she sees my car parked out front, but I'm not at all sure she'll honor that."

"Hmm…" Clint had a twinkle in his brown eyes. "I could probably arrange for her car to be impounded for some traffic violation."

Mom gave him a mock glare.

I chuckled. "I doubt that would slow her down much. She'd only get her fiancé to chauffeur her."

"She's engaged," Mom said, incredulous, "and still she wants to run her ex's life?"

"Um, the situation is complicated." I really didn't want to get into my client's finances. Herb had explained that he'd paid the down payment on his house from his half of the sale of the modest home they'd owned together—before Char had hit the big time as real estate agent to the rich and famous.

She had put up the rest of the funds and held the mortgage, giving him low monthly payments that he could afford with his military disability. But she'd insisted that her name be on the deed with his.

I shook my head and changed the subject. "I stopped by Becky's house this morning. You should see how the twins have grown!"

⊷⊶

A strange SUV sat in front of Herb's house the next morning. I took a deep breath, before getting out of my car. If this was

Char, perhaps in a different vehicle, I needed to keep my cool.

Yesterday afternoon, we'd focused on some of the things Dolly could do to help lower Herb's anxiety level. I really should have covered them before nudging him to go outside, but he'd been doing so well.

We had one more anxiety-reducing task to go over today. Then I'd see how he felt about tackling more doorways.

The SUV turned out to be Frank's. I could hear his voice behind the slightly ajar front door.

I was about to knock when I caught the words, "Char was pretty upset yesterday." Herb's response was too low to make out words.

"I tried to gently tell her," Frank said, "that your trainer has a point. She really is interfering."

The low rumble of Herb's voice. I only caught "...that go?"

"How do you think it went? She bit my head off."

Using hand signals, I backed myself and the dogs off the front porch and down the sidewalk a few yards. I stomped my feet as we approached the porch again. "Come on, Dolly," I said, even though the dog was right at my side.

The door swung open. "Hi, Marcia." Frank greeted me with a warm smile. "I'll be out of your hair in a few minutes. I only came by to replace some hinges on the kitchen cabinets."

Frank picked up a large toolbox, the size of a small suitcase. He noticed me eyeing it. "It was my father's. He was a carpenter, worked construction. If it was made of wood, he could build it or fix it."

I nodded. "And he taught you…"

"Yeah," Frank said, "but he wouldn't let me work construction, not even as a summer job. He said he hadn't worked hard all those years to put me through college to have me doing physical labor for a living. But he was okay with me doing it as a hobby."

It was the most I'd ever heard Frank say. I'd assumed he was the quiet type, but apparently that was only when Char was there to hog the stage.

Frank had used past tense. I felt for him. I'd lost my own beloved father almost a decade ago.

Herb and Frank were now discussing the hinges that needed replacing. "You could've just brought me the new ones." Herb's voice had a slight chuckle in it. "I know how to use a screwdriver."

"I don't mind installing them," Frank gestured toward me and the dogs, "and you've got better things to do today." He headed to the kitchen with his toolbox.

I told Buddy to lie down out of the way and began to explain to Herb about deep-pressure therapy for anxiety.

His face brightened. "I know about that. My counselor suggested I get a weighted blanket. It does help me sleep."

"Good." I gestured toward the armchair. "Let's start with sitting up. The verbal signal is 'Dolly, up.'"

Without being prompted, Herb gave her the on-duty signal. Then he sat down in the armchair. "Dolly, up."

The dog immediately jumped into his lap, draped her front legs over his shoulders and leaned her weight against his chest. She laid her head on one shoulder and whined.

He laughed. "It's like she's giving me a hug."

"Kind of," I said. "It works even better if you're lying down. She'll stretch out full-length on top of you."

"Why is she whining?"

"Her whining is actually a signal for you to pet her, remember? To help you calm down. If you say, 'It's okay, girl,' she'll relax."

He ran a hand over the top of her black and white head. "It's okay, girl."

"Dolly, down," I said. The dog complied but sat at Herb's knee.

Frank came back around the breakfast bar. "All done."

"That didn't take long," I said.

Frank shrugged. "I couldn't help but overhear." He gestured toward Dolly. "That's pretty amazing. How did you teach her to detect anxiety?"

I grinned. "I merely recall what it was like when my ex-husband and I were breaking up." That had also happened a decade ago, but I could still conjure up the feelings as needed.

Both men snorted, which led me to believe that Frank too had an ex in his past. I would've loved to ask what he saw in Char but kept my mouth shut.

"And that deep-pressure therapy," Frank said, "I'd never heard of that before. That's pretty interesting." He grabbed up his tool-box. "Well, I'll let you guys get on with it." He went out the door.

"Hmm, I forgot something in my car," I said to Herb. "Be right back." I signaled for the dogs to stay.

I caught up with Frank at the curb. "Do you think it's safe to assume that Char won't come by today, since you already have?"

He gave me a small smile. "Don't worry. She's out of town—left last night on a business trip."

I smiled back. "Thanks."

"She doesn't mean any harm, you know. She's just used to Herb being part of her life, even though they're not a couple anymore."

"She thinks he won't be if he becomes more independent?"

He sighed. "Maybe not consciously, but yeah."

"She could talk to him about it. I'm sure he's used to having her around as well."

Frank let out a short bark of laughter. "Char doesn't talk about feelings."

Sounds like they've got their roles reversed, Ms. Snark commented internally. *Char's more of a 'guy' than he is.*

I silently agreed but kept those thoughts to myself.

Frank sketched me a small salute and climbed into his SUV.

⬚

We started over, in the kitchen area. I wanted to give Herb some positive experiences with clearing rooms, before we tackled going outside again.

Every time I thought about what Char had done my blood boiled. How could she so blatantly sabotage him like that? And he either didn't realize she'd done it on purpose, or he was ignoring that reality.

I moved us to the hallway. Herb did fine there, and even managed to go into the hall bathroom after Dolly had cleared it. I called for a break.

"Do you mind if I get on the computer for a few minutes?" Herb said. "I need to order some groceries so Char can pick them up for me tomorrow."

"No problem," I said. "I'll take the dogs out back for a bit."

As I walked through the dining area, my foot landed on something small and hard. I stepped back, scanned the multicolored braided rug that covered most of the floor, and spotted a small, black object.

I picked it up, realizing it was plastic. Other than that I couldn't tell what it was. It looked like it might have broken off of something.

I scanned the dining area for a trash can. Not seeing one, I stuck the bit of plastic in the pocket of my capris.

My phone vibrated in my back pocket as we stepped out into the fenced-in yard. I gave the release signal. The dogs trotted away, and I pulled out my phone. "Hello."

"Hey, Marcia." The voice of Elise, the owner of E&R Electronic Investigations, the background check company we use.

"Hey, Elise. What's up?"

"I tried to reach Will, but it went right to voicemail."

"That usually means he's in the middle of something tricky, like he's about to arrest a bad guy."

"That's what I figured. I have the preliminary reports on the background checks he requested."

"Um…" I hesitated, curiosity doing battle with integrity. The latter won, surprisingly. Or maybe it was more expediency. If I wanted our fledgling agency to survive, I needed to honor the wishes of our first client, strange as they were.

"The client has asked for total discretion." I sauntered along the wall of the house. "You should really wait until Will calls you back."

I stopped at a window a little past the kitchen one.

"Okay," Elise said, "but there's something strange here."

There was a narrow opening between the curtains over the window. I glanced through it, and froze.

"These people…" Elise's words blurred into gibberish, as I stared at the queen-sized bed dominating the room behind those curtains.

On that bed were legs—female, ending in stiletto-heeled pumps with red soles.

CHAPTER FOUR

I moved back and forth, trying to get a better look at the owner of those legs through the narrow opening between the curtains. The only new information gleaned was that she wore a knee-length black skirt.

The legs hadn't moved.

"Elise, I gotta go. Try Will again." I stuffed my phone in my pocket and darted back inside.

Herb was squinting at his computer, on a desk in one corner of the living room.

"Gonna use the restroom," I muttered as I went by.

At the door leading to the hallway, I eased the slide bolt open. I slipped into the hall and tried the first door on my right, which should lead to the bedroom I had seen through that window.

The knob turned but the door wouldn't open. I pushed a little harder, but it didn't budge.

Crapola! Up to this point, I'd been telling myself that the woman in that room was only taking a nap. I was pretty sure it was Char.

I quickly walked through the house again to the back door.

Herb was still scrolling through pictures of loaves of bread and cartoons of milk.

I went out back and peeked through the window. The legs hadn't moved.

Reality asserted itself. My heart rate, already accelerated, shot even higher. I ran back into the kitchen. The dogs had sensed something was wrong. They were on my heels.

"Herb!"

"Hunh." He whirled around on his desk chair. "What?"

"The bedroom on the back of the house, that's the master, right?" My voice was shaky.

"Yeah, why?"

I wasn't sure why that mattered. It didn't really. I was stalling, not wanting to tell him. Not wanting to make the horror that was about to descend real.

"There's someone in there, a woman. The door's locked. I think they're hurt."

Herb stared, eyes wide. "A woman… in my bedroom?"

I nodded mutely.

Despite the urgency of the situation, we had to wait while Dolly cleared the hallway, before Herb could enter it and try the bedroom door. "That's weird. The knob should be locked. It's not, but the door still won't open. Whoever's in there must have thrown the slide bolt."

"Why the heck do you have a slide bolt on the *inside* of the door?" I should've phrased the question a bit more diplomatically, but I was a tad rattled.

"Uh, back when I still slept in there, the only way I could get to sleep was if the door was bolted."

"What about the windows?"

"They've got keyed locks on them. Can only be opened from the inside."

"Do you think you could handle coming outside with me?" I hadn't planned on tackling the backyard today—had wanted to let some time pass, after yesterday's debacle—but under the circumstances…

Herb swallowed hard, then nodded.

The dogs and I led the way to the back door. I opened it and signaled Dolly to clear the yard.

She was back in the open doorway, sitting, in a few seconds. Still all these delays made my stomach queasy.

I went outside first and reassured Herb that the yard was empty. I even stood on tiptoes and peeked over the top of his wooden gate to guarantee no one was waiting there.

Herb took one step through the doorway. He looked like he might faint but he resolutely took another step.

I gestured toward the bedroom window.

Keeping his back to the house wall, he eased over to it and peeked in.

"Char," he gasped, swaying on his feet.

"Buddy, brace," I said.

Buddy was beside him in a second, stiffening his legs. Herb put a hand on the dog's back to steady himself.

Dolly gave me a confused look, whining. She didn't know that command, but she knew that both of her humans were anxious.

"We need to call 911." I pulled out my phone.

Herb suddenly slid down the wall and sat on the ground. Dolly was in his lap in an instant, draping herself over his torso.

⟵——⟶

The horror I'd imagined descending on us was worse than I'd thought. It wasn't just that Char was dead, but it appeared that she had committed suicide.

And yet Clint's successor as sheriff, Rick Young couldn't seem to decide for sure if that was the case. He'd been a detective when I'd locked horns with him a few years ago over the flea market murder. Those years had left their mark. He now had flecks of gray in his dark hair and a slight paunch.

He kept pointing out that Char was found in a locked room, with a suicide note on the bed beside her. But the questions he aimed at Herb and myself implied that we were potential murder suspects.

My client was pale and shaking slightly—sitting on the edge of his sofa bed, Dolly leaning against his knee—as sheriff's deputies and crime scene techs swarmed around him.

Well, they weren't really swarming. There were only about five of them, but it seemed like a swarm to me. And if I perceived them that way, how must Herb be experiencing them?

I needed an ally to help me protect him from being forced to do something that would aggravate his phobia.

Standing near the sofa bed, I surreptitiously pulled out my cell phone and hit the speed-dial number for Clint and Mom's house, then lowered the phone to my thigh.

"Hello." My mother's voice, muffled.

I stealthily moved it to my ear and whispered, "Tell Clint to come to my client's house, quick." I gave her the address. "The ex is dead."

"What?" Mom yelped.

Sheriff Rick whirled around, narrowing his eyes at me. Apparently, he has good hearing.

I quickly lowered the phone beside my thigh again, the line still open.

"Ms. Banks-Haines, what are you doing?"

I slid the phone around to the back of my thigh, out of his view. "Nothing."

"Did you take pictures of the crime scene? Let me see your phone." He held out his hand.

How could I have taken pictures? I hadn't even been *in* the master bedroom. The first sheriff's deputy on the scene, who'd arrived seconds before an ambulance, had ordered us to sit tight in the living room. We'd both winced at the smashing sound of the master bedroom door being kicked in.

My phone?" I said now, the epitome of innocence.

"Your phone!" His face reddened. "Hand it over."

I stood up straighter. "Do you have a *warrant* for my phone?" I said in an overly loud voice.

A faint gasp emanated from behind my thigh.

I hoped my mother wasn't just listening, but had actually summoned Clint.

The sheriff glared. "I see any pictures leaked to the media, I'll know where they came from." He turned back to his people.

Clint arrived fifteen minutes later. The deputies and techs greeted him with pleasure and respect.

He sauntered across the living room to Herb, still sitting on the sofa bed. Buddy and I stood nearby. "Y'all okay?" he asked in a low voice.

I glanced at Herb. He'd stopped shaking but his face was still pale, and his fist was curled in the fur of Dolly's ruff.

"For now," I whispered back, my tone implying the situation was touch and go.

Clint looked up, surveyed the scene. "Best place for y'all to wait?" he asked under his breath.

Warmth spread through my chest. *He gets it.* Perhaps Mom, a retired nurse, had given him the scoop on the likely psychological state of my client. Or maybe he'd seen PTSD in his department in the past. But either way, he got it.

"Backyard," I whispered back.

"Be right back." He sauntered nonchalantly over to one of the deputies, put a hand on the man's shoulder, said something to him.

The deputy broke out a smile. The two men shook hands, exchanged a few more words. Then Clint moved leisurely back toward us, smiling and nodding at the deputies and techs.

"It's okay," he said. "Go out back, but stay there."

With a head gesture, I conveyed to Herb we should move. The dogs stuck close without prompting.

At the kitchen door, we paused. It was sitting open, allowing the law enforcement horde to come and go.

I pointed out the door. "Clear." Dolly darted out into the yard.

Unfortunately, the backyard held several more deputies and techs, checking for evidence of an intruder. All the people coming and going confused the dog. She tried to sit in front of them and bark to indicate she didn't know them, but most of them kept moving, intent on their jobs.

Dolly looked my way and whined, but I was more worried about Herb. Beads of sweat peppered his forehead. I doubted they had much to do with the summer heat.

"They're all law enforcement," I said in a low voice.

His face grim, he forced himself to step over the threshold onto the back stoop.

One of the techs noticed us. I pointed to a pair of Adirondack chairs, about twenty feet from the house.

He nodded. "We've already searched back there."

Once we were in the middle of the yard, where there was no place for the enemy to hide and ambush us, Herb relaxed some.

The chairs were covered in pollen and leaves. I dusted off the worst of nature's debris and sat down in one of them. Herb hesitated next to the other.

I was trying to decide the best next move. *Again, why am I making the decision?*

"Which would help more," I said out loud, "Dolly in the cover position next to the chair, or on your lap to help with the anxiety?"

"Cover."

"Dolly, cover." I pointed to the side of the empty chair. She sat down, facing the end of the yard.

Herb gave me a small smile and gingerly lowered himself into the chair. "Is it okay to pet her while she's in the cover position?"

"Sure." Normally, it would not be ideal, as it would distract the dog from watching for someone approaching. But in this case, the issue was Herb's anxiety, not the actual possibility that someone might come up behind us. There was no one there. All the action was in front of us.

Roughly ten minutes later, Clint came out the back door and headed our way. He loomed over us.

I frowned up at him.

He got the hint and crouched down in front of our chairs. "The sheriff wanted to take y'all to the department. I explained that wasn't feasible. He's willing to officially interview you here instead." He glanced my way, a question in his eyes.

"We're kind of settled out here," I said by way of an answer.

He nodded. "He'll be out in a little bit." He paused, looked around. "Got anywhere that an old man can sit while we wait?"

It took me half a beat to get it. Clint wanted to be comfortably ensconced when Sheriff Rick came out to start his "official" interview. It was unlikely the man would have the nerve to tell his former boss to get lost.

I jumped up, gestured toward my chair. "I need to stand for a while," I lied. "Stretch my legs."

Sheriff Rick did chase *me* away, but he let Clint stay. According to Herb, the official interview was relatively benign—mostly the same questions he'd been asked before, only recorded this time.

But then came the bigger issue. The sheriff did not want Herb staying at the house tonight.

When we expressed resistance, he said, "You can't stay with friends, or at a hotel?" His tone was genuinely bewildered.

Herb and I locked eyes. He looked utterly lost.

My heart ached with grief for the first time since I'd seen Char's legs through the window and suspected she was dead. For all her flaws, she'd been Herb's protector and advocate. Now that buffer between him and the world was gone.

CHAPTER FIVE

My brain cast about for a solution. "Sheriff, will you be leaving a deputy to preserve the scene?"

He nodded.

"Instead of having him sit out front in his car, could you have him sit at the master bedroom doorway? That would be more comfortable for him, as well as allowing my *agoraphobic* client to stay in the environment where he feels safe." I came down hard on the word *agoraphobic*, reminding the sheriff that Herb's diagnosis qualified him for disability accommodations.

At the same time, I was cringing inside. Talking about a client's diagnosis—in front of said client, no less—violated everything I'd been taught about confidentiality in the mental health field.

Herb, however, was giving me a grateful look.

Meanwhile, Sheriff Rick was grumbling under his breath, but he agreed to the plan.

⊷———⊶

An hour later, the crowd of county personnel had thinned out some, and Frank had arrived, his expression stunned.

Before I could offer my condolences, Sheriff Rick whisked him away for questioning.

Herb was now sitting in his living room, a far away look in his eyes, and Clint was chatting with one of the deputies in a corner of the room.

The adrenaline had drained away, and I was exhausted. Telling Herb I'd touch base in the morning, the dogs and I made our exit.

When I stepped into my mom's kitchen, I must have been a little green around the edges, because she immediately sat me down at her kitchen table with a cup of her "special" herbal tea. I politely sipped the stuff—that tasted like flowers and dirty socks, not my fave combination—while telling her what had happened.

Her mouth dropped open when I got to the part about finding the body.

"It wasn't that bad," I quickly said. "I only saw her legs through the window." And honestly, I'd seen worse in the past, but I didn't tell my mother that.

"I can't say I've always liked Rick Young," I added, "but my impression is that he's a good investigator, so hopefully he'll figure this out quickly."

Mom looked confused. "I thought it was suicide."

I sighed. "That's what it seemed like on the surface. There was even a note next to her on the bed. But it was printed out, from a computer. The sheriff was asking questions as if he wasn't sure which way to go with it."

"What do you think?" Mom asked.

I gave her a wan smile. "Thanks for the tea. It's helping my queasy stomach." Which it was, despite its obnoxious taste.

She took the hint and jumped up to start dinner, waving aside my half-hearted offer to help.

While she worked, I described the room where Char had been found, with locked windows and a slide bolt thrown on the inside of the door. "There's no way anyone could have been in there with her, unless they evaporated through the ceiling."

"And yet you have doubts," Mom said, glancing up at me from where she was expertly chopping vegetables.

I gave her another half smile. She was excellent at hearing what one wasn't saying. A trait I had found exceedingly annoying as a teenager, but it made her a good sounding board now.

"I didn't know the woman well," I said, "but I find it very out of character that she would commit suicide. She was too…" I paused, searching for the right word, "…self-righteous."

Mom turned from a pot on the stove that was starting to steam, her eyebrows arched.

"What she wanted was more important than others' needs," I explained. "And if something went wrong, she struck me as the type who'd blame it on someone else, not herself."

"In other words, a narcissist."

"And a control freak," I added.

"Maybe she saw your client slipping away from her control and couldn't take that."

Her words echoed what Frank had said this morning, but still…

"She wouldn't have given up so easily. She would've fought to regain control." I sipped my tea and grimaced. It tasted even worse cold. "I can see her killing someone else, but killing herself?" I shook my head.

"What did the note say?"

"The sheriff wouldn't let us see it. I only caught a glimpse of it and saw that it was typed. I guess eventually he'll have to tell Frank, her fiancé, what it said."

"Why does your client have his bedroom set up like a fortress?" Mom asked.

"Um, I can't get into details, but let's just say, that was the only way he could sleep in there."

She raised her eyebrows again, but then nodded. As a nurse, she'd no doubt seen more than one case of PTSD.

A delicious fragrance wafted toward me. My stomach rumbled, but in a happy, I'm-hungry way this time. I made a mental note to get Mom's chicken vegetable soup recipe.

Ready to change the subject, I said, "So, do you like it down here, Mom? Do you miss the North?"

"Not much to miss except ice and snow, and your brother and his kids, of course." Notably, she'd left out my sister-in-law whom she didn't particularly like.

"Most of my friends are retired now and have moved elsewhere," she added. "I'll be happier down here, though, when we can find a house farther away from the county seat. As the wife of the former sheriff, I feel like a bug under a microscope. I got enough of that while married to your father."

My father had been the rector of an Episcopal church. And out of loyalty to him, she'd never let on that being a minister's wife, after having been a minister's daughter, was not her favorite thing.

"Speaking of which," she said," I found some houses online that seem promising. Take a look for me and tell me what you know about the areas they're in." She stepped over to where her laptop sat open on the table and scooted it around for me to see the screen.

And there at the top of the page was a banner for the Reynolds-Mathers Real Estate Agency. "Mom, that's the lady who died today, Charlene Mathers, the owner of this agency."

"Really? They're huge. By far, they have the most listings."

"They're into commercial property too," Clint said, his big frame filling the kitchen doorway.

I hadn't even heard the door open. He dragged himself past me, looking as tired as I felt, and flopped into the oversized armchair in one corner of the country kitchen.

"Frank Hawkins heads up the commercial branch of the agency." Clint's Florida Cracker accent was thicker than usual. "They've brokered quite a few deals 'round here lately."

"I'm sorry to hear that," I said. "It used to be a real pretty area, but now there are a lot of ugly commercial buildings."

He nodded. "Sadly, the county council cares more 'bout tax revenue than aesthetics."

I hid a smile. Every time Clint's accent misled me into thinking he wasn't all that well educated, he'd slip in a word like *aesthetics*.

"Another good reason to move farther out," Mom said as she brought over two bowls of soup. She went back for hers. "We'd like to find a place about halfway between here and Mayfair, so it's only an hour's drive each way."

Made sense. All but one of Clint's children and step children lived in Crystal County, and the other lived in Belleview, just north of us.

Clint struggled out of the armchair and sat down at the table.

Famished, I picked up my spoon, but froze when Mom cleared her throat.

Internally, I informed Ms. Snark that no, she could not roll her eyes at our mother. I quickly mumbled the grace I'd learned as a child, then ate a spoonful of soup.

My stomach gurgled happily. I definitely needed to get this recipe, because Bumpkin really liked it.

When I called Herb the next morning, I wasn't particularly surprised that he begged off from training for the day.

"Is there anything I can do to help?" I offered, as one does.

But I didn't receive the expected answer. "Uh, could you pick up my groceries? They're scheduled for five p.m."

Crapola. The thought had already been forming that I could go home for the day, work on the nursery, maybe even see my husband this evening.

Normally I take breaks every few days when training the veteran clients, so I can go home and work with whatever dog I'm currently bringing along. But I didn't have a current trainee. I hadn't even taken on a new assistant yet, unsure how much time I'd be willing and able to commit to training after Bumpkin was born and the agency was underway.

Considering the two-hour drive and the convenience of staying with Mom and Clint, I had planned to work with Herb for longer stretches of time, without breaks. But Char's death had thrown a wrench into that plan.

"Can you move the pick-up time to earlier?" I asked Herb.

"Uh, maybe. I think so…" His voice was shaky. "I'd have to check on the website." He sounded like he was hanging on by a thread.

"Never mind," I said quickly. "I'll make five o'clock work."

We signed off, and I sat back in my chair at Mom's kitchen table. *Dang!* Now what should I do with myself? It wasn't worth it to make the two-hour drive and then have to get back here by five. And Will would be at work anyway.

Maybe I could check out the local animal shelter. I'd been toying with the idea of training a new mentor dog. I glanced over at Buddy, lying on his blanket along the wall.

Sorry, boy, I silently apologized, *but you're getting old.* My heart squeezed in my chest.

He was now nine, with white hairs showing around his snout. He'd probably be with us for another couple of years, but he was starting to slow down. Sadly, large breeds don't live as long as smaller ones.

Mom came into the kitchen, and we exchanged good mornings. "When are you heading over to your client's house?" she asked.

"I'm not." I filled her in, and her eyes lit up when I got to the part about being at loose ends.

"Want to go look at houses with me? Clint was called out early to search for a little boy who wandered out of his yard."

Clint belonged to a volunteer search and rescue team that covered Crystal County plus several others in the area.

"Yeah, that would be fun," I said.

"Great. I have two houses lined up for today, with one of the agents from that agency, Reynolds-Mathers. And if we wait until tomorrow, they might be gone. The market's pretty hot right now."

"Happy to go along." *And*, maybe I could find out more about Char from her agent. They say on the TV cop shows that in order to solve a murder, you need to start with the victim.

Not that I was planning on solving the murder…not that I even knew for sure that it was murder…

I'm sure I could've come up with some good reasons, like my client needed resolution, but in reality, I was plain old curious. Was Char the type who would kill herself, and if not, why would someone else kill her?

It certainly wouldn't hurt to ask a few questions, right?

◄────►

The real estate agent's name was Merrilee Brooks. She was a blue-eyed blonde and drop-dead gorgeous, with the kind of bubbly personality that brought out the worst in Ms. Snark. I'd have to keep a tight rein on her.

The first house was a small rancher in a farm community, almost exactly halfway between Clint's son and stepchildren in Crystal County and his daughter and us in Marion County. And it backed up to a wildlife preserve.

"Location, location, location," Merrilee chirped.

True, but size mattered also. The house was billed as three bedrooms, two baths. The main bath had a new jacuzzi tub, but the second bath was a shower stall and toilet stuck into a tiny space off the master bedroom that had probably been a closet in a previous lifetime.

Mom had already wrinkled her nose at the small galley kitchen adjacent to the dining room. Now she didn't even bother to look in the other two bedrooms.

"Too small," she declared, and Merrilee's perpetual smile sagged some.

The second place was only a few minutes away, and as we drove up to it, Mom sighed. The large Cracker-style house was surrounded by two sprawling acres.

"That's a lot of land to take care of," I said.

"We both like to garden," Mom said, "and Clint has a small tractor."

We piled out of the car, with Buddy in tow. I'd left Dolly snoozing in Mom's kitchen. She deserved a day of rest.

Merrilee eagerly led us up the walk, babbling about the merits of the house, which had been renovated recently.

When she paused for breath, I said, "Hey, sorry about your boss. That must have been quite a shock for everybody at your agency."

Merrilee rounded on me in the middle of the walkway, eyes wide and face pale. "How'd you know about that?"

"Actually, I was there, visiting her ex."

"What the heck happened?" she demanded. "Did he kill her?"

"Of course not. What did the sheriff's department tell you all about it?"

She shook her head slightly, seeming to realize she might be alienating a customer.

I felt a little bad for upsetting her.

She took a deep breath and squared her shoulders. "That they were treating it as a suspicious death until the autopsy was done."

I nodded. That made perfect sense. I only wished the sheriff wasn't so quick to cast those suspicions onto Herb and me.

"I feel really bad for Frank," Merrilee said. "He's pretty torn up about it."

"I can imagine."

Mom cleared her throat and tilted her head toward the inviting front porch of the house.

"Oh, yeah." Merrilee turned and scampered up the steps, resuming her litany of delights the house had in store for us.

And the house was delightful. Lots of windows to give the rooms a more open feel, and a large, fully renovated kitchen with modern appliances. And best of all, a covered lanai out back with a small in-ground pool.

Pointing at it, I said, "Those can be a pain to take care of."

"Yes," Mom said, "but it would be worth it."

That's what I'd hoped she'd say. I was fantasizing about cooling off in that pool, when Mom asked, "How likely is it that this place will still be available tomorrow?"

Merrilee shrugged. "It's only been on the market for a couple of days, but it is priced to sell."

"I've never lived in the country," Mom said. "I would love

having all this space. Excuse me." She walked away, poking her phone's screen.

"So, was this Char the type who would commit suicide?" I asked.

Merrilee turned, giving me a deer-in-the-headlights stare. She blinked once. "No."

"If it turns out her death is a homicide," I was trying to avoid the jarring word *murder*, "is there anyone at the agency the sheriff should be looking at?"

Merrilee paled again, and a twinge of guilt tightened my chest.

I expected a denial, but after a beat, she said, "Pretty much everyone. I shouldn't speak ill of the dead, but she wasn't an easy person to work for."

"Anyone in particular who hated her?" I tried for a casual tone, as if I were only passing the time while Mom made her phone call to Clint.

Merrilee's face went from ghost pale to a rather attractive rosy color, then moved on to an angry red. "Just me. I hated her guts."

Even though I'd asked the question, I was taken by surprise. "Why?" I blurted out.

"She took Frank away from me."

Whoa, Nellie! Ms. Snark exclaimed internally.

I wondered when you'd show up, I replied.

CHAPTER SIX

Mom and Clint ended up making an offer on the second house, for full price.

I'd picked up Herb's groceries and stashed the perishables in Mom's fridge. I would take them to him in the morning, and hopefully he'd be up for some training.

After dinner, Mom, Clint, and I made idle chitchat, pretending that we weren't on pins and needles, waiting for the phone to ring.

Gone are the days when sellers only considered one offer at a time. In the current market, one could easily end up in a bidding war. And I could tell Mom really wanted that house.

"So, what happened with the little boy?" I asked Clint.

He chuckled. "We found him three houses away. He'd followed a neighbor's dog down the street–"

The house line rang and Mom jumped up to answer it. She listened, grinned, and then frowned. "I'll call you back."

She turned to Clint. "They're fine with the contract, except they want us to take out the contingency for the sale of this house." She paused, took a deep breath. "But we've got enough savings to cover a down payment."

Clint nodded. "This place is paid for, and it'll probably sell fast."

I stared at their ancient, avocado green refrigerator and kept my doubts about a quick sale to myself. After all, it was a hot market.

Mom grinned again as she hit redial. A short chat with Merrilee and she disconnected. Then she grabbed me out of my chair, and danced me around the living room.

I was thrilled to see her so happy.

⋆━━━⋆

The next morning, I didn't call ahead. I didn't want to give Herb the chance to bail on training again. At his house, I tensed at the sight of a small horde of reporters, camped on the side-walk by the street.

I texted Herb. *We're here. Got your groceries.* I meant it as a heads up, so he'd know it was me knocking, not a reporter.

Herb replied. *Front door's unlocked.*

Ignoring reporters' questions being thrown my way, I got the dogs and the groceries out of the car. Lumpy plastic bags dan-gling from each arm, I plowed forward. The reporters did not follow. On the porch, I opened the door, and stepped back to let the dogs in first.

"Hurry! Close it and bolt it." Herb's voice, shaky, from a distance.

I quickly slipped through the doorway—the grocery bags banging against the jamb—got the door closed and turned.

Herb stood on the braid rug next to his small dining table. Almost as far away from the front door as he could get. This did not bode well.

His eyes were red-rimmed, his face pasty.

"How'd you sleep last night?" I asked, for lack of anything better to say.

He let out a short bark of humorless laughter. "Not much."

I tried to think of a way to reassure him that his ex-wife being found dead in his house didn't make it unsafe. I couldn't come up with a dang thing.

"Is the deputy still here?" I asked.

He shook his head. "The sheriff's released the room."

I nodded.

Dolly trotted over and sat in front of Herb. She whined softly, sensing his anxiety.

He crouched down, started to give her an ear scratch but ended up burying his face in her ruff. I slipped past them with the grocery bags.

When I came back from putting the perishables away, Herb was sitting on the floor, Dolly in his lap. He stroked her head, avoiding eye contact with me. "If you and Dolly weren't here, I don't know what I'd do."

I opened my mouth but nothing came out. Herb's reality slammed into my chest like a brick wall. Char had been his life-line to the outside world. Without her…

"Well, we *are* here, and we're going to…" I trailed off. I'd been about to say, *teach you how to do things on your own.* But somehow that seemed harsh right now, judgmental toward Char.

My voice softer, I said, "We're going to support you."

Rule of thumb when training the anxiety-ridden veterans who receive our dogs—if things get tense, fall back on the basics. We spent the first part of the morning reviewing the on-duty and release signals and the anxiety-reducing tasks.

Perhaps I was projecting my own feelings onto the dog, but Dolly seemed worried to me. I called for a break and gestured for Buddy to lie down with her. Maybe his familiar companion-ship would soothe her.

The dog was supposed to pick up on her owner's anxiety, but not absorb it as her own.

And yet I couldn't blame her. Herb's grief and stress were palpable. It was hard not to get sucked into it.

He perched on the edge of his bed. I noted the bedding wasn't as taut, the corners not as precise as usual. I sat in the armchair that Char had occupied just three days ago.

Herb's military-honed posture was gone as well. He slumped forward, his head down.

I resisted the urge to fill the silence.

Finally, he spoke. "Char was invincible. I never, in a thousand years, would've thought anything could happen to her."

And that was the absolute crux of trauma. The unexpectedness of it, like the attack in that supposedly-empty house in Syria. I knew enough from my grad-school classes in abnormal psychology to get that much, but I had no idea what to do with it. My throat ached.

I cleared it. "This training involves a lot of repetition. Let's work on clearing the kitchen and powder room again."

I stood and led the way to the opening next to the breakfast bar, the "doorway" into the kitchen.

But halfway there, Herb stopped, blew out air. I turned.

His shoulders were back, his spine straight. "It doesn't require *this much* repetition, does it?"

I shook my head slightly.

"Don't treat me with kid gloves, Marcia. I…I need to learn this, so you can get back to your life."

A sense of proud recognition washed over me. *This* man in front of me was the Marine who'd served his country without hesitation. This was the way of the military—you did what needed to be done, no matter what.

I gave him a small smile. "Then, let's work on going outside." I headed for the back door.

By the end of the day, Herb was comfortable going into the backyard and back into the house, with Dolly clearing the space ahead of him. And we'd even spent some time on the cover task, another one that would be essential if he was ever going out into the world again.

As the dogs and I were by the front door, about to leave, Herb held up his hand in a stop gesture. "Marcia, I have something to ask, but it's okay if you say no."

My chest tightened slightly. I hoped it was something simple.

I was tired.

"You said you and your husband were starting a private investigation company."

"Yes." My chest tightened a bit more.

"I don't have any money now, but Char said she would leave me some in her will. I can pay... But down the road, when I inherit..." He trailed off.

If *he inherits*, Ms. Snark said inside my head. *If he killed her, he gets nothing.*

That was assuming Florida laws were similar to Maryland's on that, which they probably were. One wasn't allowed to profit from one's crimes.

Herb sucked in a big breath. "Could you two investigate for me, find out what really happened to Char?"

Excitement bubbled in my chest—permission to investigate would mean I wasn't merely being nosy—but at the same time a lump of dread was growing in my stomach. "Um, it's an open police investigation. We could get in trouble for interfering."

His face sagged, but he nodded. "It's only that... I can't bear the thought of her killing herself. What if it was because I told her not to come around? I mean, she puts on a good show, but inside she's pretty insecure." He didn't seem to notice that he was using present tense.

Okay, I said internally to Ms. Snark. *He wants us to investigate. Doesn't that convince you that he didn't kill her?*

No response.

Out loud, I said, "Tell you what, I can look into a few things discreetly, behind the scenes."

He gave me his first full-blown smile since we'd found his ex-wife dead in his bedroom.

⊷———⊶

On the way back to Mom's, I called Elise. "Hey, did you catch up with Will okay?" I asked by way of an opening.

All I heard was heavy breathing.

Huh? I glanced at the dashboard screen. *E&R Electronic Investigations.* Yup, I'd called the right number.

"Yes, but he didn't seem concerned about what I found out." Elise's voice was wheezy.

"You okay?"

"Yeah… I, uh…just need to catch…my breath."

"Elise, what's wrong? This is like the third time you've sounded as if you're dying when I've called."

It was at least twice last spring, when I'd called for background checks, that she'd been out of breath and wheezy. She'd said she'd been exercising, but that had sounded off at the time.

Soft snuffling sounds in my ear. Was she crying?

"What's wrong?" I said again, in a softer tone.

"I was trying to have a good cry…and it set off an attack."

"Good cry about what?" I blurted out, then realized I was being a tad too nosy.

While you're at it, find out what kind of attack, Ms. Snark added unhelpfully.

My heart squeezed in my chest. Was something seriously wrong with Elise?

"I think I told you, didn't I, what the R stands for in E and R?"

"Yes, your dog Rocket."

"He died a few months ago."

Back around when she'd started sounding out of breath. I'd caught her crying for her dog. My heart ached worse at the same time as relief washed through me. She wasn't seriously ill.

"I'm so sorry. Does crying set off asthma attacks?"

Thank you, Ms. Snark said, her tone snide, of course.

I ignored her.

"Not asthma… You train service dogs, right?"

"Yeah, for veterans with PTSD."

"So there's things they can do for anxiety?"

Ah, anxiety attacks.

"Yes, definitely. Rocket wasn't a service dog, was he?"

"No, but he and I were…in sync, I guess you'd call it. He knew when an attack was coming on and would climb up into my lap or lay on me if I was lying down."

"Two of the very things service dogs are taught to do. How bad is the anxiety?"

"Pretty bad. I can't leave the house."

My mouth fell open. *Wow, another agoraphobic.*

"I've had bad anxiety since I was a teenager," Elise was saying, "but it's gotten worse over the years. And then I got Rocket." There was a slight hitch in her voice when she said her pup's name. "He's helped me keep it in better check for the last decade. Um, could you possibly... I mean I know it's a lot to ask, but could you train a dog for me?"

She'd caught me off guard and I didn't answer right away.

"I can pay," she quickly said. "How much do they cost?"

"The agency I train for charges ten thousand."

"Dollars?" she gasped out.

"Yes, but... Well, I'm not supposed to freelance, but since you're not a veteran, I can probably get permission from the director to make an exception."

The clause was in the agency's contract only because Mattie Jones wanted to maintain control over the screening of the veterans. Ones that were irresponsible, used drugs or drank too much, or were too volatile could end up harming the dogs. And for Mattie, the canines were always more important than the *homo sapiens*, as she called people in general.

"If I do it outside the agency, it would be five thousand, plus expenses." That was two thousand dollars less than I usually got, but the training would be simpler.

"Can I maybe give you free services until it's paid off?"

Oh yeah! I jumped on that idea. "That would be perfect. That would help us get the PI agency off the ground."

We talked a bit about breeds. Rocket had been a German Shepherd mix.

"That's a big dog to be a lap dog," I commented.

Elise chuckled. Her breathing had evened out as we'd talked. "I've got a big lap."

I adjusted my mental image of her. I'd always imagined a thin, young, blue-eyed blonde, sitting at her computer working her magic. But she'd said she'd had anxiety "for years" and Rocket had made it somewhat better for the last decade. I visualized a rather large, middle-aged woman.

"Sorry, why were you calling?" Elise asked.

"Oh, I may have a new case. At least I have a couple of people for you to run background checks on. Charlene Mathers and Merrilee Brooks." I gave her as much info about them as I had, which wasn't much. But knowing where they were employed would help Elise narrow things down.

I considered having her do a check on Frank Hawkins as well, but decided to wait. I didn't want to run up the expenses for Herb. One step at a time. Get to know the victim first, and the woman who said she hated her.

As we disconnected, I pulled into the driveway at Mom and Clint's house and was happy to see the latter's light blue pickup parked next to Mom's compact.

They were at the kitchen table, steaming cups in front of them—Mom's would be her vile herbal tea, and Clint's would be the last coffee he allowed himself for the day.

A delicious fragrance, emanating from the oven, had my mouth watering and my stomach gurgling. Not sure if it was a happy gurgle or not, I grabbed a saltine from the box Mom was now keeping on the counter for me.

We exchanged some small talk, and Mom gave an excited report on the progress made toward buying the new house— an inspector was lined up to look at it and a mortgage had been applied for. When there was a lull in the conversation, I asked Clint, "You didn't happen to hear anything about the autopsy of Charlene Mathers, did you?"

He eyed me warily. "Yes, but it's only a preliminary report, and the findings were inconclusive."

"How'd she die?"

A slight pause. Mom was giving me a pointed look.

"Tox screen's not back yet," Clint said, in a matter-of-fact voice. "But signs point toward it bein' an overdose of a drug she had a prescription for."

"What signs?"

He sighed. "Empty pill bottle in her purse. It had just been refilled a few days ago."

"And she was in a locked room," I said. "So why inconclusive?"

"The suicide note was strange."

"Strange how?" I was really curious about how he'd found out all this, but I didn't want to stop the flow of info.

"My source—and by the way, Marcia, you cannot let on to anyone that you know even this much. My source said it sounded more like a business letter. They're getting a handwriting expert to examine the signature."

"You didn't see the note?" I asked.

"No, and they aren't likely to show it to anyone who hasn't been ruled out as a suspect."

"I take that to mean that I haven't been ruled out."

"They can't think Marcia did in the poor woman!" Mom protested. "She hardly knew her."

"But she was there," Clint said, "and she found the body."

And Frank, no doubt, had told the sheriff by now that Char and I'd had words the day before her death. I didn't have a strong motive, but yeah, I would still be on the suspect list at this point.

"And don't ask me to try to get a look at the note," Clint said to me. "I only know this much because one of my dep… one of the deputies called me. He thought I'd want to know about the autopsy findings."

"So why are you telling me?"

Clint let out a dramatic sigh. "Because I knew you'd harass me until I gave in. I figured I'd save us both some time and stress."

Mom rolled her eyes and got up to tend to dinner.

I ate another saltine as I digested what Clint had told me.

⊷—⊶

That night, on the phone with Will, my voice broke a little as I was trying to explain how my client had seemed that day—sad and anxious, and downright overwhelmed at times, but determined to "soldier" on.

"Marcia, are you okay?" An edge of worry in Will's voice.

"Ye…yes." *Dang hormones.*

"Her…" I quickly swallowed the *b*. "I mean, *my client* will be a suspect, if the sheriff decides it's a homicide."

I'd almost slipped and said Herb's name. But then again, Will probably knew who he was by now. No doubt the whole mess had been all over the news, thanks to the reporters camped outside Herb's house.

One advantage to agoraphobia—he hadn't had to get past them to go in and out of his home. And they had behaved, stayed out front on the sidewalk.

"But what bothers my client more is that he doesn't believe she would commit suicide."

"Most family members of suicides struggle with that," Will said. "People are good at hiding their pain sometimes."

"True, but I have to agree that she wasn't the type."

"You're not nosing around in this, are you?" Will's tone was a bit sharp. He knew me way too well.

"No," I said, perhaps too quickly. "My client actually asked if we could investigate. I told him no, but I did say I'd check some things out behind the scenes." I took a deep breath and told him about the background checks I'd ordered.

"Okay," he said, "but beyond that, we can't get involved in this. It's an ongoing police case, and I *am* still employed as a law enforcement officer."

He paused. "And anything worthwhile that Elise digs up, you turn it over to the sheriff."

I made a face at the phone. I could imagine that conversation with Sheriff Rick, and it did not go well inside my head.

"Of course I will, if it's relevant."

Another pause. He knew darn well that what I would define as relevant and what the sheriff would were likely to be very different things.

"And won't the sheriff's department be running their own

background checks?" I asked.

"Yes, but they're not Elise."

We both chuckled, and my insides relaxed.

"She is a marvel," I said. It was incredible what info Elise could dig up from the comfort of her desk chair. "By the way, she seemed to have some concerns about your case?"

"Yeah, I told her that sometimes 'it is not ours to reason why.'"

Hmm, that didn't sound all that reassuring to me, especially since the rest of that Tennyson quote was, "ours but to do and die." And it was from a poem about the Charge of the Light Brigade, which did not have an auspicious ending.

But I didn't know what Elise's concerns were. Maybe they were no big deal. I was tempted to push Will to tell me what was going on, but I resisted. The client had demanded strict confidentiality, and we couldn't afford to piss off our first paying client.

I started to tell Will about the deal I'd made with Elise, but hesitated. I should ask her first if it was okay to share her diagnosis with him.

We chatted about other things for a few minutes, including Mom's excitement regarding the new house, and signed off.

I got ready for bed and, as I climbed under the covers, I realized I felt much better than I had all day. I started to drift off with another saying running through my head, one that Mom likes to quote. *A sorrow shared is half a sorrow, a joy shared is doubled.*

I snuggled down into the mattress, glad that I had Will to share both.

A pang of guilt tightened my chest. Poor Herb didn't have anyone. Not even an *ex*-wife anymore.

CHAPTER SEVEN

During a mid-morning break in our training, I asked Herb to tell me more about Char's agency. "I guess she'd been selling real estate for a long time, to have her own brokerage."

"Not a real long time," he said from the side of the sofa bed. I sat in the lone armchair.

"She was working for a mortgage company when I met her. She was gorgeous, a natural beauty. I never guessed she was ten years older than me, until she finally told me on our third date." His face had a wistful look, then he shook himself slightly.

"She got her real estate license shortly after we married. She was really excited. She started doing that part-time, but kept her day job for a while. The owner of the agency, John Reynolds, took her under his wing. When I got my orders for Syria, I was glad she had something that would keep her occupied while I was away."

I nodded, mentally doing the math as I stroked Buddy's head in my lap. Ten years older than Herb. She was forty-five.

Or rather, *had* been forty-five. A sadness washed over me. That was only a year older than Will—way too young to die.

"How'd she end up the broker so quickly?"

"She really took to it, like a duck to water." He smiled a little. "I got a letter a couple of months into my deployment that she'd decided to quit the mortgage company. John had made her his assistant."

"That doesn't sound like a promotion."

"No, it wasn't like a clerical assistant. They worked together on the bigger deals, rich people's houses and commercial properties. Clients who expected the boss to work with them, not just some agent. But Char did most of the work behind the scenes. And he split the commissions with her."

That would explain how she could afford red-soled designer pumps.

"John died shortly before I came home," Herb was saying, "and she found out he'd left the agency to her."

"That was very generous of him." Hmm, could be another reason why Merrilee, and perhaps other agents as well, would hate Char.

When Herb didn't elaborate, I said, "Well, I guess we should get back to work."

We'd been at it for about an hour—Herb was able to enter the guest room and the hall bath again—when his phone pinged. He pulled it out and glanced at the screen.

"It's Frank. He's on the front porch. Says he has some news, but didn't want to interrupt us."

Which had already happened, but under the circumstances, I couldn't get too upset about it.

Frank gave me a wan smile when I answered the door. I gestured for him to come in.

"Sorry to interrupt." He stood in the middle of the living room, a manila envelope in his hand. He took a deep breath. "I've got news, and I'm not sure if it's good or bad."

"What?" Herb said, slightly impatient.

"The sheriff has declared it a suicide, based on the note and the fact that she was in a locked room."

Herb sank onto the corner of his bed.

"Well, it's good news in a way," Frank said, "because it means all three of us are no longer suspected of murder. But..." He trailed off, his face sagging.

"But it's hard to cope with," I said, in a low voice.

Herb nodded, his eyes shiny.

Frank held up the envelope. "The sheriff gave me a photocopy of the suicide note. Their handwriting expert confirmed it's Char's signature. I haven't had the nerve to look at it yet."

He undid the clasp, took another deep breath and pulled out a sheet of paper. He read it, turning a little gray, then passed it to Herb.

Herb's face paled as he read. He threw the paper on the floor, covered his face with his hands.

I tried not to seem too eager as I moved to pick up the note. I read the words twice, trying to make sense of them.

I'm sorry. I do love you. But what's been put into motion because of your actions is intolerable.

I don't see any other way forward. This is my only option.

I know it's harsh to just leave this note for you like this. But face-to-face, it would only get ugly.

Take care of yourself.

It was signed simply *Char*.

I looked up, glanced at Frank. His expression was self-absorbed, as he stared into space.

But Herb was glaring at me. "This is because I sent her away, because you confronted her."

Frank was shaking his head slowly. "She could be insecure about certain things, but..."

Something about the note was bothering me. Indeed, several somethings. My first take was that she was breaking up with someone—a love interest?

"This is the first you've seen this?" I said to Frank.

He nodded.

"Do you know what she's talking about, 'what's been put into action?'" I made air quotes.

"No clue–"

"If you hadn't got in her face," Herb interrupted, "if we hadn't made her leave."

"Herb, that's crazy," Frank said. "She killed herself because the dog trainer got mad at her?"

Herb jumped up and raced to the back door, flung it open. "Dolly, clear." He barely waited for her to return to the doorway before taking off out into the yard.

My mouth fell open. *What the…?* Herb was blaming me for his crazy ex-wife's suicide?

And what happened to the gratitude for my support of a few hours ago?

"Maybe you'd better go for now," Frank said in a low voice. "I'll talk to him when he's calmed down."

A bit shaky, I went to the door.

Herb had turned one of the Adirondack chairs toward the back fence. He was slumped in it.

I called Dolly's name. Sitting beside him in the cover position, she looked toward me but didn't move.

My heart ached and my stomach clenched. This was not good on so many levels. The dog had begun to transfer her attachment to Herb. And now I had to make her choose between us.

But I wasn't about to leave her here, with this out-of-control client. I called her name again, and she came to me.

"Herb, I'm gonna go. I'm taking Dolly. Will you be okay getting back inside?"

Frank stepped up beside me. "I'll help him."

I debated for a moment, not sure what to do. Ultimately, I decided I should leave these two men, who'd both known and loved Char, to deal with their grief together.

The dogs and I left the house. Then I sat in my car for a few minutes, trying to digest what had just happened.

Grief could make people irrational, but this was crazy.

Aren't they the same thing? Ms. Snark said. *Irrational and crazy?*

Shaking my head, I started my car and drove us to Mom's house.

"What are you doing home so early?" Mom blurted out as I walked through the door.

I didn't respond, not knowing where to begin.

"I was about to make lunch," she said. "Are you hungry?"

I wasn't, for a change, but I said, "Sure."

She gave me a worried look. "I'll warm up the soup from the other night." She pulled a plastic container out of the fridge and dumped its contents in a pot on the stove. No microwave for my mother, even to reheat things.

"Where's Clint?" I asked from the kitchen table where I'd settled.

"Would you believe he's taken up golf?"

I snorted. "No, not really."

She gave me a small smile and came over to sit at the table. The dogs had made themselves at home on their respective blankets along the wall.

"Now, tell me what's wrong," Mom said.

So I told her. "I've had a lot of strange things happen," I concluded, "since I started training service dogs, but never anything quite like that scene."

She reached out and squeezed my hand on the table. "Grief makes people a little crazy sometimes."

I squeezed back, then let go to get a saltine out of the box she had thoughtfully brought to the table. Now that the soup was warming, and putting off what should be a delectable fragrance, my stomach was rebelling.

"I know that grief is irrational, but still… It sounded like he was blaming me." I paused, my chest tight as I debated how much to tell her.

Crapola. A woman was dead. That was the bottom line. Sheriff Rick might want to believe it was suicide, to protect his case clearance record, but…

"The suicide note was weird." I repeated its wording, as best I could remember, wishing I'd had the presence of mind to take a snapshot of it with my phone.

"Sure sounds like she was breaking up with someone," Mom said, "or firing them."

Hmm, I hadn't thought of that last possibility. Were there any agency employees Char had been close enough to that she would say she loved them?

Honestly, I couldn't imagine the Char I had met those few times as loving anybody except herself.

The lid of the pot on the stove rattled. Mom jumped up to turn down the heat. She ladled soup into two bowls and brought them back to the table.

My stomach growled and did a back flip at the same time. What the heck did that mean?

I took a tentative sip of the soup broth. My stomach settled slightly. I ate another spoonful, this one containing a small piece of chicken and some celery.

No rebellion from Bumpkin. I ate more enthusiastically.

"What are you going to do?" Mom said, between spoonfuls of her own soup.

"I'm not sure. Will texted, while I was driving back here, that he's got a new case."

"For your PI agency?"

"No, for his day job." I'd almost said his real job. "The sheriff's department."

"So?"

"So there's no point in going home. He's not likely to be there until the wee hours of the morning, if then." Part of the appeal of becoming a PI, believe it or not, was that he could have somewhat more regular hours. Most PI cases did not require 24/7 attention, like homicide investigations often did.

Of course, if I went home I could get in a ride on my mare, Niña. I visualized her in my mind's eye, her black mane and tail flowing as she romped around the pasture.

A wave of homesickness engulfed me. But I knew I wasn't going home, at least not yet.

I finished my soup, got up and kissed my mother on her cheek.

"Mind if I leave Dolly here?"

"Of course not. She's a sweetie." She gave me a critical once-over, like only a mother can do. "You coming back for dinner?"

"Probably."

I called Buddy to follow and headed out the door.

I had a mission. To find out if Char Mathers killed herself or was murdered. And if it was the latter, by whom.

CHAPTER EIGHT

As I drove to the real estate agency, I debated what approach to use. I could pretend to be shopping for a house myself, but if Merrilee was there, she might claim me as hers. I really wanted some input from a fresh source.

I didn't see Merrilee's white Acura in the parking lot, so I was hopeful. Buddy and I entered the sprawling one-story building.

A young man sat at a large desk, in front of a small bullpen of other slightly smaller desks. Around the perimeter of the room were cubicles with frosted-glass partitions. A half dozen well-dressed people, male and female, sat at various desks, inside and outside of the cubicles, squinting at computer screens. A few of the cubicles also had one or more people sitting in front of the desks—customers, I presumed.

Or maybe they called them clients. What did I know? It had been over a decade since I'd dealt with a real estate agent. When I'd bought my cottage in Mayfair, it had been a sale by owner, the owner being Edna Mayfair herself.

"Can I help you?" the young man said, one eyebrow in the

air as he eyed Buddy.

"Yes, I'd like to look at some houses in the area. Um, something with a yard."

"How big?"

"The yard?" I said, a bit distracted as I tried to sort out the pecking order of the agency employees in the room.

"No, the house."

"Oh, at least three bedrooms, and a decent sized family room."

The receptionist flagged a young man walking by. "Davis, this lady would like to see some houses, three and two, with a family room and a yard."

"Sure." The new young man, Davis, gave me a toothy smile. "Come this way." He led me to an unoccupied cubicle and gestured toward the chair in front of the desk.

I sat and Buddy settled at my feet.

"Will your husband be joining us today?"

"No, um, I thought I'd see what's available first."

"Sure." He tapped keys on the desktop computer in front of him. "Do you have a price range in mind?"

"Under two-hundred-fifty thousand." The ones Mom had been looking at were in that range.

Davis—I had no idea if that was his first name or last—nodded and tapped more keys. "Okay, I'm finding three houses that might work, two that are the best matches."

"Can we go see them now?" I asked. I was getting antsy, afraid Merrilee would come in and insist I was her client...customer, whatever.

I did want to talk to her again, but first I wanted to find out more about the agency and Char, from this poor guy whose time I was about to waste. I felt a little guilty, but only a little.

Davis declared that he was happy to show me some houses. Soon we were in his silver Prius, Buddy's safety strap transferred to his backseat. The car looked to be several years old, but he kept it shiny and the interior neat.

First order of business, get him talking.

"So, is Davis your first or last name?"

"First. Davis Brown." He gave me another toothy smile, but nothing else.

"How long have you been an agent?"

"Not quite a year."

"At this agency that whole time?"

"Yes." A quick smile, then his gaze was back on the road.

"Do you like it?"

"Yes."

Internally, Ms. Snark rolled her eyes.

"Uh, I'm thinking about becoming a real estate agent," I said. "What all is involved?"

"In becoming one?"

"No, I mean, how does it all work? Is it hard?"

He turned his head toward me. "No, but it's fairly time-consuming." He dropped his gaze to my baby bump, then looked back out the windshield.

"What's the deal at an agency like yours? I mean, is there a hierarchy of agents or something?"

"Yes and no. Of course there's the broker, and the manager of the commercial division. He's the broker's fiancé, or was. Among the agents, those who are well established get a lot of their listings from word-of-mouth referrals. Those getting started, like me, deal with the walk-ins, like you."

Another quick smile, and he clammed up again.

"A woman named Merrilee something helped my mom find a house recently. That's how I knew about your agency."

Davis glanced my way, not smiling this time. "Oh, I wish you'd told me that before."

"Why?"

"Well, she might think that you should've been her client." He squirmed some in the driver's seat.

"But you've already looked up the houses and we're on our way."

"True, but..."

"Will she give you a hard time?"

"Oh, no," came out of his mouth, but he grimaced.

"Actually, I'd prefer if you didn't tell her about me," I said. "I didn't really care for her… I'm not sure what to call it?"

"Her somewhat intense sales pitch?" His grin seemed much more sincere this time.

I chuckled. "You don't like her either?"

"Oh, I wouldn't say that. But her style is not mine. I like to be more low key. If the house is right for the buyer, no sales pitch is needed."

"I agree. I take it she's one of the established agents."

"She's more than that. She's got an in with the bosses. So please don't repeat any of this conversation to anyone from the agency."

"Oh, don't worry." I paused. "She has an 'in.' How so?"

"Well, she used to, and I think she may again."

"Oh, that's tantalizingly vague," I said with another chuckle. Finally this guy was loosening up, and I was praying he'd keep talking.

"She was engaged to the commercial properties manager, but then they broke up and he started dating the big boss, the broker." His face sobered. "You might have heard of her. She died recently. Charlene Mathers."

"I think I did hear something about that. Was she ill?"

"No, not at all. And she was old but not that old, about fifty."

Poor Char would have been devastated. I'm sure she'd thought she appeared to be younger than her forty-five years, not older.

But this guy was only a kid, mid-twenties, if that.

Gack! When did I begin to think of mid-twenties as a kid?

"She committed suicide," Davis was saying.

I tried my best to look shocked without overdoing it. "Oh, no. Why?"

"No one knows."

"Did she and her fiancé have a fight, maybe break up?"

"I don't think so. There didn't seem to be any tension between them. Not that I saw, at least."

"How about other people at the agency? Had she had a falling out with someone else close to her?"

Davis gave me a sharp glance.

Oops, I needed to back off some.

But he answered me. "Merrilee. They used to be best friends, until Char stole Frank from her. Frank's the commercial division manager. Well, now I guess he's the broker."

"Stole him? He didn't have any say in it?"

"Well, of course he did. But that's how Merrilee saw it, that Char stole him. In fact, he was the one who pursued Char."

"In what way?" I gave him a wide-eyed, curious look.

"He was always finding an excuse to go into her office. And if anybody moved toward Char's office, he'd intercept them, ask them what they wanted to see her about, then he'd tell them he'd talk to her on their behalf."

Hmm, that seemed to be a pattern with Frank, playing the go-between. "In other words, he made himself her *de facto* second in command."

"Yeah, I guess that's what you'd call it." He pulled to the curb in front of a white cement-block rancher. "Anyway, he made himself seem indispensable. *And* he started sending Merrilee home without him, saying he needed to work late."

"They were living together?"

"Yes, and then one day he was living with Char instead."

"Did this Char have any other enemies at work?"

Davis thought about that for a beat. "Not really. She wasn't an easy woman to work for. But real estate agents, we're semi-independent, as long as we're bringing in commissions..." He trailed off, implying that the broker would leave you alone if you were making them money.

"Anybody she was particularly close to, besides Merrilee and this Frank guy, that she might have had a falling out with?"

He looked at me funny.

"Sorry. I'm just nosy. Drives my husband nuts."

"No, not that I know of." Davis pointed to the house. "This is a sweet little place. Shall we check it out?"

The toothy smile was back. He had gone into salesman mode, so I needed to switch to pretend-house-buyer mode.

I opted to go home for the evening. I told Mom that my back was bothering me and I wanted to sleep in my own bed for a night. It was the truth. And Bumpkin was now big enough that his/her weight, pushing down on my spine, wasn't helping.

The main reason, however, that I wanted to go home was to have the evening to myself so I could think. Did I really want to pursue this case any further?

I'd been gung-ho earlier, but I hadn't really gotten anything all that new out of young Davis. And I wasn't even sure that Herb wanted us to continue investigating, or that he would pay for it eventually. It had also occurred to me that this morning's events gave me the perfect excuse to bail out of an increasingly stressful situation.

But I couldn't gather my thoughts with Mom hovering, wanting to know what I'd like for dinner. So I gathered my things instead.

"Are you coming back?" Mom asked.

"I don't know. I'll call my client in the morning and see where things stand."

If there was continued tension between Herb and me, it would even be hard to finish the training. Maybe I could get Carla to do it. She knew Dolly and the tasks she could do as well as I did. We'd put the final touches on her training together last spring, when Carla had to stay isolated due to Covid—she's a cancer survivor—and she'd stayed in our guest suite for a while.

But that would mean giving her a bigger cut of the training fee, a loss of income that I could ill afford right now.

"Well, you're welcome back any time," Mom was saying. She gave me a hug.

I clung to her for a moment, fighting tears.

Dang hormones, Ms. Snark said internally.

I was pretty sure she was making fun of me.

CHAPTER NINE

Driving home, I contemplated the strange turn of events of today. The last thing I'd expected was that Herb would get mad at *me*.

Ah, the unexpected, that was the crux. It was even part of the definition of trauma—an event, usually sudden and unexpected, that is so overwhelming it cannot be processed emotionally or cognitively at the time.

Okay, by comparison to the attack on Herb in Syria and Char's sudden death, my "trauma" was minuscule. But still, the unexpectedness of it made it more stressful.

And I had enough stress in my life right now, what with the start-up of the agency and Bumpkin coming, plus trying to decide just how much training I would do in the future.

I impulsively swung north to the Marion County Animal Services shelter. Maybe searching for a potential service dog for Elise would distract me.

The staff behind the counter waved as Buddy, Dolly and I walked through. They knew me.

We strolled the outdoor cement corridors where chain-linked kennels housed dogs of pretty much every size, breed and color.

Buddy and Dolly were the litmus paper. Most of the dogs barked at them and some lunged against the mesh of their cages.

Those who only yipped a greeting and/or wagged their tails, they had potential.

One such pup, medium-sized, had a red, wavy coat. I stopped to peruse his statistics on the laminated sheet attached to his kennel door. He was a stray. The staff had estimated his age at two years and had listed his breed as a Cocker Spaniel mix.

I looked down at him. Maybe some Cocker Spaniel—definitely cute. The staff had dubbed him Cinnamon.

I snagged a volunteer and asked to take the dog into a play area. She looked skeptically at Buddy and Dolly.

"He's gotta get along with them for it to work," I said, not up for the long explanation that I was a trainer, searching for potential service dogs.

She brought the dog out on a leash and led the way to a fifty-square-foot fenced area.

Cinnamon not only got along fine with Buddy and Dolly, but he ignored the distractions around him. Dogs barked in their kennels. Volunteers shouted back and forth. But the dog stayed focused on me as I asked him to sit, lie down and stay. He knew all of those commands.

I didn't have any treats handy, but he seemed content with ear scratches and "Good boy."

I was about to go ask the office staff to let me take him as a "foster," the arrangement I had with several shelters to allow me to try out dogs. Then it dawned on me that if Herb came to his senses, I would be in Crystal County for the next week or so.

I called Carla, who was now training dogs for Mattie on her own, as well as working at the Mayfair Diner. I described Cinnamon to her and explained the situation. "Can you take him for a while? I'm in the middle of working with a veteran."

"No problem. He sounds like a sweetie. If he isn't a good fit for your new client, maybe I can find him a home."

I smiled at the phone. Carla came across as a hard-nosed, take-no-prisoners kind of person. But those of us who'd gotten to know her, we saw the animal-loving, soft-hearted woman that she was.

I was pretty sure Cinnamon would work out for Elise, but if he didn't, his new home would likely be with Carla.

I made the arrangements to foster Cinnamon and still made it home by six.

I settled the new guy in one of the dog crates in the training center, with a chew stick and a bowl of fresh water.

He laid down and started gnawing on the stick.

I texted Will but wasn't up for getting into what had happened at Herb's. I left it that I was home for a short break.

As I'd suspected, he texted back that he was working late on his new case. I sighed. But this was exactly what I'd wanted, a good stretch of alone time to think.

It was still stinking hot at this hour on a July day, but I wanted to check on my horse.

Buddy had flopped down on his bed under the window in the living room, and he didn't make a move when I called Dolly over and clicked her leash onto her collar.

"Buddy?"

He lifted his head but didn't get up.

"Are you tired, boy?"

He laid his chin back down on his paw.

I guess that's my answer. My heart squeezed in my chest. I would need to train another mentor dog soon, so Buddy could retire.

Might as well check out Cinnamon a bit more.

He was still working on his chew stick, but when I said, "Walk," he jumped up, tail wagging. A good sign that he was both energetic and people-oriented.

Unfortunately, walking the dogs around the town of Mayfair was not a great idea, from the alone-time-to-think standpoint.

First, I ran into Susanna Mayfair at the riding stable across the street from my house. "Sorry I haven't been around," I said, "to help with the chores and feeding in the mornings." She and I usually alternated mornings caring for the horses, our own and several boarders.

"Not a problem. I may get you to pay me back soon. Truman and I are talking about taking a little vacation. A romantic getaway to celebrate my birthday."

I smiled, delighted to hear that. Susie—her Aunt Edna's nickname for her—was mid-sixties, although she didn't look it. Life had not always been kind to her. But she'd begun to blossom a couple of years ago when Edna and I had located a comfort animal for her, a miniature palomino horse. And then she had met Truman Samuels, now her husband.

We chatted for a few more minutes, while petting our respective horses, Susie inside the small paddock we'd built for her Queenie and me leaning against the outside of the fence, stroking Niña's velvety black nose.

Finally, the dogs and I moved on, after I'd promised Niña I would remember to bring carrots tomorrow morning.

Next we ran into my neighbor, Sherie Wells, also out for a walk. Sherie was Susanna's contemporary, but she too did not look her age. Her smooth brown skin had almost no wrinkles.

I swear it's something in Mayfair's water. I was hoping it would help me age as graciously, even though I hadn't grown up in the town like Susanna and Sherie had.

Sherie's hair, pulled back in her usual chignon on the back of her head, was now more silver than black. She tugged at the front of her sleeveless white shirt. "Phew, it's hot today."

Then she spotted the new dog. "Who's this guy?"

"His name is Cinnamon," I said. "Although I'm hoping the person I'm training him for changes that. It's not very masculine."

Sherie grinned at me. "But it's a cute name, which matches his cuteness."

I smiled back. "True." Realizing alone time was a lost cause for now, I fell into step with her. She had always been an excellent source of advice, so I laid out the whole sorry story about Herb and his dead ex-wife, leaving out any identifying details, of course.

"Glory be, child!" she exclaimed when I'd finished. "You've landed yourself in quite a mess there."

"Yes, and I'm feeling pretty conflicted about it now. Do I continue to investigate, like my client originally wanted me to? Or do I take advantage of today's events to get out of said mess? And before you ask, I haven't talked to Will yet about today. He's working a new case."

"Okay, tell me again why it might be suicide," Sherie said.

I went through it all again—Char seeming to be upset that Herb might not need her anymore, the locked room, the suicide note, and she'd apparently died of an overdose of her own medication.

"And since the sheriff decided it's suicide," Sherie added, "you and your client are no longer murder suspects."

"True," I said. "So you're saying I should let it go?"

She shook her head. "I'm not saying anything yet." We'd reached the corner of Main Street and Mayfair Avenue. Sherie turned left, toward the Methodist church. "What points to it not being suicide?"

"She wasn't really the type who would do that, and the strange wording of the note."

"And?"

"The fact that a lot of her employees didn't like her much."

"Quitting would make more sense than murder," Sherie pointed out.

"Her fiancé's ex-girlfriend hated her guts." I paused. "But if she'd killed the woman, I doubt she would've volunteered that information to me like she did."

We had reached the edge of the church's parking lot. Sherie stopped in the shade of a live oak tree and turned to me. "Anything else?"

I thought for a moment, then shrugged. "My client wasn't coping well with the idea that she'd killed herself."

Sherie raised her eyebrows.

"Yeah, okay," I admitted, "that's a pretty normal reaction on the part of a loved one."

While silently moving her lips, Sherie ticked off items on her fingers. I suspected she was running through my lists again.

I was right.

"I count four good indicators that it was suicide," Sherie said when she reached her little finger. She tapped her thumb. "And a very good reason for leaving it alone. *You* are no longer a suspect."

I nodded. "And only one truly solid indicator that it wasn't, the strangeness of the suicide note." I blew out a long sigh. The tension in my chest and shoulders, that had been there all day, relaxed some.

"Has this helped?" Sherie asked with a smile.

"Yes. I'm still not totally sure what I'm going to do, but this has helped. A lot."

"Good." She pointed toward the church. "I need to talk to the reverend about using the church hall for this month's meeting." Sherie was the chairperson of our local Chamber of Commerce.

"Thanks."

"You're welcome." She started to turn away.

"Uh, is it too hot for a hug?" I asked.

She turned back. "It's *never* too hot for a hug."

◆———▶

"Mar-see-a!" Edna Mayfair called out from the Mayfair Motel's porch, as the dogs and I walked past.

Apparently my adopted hometown wasn't done with me yet. I plastered on a smile, turned, and waved to my octogenarian friend.

"Hold on. I've got somethin' for ya." She darted into the Victorian-style building.

The dogs and I went up the motel's porch steps to wait for her.

A minute later, she came out, carrying a paper shopping bag with a name imprinted on it—of a department store chain that had gone out of business two decades ago.

Edna ducked her head, a gesture a little out of character.

The muumuu covering her plump frame today was black with bright red hibiscus flowers on it, my favorite of her multicolored collection.

"I made you some things. I hope you like 'em." She eyed my expanded stomach under my tee shirt. "I mean, I know you youngsters don't mind your baby bulge stickin' out, but I thought maybe…" She trailed off and thrust the bag toward me.

She leaned down to introduce herself to Cinnamon, who sniffed and then happily licked the fingers she extended.

I peeked inside the bag, lifted the contents out, one garment at a time. They were oversized camp shirts, four of them of various colors, with carefully stitched collars and breast pockets. The workmanship was meticulous.

"They got three-quarter sleeves," Edna said, straightening, "but they roll up easy to short-sleeved. So you can wear 'em now and into the fall, either over your tees, or by themselves."

I opened my mouth, but a lump had formed, not letting words out. My eyes stung. I cleared my throat. "They're gorgeous. Thank you."

Edna's body visibly relaxed. "I hope you don't mind, but I kinda think of your little one as another grandbaby."

My chest ached. Her only "grandchild" was her great-nephew, Susanna's son Dexter, who'd suffered prenatal brain damage at the hands of his wife-battering father. Dexter, now grown, held a job, but he still lived with Edna and he wasn't likely to ever marry or reproduce.

"I don't mind at all," I managed to choke out. "And thank you for these. I love them."

At home, I laid the shirts out on my bed. There was a white one and a black one. The other two were my favorite colors, red and turquoise. The fabric was a lightweight cotton that would breathe on the hottest of days.

I was thrilled to have the shirts but also to see Edna in such a good mood. For a while there, both Susanna and I had feared that she might not pull out of the depression she'd sunk into during the worst of the Covid pandemic. Even after the motel was allowed to reopen, she had let Susie and Dexter continue to do most of the work. Susie had been fine with her Aunt Edna retiring—she'd hired extra help for the motel—but it was so unlike Edna to be idle.

I was happy to see that she was sewing again, and that the idea of a new baby she could spoil was lifting her spirits.

After hanging the shirts lovingly in the closet, I went out to the newer part of the house. Our home was a bit of a patchwork quilt, with my old cottage on one end—now my training center and the guest suite—and Will's former house on the other end, where our study, bedroom, and the nursery were located. In between, we'd had a modern section built to connect the two older buildings, with the kitchen and a big living room/family room.

I sat at the breakfast bar and grabbed the pad on which we wrote our grocery lists. Again, I wrote down the points I'd run down for Sherie—one list titled *Reasons to Leave It Alone* and the other *Reasons to Investigate*.

And again, the *Leave It Alone* list was longer and more convincing, especially when it occurred to me to add *Herb may not pay for investigation; he thinks it's suicide.*

Crapola! I might already be out several hundred dollars for the background checks I'd already ordered. I could probably make them part of the barter arrangement with Elise, but still that meant fewer free background checks in the future.

I booted up my laptop to check my email, hoping to be able to cancel the background checks, if Elise hadn't done them yet. But she had. There were two emails from her, labeled *preliminary report–Charlene Mathers* and *preliminary report–Merrilee Brooks*.

The report on Char confirmed the history of her career that Herb had told me. But Elise had also discovered that she'd been hospitalized briefly, in her early twenties, after a suicide attempt.

My stomach clenched.

I opened the email regarding Merrilee. Elise asked, *Do you want me to dig deeper into this lady's finances?*

I skimmed the report. Merrilee was thirty-two and had never

been married. She made, on average, sixty-five thousand a year in real estate commissions, which was more than a decent income for this rural area of Florida, where the cost of living was relatively low.

My gaze caught on the phrase, *She bought a house last year, for $700,000.* I gasped.

No wonder Elise had made the price bold. That was almost three times the cost of the house Mom and Clint had a contract on, and of the ones I'd seen earlier with Davis. All of which were in nice areas and would be perfectly adequate for a single person or couple.

How in the world could Merrilee afford the mortgage on a house that expensive?

I so wanted to tell Elise yes, dig deeper. But I didn't. Reluctantly, I emailed her to put things on hold for now. And I asked her if it would be okay to tell Will why I was training a dog for her.

She responded with *Sure you can tell him. Let me know when you want more info.*

Curious, as always, I looked up Merrilee's house on Google maps and switched to street view. It was a mini-mansion, on three acres in one of the few truly swank communities in Crystal County.

⊷——⊷

The next morning, I was leaning toward ditching the investigation but was still a little ambivalent. I had decided on one thing, however. I was going to enjoy this mini-break from the training.

I'd promised Susanna I'd take care of the horses this morning, so I dragged myself out of bed way earlier than I would've liked.

Will had come and gone during the night, catching a few hours of sleep. He'd left a note on the breakfast bar that said only, *Love you!*

A ride on Niña around the fields behind our house went a long way toward restoring my emotional balance. After hosing the sweat off my horse, and chuckling as I watched her roll in the dirt—the only way horses can scratch their backs—I headed home for a shower of my own.

A text came in from Will while I was out back playing with Cinnamon, getting to know him better.

I may get home early today. Caught my bad guy. Wanna paint the nursery later?

I called him. "Can you talk?"

"Yeah, my perp's being processed over at the jail. I'm gonna talk to him again and write up my report. Hopefully I can be home by around two. So, why are you off today? I thought you weren't taking any breaks with this client's training."

"I wasn't planning to." I took a deep breath and told him about Herb's strange reaction to the suicide note.

"Grief makes people crazy sometimes," Will said. "He'll come to his senses. But that note definitely sounds hinky. I wouldn't be closing the case that quick if it were mine."

Dang! He had to say that. Now I was back to wanting to get to the truth.

"Would you be okay then with continuing to look into this?" I asked, not sure which way I wanted him to answer. "I mean, if it's been ruled a suicide, then we're not interfering in an active case anymore, right?"

"Theoretically. Is this guy willing to pay us?"

"He was, out of what he's supposed to inherit from the woman. But after yesterday, I'm not sure where things stand."

"And if we happen to uncover that he killed her, he won't inherit."

"I can't begin to imagine this guy killing anyone, much less the woman he needed to bring him stuff from the outside world."

"But with Dolly, he'll be able to go out again."

"Theoretically." I tossed his word back at him.

"Maybe he decided she was now worth more to him dead than alive."

"I still don't see it. He's a gentle soul."

Will snorted. "An ex-Marine who's a gentle soul?"

"Former Marine. They don't like 'ex.' And yes, he's your quintessential nice guy."

"Nice guys occasionally turn out to be axe murderers."

I stopped arguing. Will was your quintessential cynical cop, and there was no getting him to assume people had a better side until he saw it for himself.

"So what are you going to do about your client?" he asked.

"Not sure. I think I'm gonna give him today to contact me. Maybe I'll call him tomorrow, if I don't hear from him. He needs to finish his training in order to get Dolly…" I trailed off.

"In the meantime, have you decided on a color for the nursery?"

I smiled at the phone. Will often seemed to know exactly when to change the subject. "How about the light green. I saw some cute Winnie the Pooh curtains that would go with that, regardless of the baby's gender."

"I'll pick up the paint on my way home," Will said, and we signed off.

I walked into the nursery and stared at the paint splotches on the wall. The green one was called *Spring Lawn.*

Why can't they just call it light green? Ms. Snark complained.

Good question. I began prepping the room for painting.

━━━━

Herb called at one-thirty. "Marcia, I'm sorry," he said before I'd even said anything. "I overreacted. Can we start up the training again this afternoon?" His voice was rushed, anxious.

I quietly blew out air. "I can't today, Herb. I've made other plans. But I can come over in the morning."

The sound of heavy breathing in my ear. Was he hyperventilating?

"Herb, are you okay?"

"Yes… Well, not completely."

"What's going on?"

The heavy breathing again.

"I think I might…uh, maybe…" He stopped. The sound of air being sucked in. "I may be losing it. I'm hearing voices."

CHAPTER TEN

Herb was hallucinating? *Double crapola!*

Was he more unstable than I'd thought, beyond the PTSD and agoraphobia? Hallucinations were a symptom of psychosis, a complete break with reality. My stomach tensed.

Then I gritted my teeth, as anger swelled in my chest. Talk about mixed emotions.

Herb has a counselor, I reminded myself, *assigned by the Veterans Administration. It's her job to sort this out, not mine.*

And I *did* have other plans now for the afternoon, with my husband. Plans I really, really wanted to keep.

"Herb, you should talk to your counselor about this."

"I called her, got her voicemail."

"Is she good?"

"Oh, yeah, I really like her. You're right. I should wait for her call back." Silence, but no heavy breathing now.

"I wish we were farther along," he finally said, "and you could leave Dolly with me. I'm between a rock and a hard place here. I can't leave this house, but now I can't stand being in it either."

My heart felt like the rope in a tug of war. I felt bad for him, but no, I wasn't going to leave Dolly with him yet, without my supervision. And no, I did not want to spend my afternoon with this neurotic, perhaps psychotic, man instead of my husband.

But an idea was forming in my brain, a possible solution.

"Hey, do you remember Carla?"

"The woman who was with you some of the times we Zoomed last spring?"

"Yes. Let me see if she's available to bring Dolly over and work with you some today. You can just review basics, get back into the swing of it. But I need your permission to tell her what's going on, and maybe tell her boss too, so she can get off work. Her boss is a friend of mine, and she's not a blabbermouth. She'll keep it confidential."

As I said all that out loud, I was thinking, *This is crazy.* But it might work out. It was worth a try.

Herb agreed. I left a note for Will and hurried over to the Mayfair Diner.

Where I had a stroke of luck—both Carla and Jess, the diner's owner, were there.

The diner had opened for dinner a couple of months ago, and Carla was the new evening manager. Plus, she was renting a room from Jess, who lived in a big old farmhouse by herself, except for her dog Biscuit.

I told Carla I needed to speak to both of them, if possible. I really didn't want to go through the whole explanation twice.

She scanned the diner. The lunch crowd was thinning out. "We should be able to pull that off in a few minutes." She gestured toward a corner booth. "In the meantime, lemme bring you a new soup we're trying out, on the house." Her eyes shifted, breaking contact.

What's that about?

A few minutes later, Lisa, Jess's waitress of long standing, brought me a bowl of soup. It smelled delicious, the fragrance reminding me of something, but I couldn't pin it down.

It was rich with chunks of tomato and bits of celery and

something that tasted like seafood. I'd already had lunch, but I scarfed the soup down anyway.

When things had calmed down to the point where Lisa could handle everything for a bit, Jess and Carla sat down across from me in the booth.

Carla was taller and thin, with a more angular face. Jess was petite, only five-four, and despite being such a great cook, she never gained weight, which made me extremely jealous. Both had their medium-length dark hair up in short ponytails and covered by hairnets, and they wore matching white aprons over their tee shirts and jeans.

I noticed that Jess no longer wore the chef's jacket her late fiancé had talked her into, saying it added class to the place. She'd continued to wear it for a while after he'd been killed two summers ago.

But the jacket had always seemed out of place to me. A diner in a rural community isn't supposed to be classy.

"What's up?" Carla asked, eyeing my already empty bowl over the mask she still wore because she was immuno-compromised.

I filled them in as succinctly as possible.

"Wow, that poor guy," Jess said.

"What a double bind," Carla said. "He's afraid to be in the house by himself—and I can't say as I blame him—but he can't leave."

"Exactly. I'm pretty sure the voices are his imagination, but I'm really worried about his mental health right now." Actually, I was terrified that he'd become suicidal.

"What's the set-up of his house?" Carla asked.

I wasn't sure why she was asking, but I filled her in on the layout. "What are you thinking?"

"That he needs someone there with him, more than he needs to train. I can't leave until after the dinner crowd eases up some–"

Jess opened her mouth, but Carla held up her hand. "I'm not leaving you to deal with the Friday night crowd on your own."

She turned to me. "But I like Herb. I don't want anything to happen to him. Tell him I'll be there by ten, with Dolly. And we'll stay the night and do some training in the morning, until you can get there."

"That sounds like an even better plan than mine. And I'll bring Cinnamon with me in the morning. We'll trade dogs at Herb's house."

I called Herb and told him Carla's idea.

Air whooshed out on the other end of the line. "That would be terrific. Frank said he'd come over for a while this evening, so I should be fine until Carla can get here. Tell her she's a saint."

I signed off and repeated his words.

"Uh, no," she said with a chuckle. "I doubt I'm up for sainthood, but I'm glad to lend a hand. Our veterans deserve all the help we can give them."

I nodded, but guilt tightened my chest. Was I being selfish by not being willing to go over there myself?

Sometimes we have to take care of ourselves. My inner mom's voice this time. I didn't hear from her all that often anymore.

"Did you like the soup?" Jess asked, her face all innocence… a little too innocent. "It was Carla's idea."

"It's delicious. What's in it?"

"It's mock Maryland crab soup," Jess said, a sly smile on her face now.

"That was crab? I couldn't quite place it."

"But it's a fair facsimile for Maryland crab soup?" she asked.

"Oh yeah."

The sparkle in Carla's eyes said she was grinning behind her mask. "It's not crab. It's tofu seasoned with Old Bay Seasoning."

Old Bay, the seasoning that made anything crab-related a true Maryland product.

"I had you in mind as a test subject when I created it," Carla added. "We needed a vegetarian alternative on our dinner menu."

"Wow, Mayfair has vegetarians?"

"A few," Jess said, "but the Buffalo burgers are also bringing in folks for dinner from out of town." Jess raised buffalo on her farm. "And sometimes other folks in their parties want vegan."

"I'll bet Edna loves that you're bringing in people from out of town," I said. As the town matriarch, she was constantly scheming to attract more tourists.

⊷——⊷

Will was home by the time I got back, standing in the middle of the living room, a slip of paper in his hand.

Sly grins were apparently contagious because he wore one too. He turned the paper around for me to read. It was a cashier's check for three thousand dollars.

"Wow!"

"Of course, half will go to Elise. I feel a little guilty about keeping the rest, since she did all the work."

"Didn't you go talk to some of the people?" I said.

"I thought I was supposed to, but the client was happy with the info Elise came up with. Only one guy looked fishy. She couldn't find out much about him, and finally decided he was living under a false identity. I was going to go talk to him, but the client said the fact that he gave a false name was enough to disqualify him from employment."

"Well, that case was sure easy," I said, now grinning myself, "and over quick."

"Yup. The check came just after I got home, by private courier."

"This client must be loaded. I hope he needs our services again."

"Me too. Let's paint."

"In a minute." I gestured for him to follow me into the training center and introduced him to Cinnamon. While Will scratched behind the dog's ears, I explained the arrangement I'd made with Elise.

Will loved the set-up. "That'll give us some breathing room financially, as we get the agency started."

"Exactly what I thought."

⊷——⊷

I woke up the next morning feeling optimistic, if not well rested. It had been a challenging night.

I had felt the baby move for the first time, and in true Bumpkin form, it wasn't a gentle flutter but a swift kick to one of my kidneys.

I'd laid still in bed, holding my breath, until I felt it again. Then I woke Will up and placed his hand over that spot. Bumpkin obligingly kicked his palm.

We'd laid there, grinning at each other, for the longest time, before I drifted back to sleep.

On the way to Crystal County, I tried to evaluate my feelings about Herb. I was starting to get what Char had implied that first day.

It wasn't so much that Herb had "special needs" or that he was a "sensitive soul." But perhaps he hadn't been quite hardened enough before being deployed, and the horrors of the war in Syria and the resulting agoraphobia had left him a needy person. It wasn't necessarily his natural personality, but it was where he was now, thanks to those life events.

I had to decide how far I was willing to be sucked into that neediness. It would be too easy for Herb to substitute me for Char.

I pulled to the curb in front of his house and texted Carla, *I'm here.*

Meet you at the door.

How did the night go?

Uneventful. No strange noises.

Carla, wearing a mask, opened the door as we reached the porch.

Herb stood in the middle of the living room, looking more relaxed than he usually did when the front door is open. Dolly stood at his knee, her tail wagging by way of greeting.

He waved at me, then said goodbye to Carla, repeating "thank you" at least a half-dozen times.

"You're welcome," Carla said back over her shoulder, as she stepped out onto the porch. She pulled the door partway closed behind her.

"This must be Cinnamon." She crouched down to the dog's level. His tail blurred, he was wagging it so hard, as she petted him.

She stood and took his leash. "I'll work with him some on the basics."

"No need," I quickly said. "He's for someone else I know, who has agoraphobia. It's not through the agency."

Carla cocked her head. "I thought we weren't supposed to freelance."

"She's not a veteran. I need to call Mattie, though, and clear it with her."

"Is she like Herb, can't leave her house?"

"Yes. Different cause, but the same issue."

Her eyes, above her mask, had an unfocused, faraway look for a moment. "As hard as things have been at times for me, I can't even imagine not being able to walk to my own mailbox." She refocused on me, her expression and voice firm. "I will work with the dog on some basics."

My chest warmed even as my stomach tightened. I was being paid for Cinnamon's training—in background checks, not money. So I should pay Carla something if she helped with the training. But cash would be scarce for the next few months.

Carla patted my shoulder. "I owe you, Marcia. Without your hospitality, I would have been homeless." She'd been fired and then evicted last spring when, because of her vulnerable immune system, she'd refused to return to her old waitressing job while Covid was still rampant.

"Plus," she continued, "you saved the man I love from a murder charge."

It was the first time she'd admitted to me that she loved Russ Fortham, the Air Force pilot she and I had trained a dog for last winter and spring. They'd been dating ever since.

I nodded, suddenly choked up. My eyes stung. *Blinkety-blank hormones!*

Without further ado, Carla and Cinnamon marched down the sidewalk to her car.

I sniffed loudly and nudged Herb's door open.

His face and voice were excited as he described how they'd been practicing going into the hallway and the hall bath again. "But I'd really like to try going out front today."

My tight muscles relaxed. It had been a good move to get someone over to stay with him last night.

"In a little while," I said. "I'd like to work on going into other rooms some more."

His expression only dimmed slightly.

After going in and out of the hallway a couple of times, we tackled the guest room.

I opened the door, and Dolly did her thing running around and into all the corners, even sniffing under the closet door.

"I, uh, know it's irrational," Herb said, from just outside the room's doorway. "But could you open the closet so I can see into it?"

"Sure." I walked over and did so. It was a standard sized bedroom closet. "Clear, Dolly."

She stuck her nose in and sniffed at both ends of the small space, ran to Herb and sat, her tail sweeping across the beige carpet.

Herb smiled down at her and eased into the room, his head swiveling as he checked the corners himself. A deep breath and a big sigh.

"Good job," I said.

He walked around the room for a moment, then picked up the stack of bed linens Carla had left on the end of the stripped mattress. "Might as well pop these in the washer."

He let Dolly lead the way and clear the hall again. But when he got to the door at the end of the hallway, he juggled the linens to free a hand to open it and stepped right through the doorway.

I was about to commend him for that, until a thought stopped me. "It's great that you didn't feel the need to have her clear the living room, but you should still let Dolly go first. Since Frank has a key and lets himself in, you don't want to be startled if he has come in while you're elsewhere in the house."

He nodded and headed for the kitchen, where he jammed the linens into the washing machine in one corner.

"Speaking of keys, Frank gave Char's back to me." He fished a loose key out of his jeans pocket. "Maybe you should have it while we're doing the training." He held it out.

I couldn't think of a way to say no without getting into the whole I-don't-want-to-be-your-replacement-for-Char issue, which would disrupt the good vibes we had going at the moment. So I took the key, reluctantly. But once the training was done, I would make a point of giving it back to him.

And by then, hopefully, he'd be able to run his own errands. We had a ways to go, though, before that point.

We returned to the hallway. With very little hesitation, Herb was able to go into the third bedroom after Dolly cleared it.

He stood near the doorway and took in the room. It was set up as a study, with bookcases and a desk along the perimeter and open space in the middle. "I used to love this room," he said wistfully.

"And you will again. It's a nice study."

"Thanks." He walked to the window, and opened the mini-blinds. "One thing that won't be the same though—I used to have a great view of an orange grove." He gestured toward the glass. "Now all I see is an ugly warehouse."

I moved over beside him and gazed out at his side yard. His was the last house on this side of the cul-de-sac, and beyond his property was a big metal one-story building surrounded by asphalt. A couple of tractor-trailers were parked nearby.

"Oh, I didn't realize that industrial park was so close to you." To get into his development, one drove past the park and made a few turns on various residential streets, before coming to his street, Paradise Court.

But it sure as heck wasn't paradise anymore with such ugly neighbors.

As we stood there, a distant rumbling reached my ears. My first thought was thunder, but it was too constant. "Is that coming from over there?" I pointed toward the industrial park.

Herb nodded. "Sometimes it gets pretty loud. And we hear it a lot at night too. Louise—that's my next-door neighbor—has filed noise complaints but the county never does anything."

I'd never noticed the sounds before, but we'd been on the other end of the house, with several closed doors in between.

Herb looked longingly at his side yard. "Can we try going out front after lunch?"

I smiled at him, relieved that our training seemed to be back on track. "Sure."

We returned to the kitchen. Herb put the wet linens in the dryer. Then he made turkey and tomato sandwiches for our lunch.

My stomach gurgled happily, indicating Bumpkin's pleasure.

"So, how is it exactly that Char ended up owning half your house?" Ms. Snark asked while I had my guard down.

But Herb didn't seem to take offense. "At the time we were splitting up, my disability paperwork hadn't gone through yet, so I had no income. I couldn't get a mortgage or even rent a place. Char agreed to hold the mortgage."

He took a bite of sandwich. I thought that was all he was going to say on the matter, but he added, "She said it appeased her guilt over our break-up."

"So splitting up was her idea?" Ms. Snark snuck another nosy question in.

"Yeah, but it was the right thing to do. I was holding her back, and…well, she had changed while I was away." He rose and took our plates to the sink.

I mentally slapped a hand over Ms. Snark's mouth, before she could push him for more. My internal image of her is my younger self—early twenties. Was I keeping her from growing up, by trying to keep her separate from the rest of me?

In my mind's eye, Ms. Snark shook her head. I tentatively removed the imaginary hand.

Harumph. Who says I want to grow up?

I shook my own head slightly.

"What?" Herb said as he returned to the table.

"Oh, nothing. I was wool-gathering."

"Can we try out front now?" he asked, an eager glow in his eyes.

"Let's do it," I said, pleased and a little surprised by the turn-around in his emotions and the progress we'd made today.

His small rancher had a long, verandah-style porch. I could've told Dolly to *clear porch*, but I had one more trick to show Herb. "Dolly, lead."

She darted out the door, looked to her left, whirled around and looked to her right, and then sat.

"That's the command," I said, "that you use when going out-side from a building, if there's no enclosed space."

Herb smiled down at Dolly, gave her a treat, and stepped past her. He turned slowly in a half circle, his smile growing. "This is gonna work, Marcia. I'm really believing now, it's gonna work!"

I returned the smile. "From here, you can see the whole front yard." There were no trees or bushes, no doubt part of the appeal of the property. He could readily see anyone approaching the house.

"Do you have a car?" I asked.

He shook his head. "I sold it a while back, since I couldn't go anywhere anyway." He grinned again. "Guess I'll need to find a new one."

"We could make that your first public outing, but not today." A car dealership would be easier to negotiate than most places. A big showroom, not a lot of people. And owning a car again would definitely improve Herb's independence.

Herb had stepped down off the porch, while I'd been think-ing all that through. He walked around the yard, beaming, with Dolly beside him.

After we'd practiced going in and out of the front door sev-eral times, I called for a break. We went back inside.

I was contemplating going home, or at least to my mother's house. I needed a nap. "I think I–"

At the same time, Herb said, "I need to ask–"

We both stopped. "You first," I said.

"Uh, I know this is a huge imposition," Herb said, "but could you stay here tonight? Last night was the first time in a long time that I didn't hear…the noises. And I was finally able to get some decent sleep."

"What noises are we talking about, exactly?" I asked. Somehow I didn't think he meant the rumbling from the industrial park.

His cheeks flushed. "Remember I said this house is haunted. I hear moaning at night, and sounds that could be voices…" He trailed off.

So he thinks the voices he's hearing are ghosts?

Or he really is *hallucinating,* Ms. Snark said, playing the devil's advocate.

"But last night," Herb shook his head, "maybe Carla being here discouraged the ghost, or something…"

I was trying to formulate a response when Dolly raised her head and looked toward the door. The low growl of an engine registered. I frowned at the dog.

She hung her head slightly but then tilted it to one side. I swear, if she could talk, she'd be saying, "But I didn't bark, Mom. I just looked up."

Our service dogs are trained to ignore random noises. They can't be barking at any old thing, since veterans with PTSD often startle easily. The dogs are supposed to lower anxiety, not make the vet jump with unexpected barking.

"That's probably the mailman," Herb said. "Can I ask another favor? Milt, the old guy across the street who usually gets my mail, he called this morning and said he's sick."

"It's not Covid, I hope."

"No, he said it was only a cold. He tested. It was negative."

I was considering suggesting that we go get his mail together, when Dolly turned her head toward the door again.

A knock a nanosecond later, followed by the rattle of a key in the lock.

"Herb, it's me, Sam." A middle-aged man in a postal service cap stuck his head inside.

No need to get the mail. It had come to us.

Herb gestured for him to come in.

The mailman stepped over the threshold, an envelope in his hand. "Um, I got one of these too. Thought you should see it right away..." He trailed off.

Herb took the envelope and stared at it. "It's from the county."

Nervous butterflies flitted inside my chest, in response to the worried look on the mailman's face.

Herb had opened the envelope and was reading the letter. He swayed on his feet, his face ghost-white. "They're taking my house."

CHAPTER ELEVEN

With a shaking hand, Herb gave me the letter. The logo was that of Crystal County, with *Planning Office* underneath it.

I skimmed through the letter, my eyes snagging on the words *eminent domain*. The signature was an illegible scrawl.

I went back and read the last two paragraphs more thoroughly.

The purpose for this seizure is confidential, but a judge has authorized it, as well as the confidentiality order.

A ten-thousand dollar bonus will be paid to each landowner who can sign over their deed and vacate within thirty days.

Strange, Ms. Snark commented.

Yeah.

"I'm calling Frank," Herb said.

Hadn't he read the next to last paragraph? I pointed it out to him.

He shook his head, his lips pressed together in a stubborn line. "I'm calling him anyway. He may be able to find out what's going on." He took the letter back.

I opted to take the dogs out into the yard for a bathroom break, carefully avoiding the bedroom window—I wasn't in the mood to find a dead body right now. But I needed some space to think.

I had to decide fairly soon if I was willing to stay here tonight. Herb had been doing so much better today, making tons of progress. And then the mailman had arrived.

If he could only stay stabilized long enough for us to get in some more training, get to the point where I could leave Dolly with him, then both his anxiety and the limitations of his agoraphobia would ease. And he'd be better able to cope with life.

The sooner the better, since said life had been lobbing curve balls at him lately.

I'd brought an overnight bag but hadn't yet called my mom about staying there. I hadn't known exactly what I would find when I'd arrived here this morning.

I felt kinda weird about staying in a client's house, even though Carla had done so last night. But maybe we were letting the boundaries get too blurry, in addition to the whole letting-Herb-get-too-dependent-on-me part. I'd only stayed under the same roof as my client once before, but she was female. And that situation had gotten quite messy, in the end.

Shaking my head, I called the dogs over to me. A clear decision felt even farther out of reach. Half holding my breath, I went back inside.

"Can everyone come here instead?" Herb was saying into the phone, one hand clutching at his hair.

A pause. His tense body relaxed significantly. "Yeah, that's great. I've got soda and coffee." He disconnected.

"Frank said he hasn't got a clue what this is about, but he's going to discreetly ask around." Herb held up the phone. "And that was Louise calling. Pretty much everyone on the street got a letter. They're holding a meeting tonight to decide what to do. Louise said she'd tell them to come here. And she's bringing brownies."

Well, that half made my decision for me. I still wasn't sure where I would sleep tonight, but my curiosity demanded that I stay for this meeting. And for the brownies.

I excused myself and went back outside to call my mom. She

reassured me it was fine if I came over later, or not. "Just call before ten and let me know."

I told Herb I would stay at least for the meeting, but I'd need a nap in the meantime.

He remade the guest room bed. I left Dolly with him but kept Buddy with me.

Again feeling a little weird about the set-up, I opted to lock the guest room door. Buddy lay down in front of it, and I stretched out on the bed.

I took a deep breath. Nothing like the fragrance and feel of fresh linens on a bed. It was my last thought for a couple of hours.

When I awoke and trundled out into the hallway, I noted that Herb had left the door to the living room open. I smiled, then yawned. He really was making good progress.

He had ordered a pizza for dinner. After we'd scarfed it down, he asked if I would man the front door when people started to arrive.

Surprisingly, Milt from across the street was the first. He mumbled his last name as he introduced himself. I didn't catch it.

"I thought you were sick?" I blurted out, wishing I had a mask with me.

"I'm doing much better. And yes, I tested for Covid. It was negative." He hobbled into the room, leaning heavily on a cane. He was a rather short but heavyset man, with almost no hair, only a white fringe that was a little too long.

After shaking hands with Herb, he said, "I came early so I could talk to you about something." He gave me a meaningful look, like he wanted me to get lost.

I tapped the knob of the front door and gave him a what-can-I-do shrug.

He frowned and hobbled toward the kitchen, Herb following him.

I could make out enough of what was being said to get the gist of it. Milt was begging off from fetching Herb's mail in the future, saying he was too unsteady on his feet to do all that walking.

"That's okay," Herb said, pointing to Dolly, sitting beside him. "I'll be able to get my own mail soon. Hey, why don't I get yours and bring it to your door?"

I didn't catch Milt's response.

A knock on the door, and the rattle of a key, even though the door wasn't locked.

I stepped over and tried to turn the knob, but the owner of the key had accidentally locked it. I flipped the lock and opened the door, and was face to face with a huge platter of brownies.

My mouth watered. Behind the platter was a tiny gray-haired lady.

"You must be Louise," I said.

"Yes, and I could really use a cup of coffee."

"Herb has it going in the kitchen."

She carried the brownies to the table.

Others arrived in clumps, and soon the living room and dining area were crammed with people. Nine households were represented by twelve people, some of them couples.

Herb had converted his bed back into a sofa and one fellow had brought a few folding chairs. Good thing, since none of these folks looked like they would be able to get up again if they sat on the floor.

I perched on a breakfast barstool, so I could keep an eye on the brownies. Dolly and Buddy settled at my feet. When a couple of people had taken some, I snagged one and took a bite.

Bumpkin was pleased—s/he gave me a friendly little kick.

The meeting quickly devolved into chaos with people trying to talk over each other, some speculating on what all the confidentiality stuff was about, but most suggesting what should be done. Some wanted to hire a lawyer. Others felt that was too expensive.

Milt had perched on one of the barstools near me. He thumped his cane firmly on the wooden floor. "Quiet!"

Most people stopped talking, more in shock, I suspected, than anything else.

"I think we should consider their offers," Milt said.

Chaos erupted again. Cries of "No way," and "Are you crazy?"

I glanced across the dining area, where Herb sat in one of the folding chairs. His face was totally white. I worried that he might pass out.

Milt thumped the cane again, twice. "Did y'all even check out the link in the letter to see what they're offering for your house? I thought it was pretty generous for mine."

"We need to be united," someone yelled from the far corner of the living room.

"Not necessarily." Sam the mailman shook his head. "Sorry, Milt, but if we sue the county to keep our houses and we win, they won't want your house alone."

"True. And I'll be happy for you all if that happens. But I've been thinkin' about movin' into one of those retirement communities. This would save me the hassle of havin' to sell my house."

More attempts to shout him down.

Another thump. "I'm just sayin' you all oughta look at what they're offering and at least consider it."

I was hoping he'd had his say and would be quiet now. With everyone staring our way, I couldn't grab another brownie without being obvious.

As others started talking over each other again, I snagged one. Then I slipped outside with the dogs to give them a bathroom break, and myself a break from the noise. It was giving me a headache.

The meeting was breaking up when we came back in. People were stopping to shake Herb's hand and thank him for hosting.

He was still way too pale. I made my way toward him, the dogs in tow.

Milt was doing the shaking-and-thanking routine as I arrived.

"This your new girlfriend?" he said, glancing my way. "She sure can put away the brownies." He looked meaningfully at my bulging tummy.

"I'm pregnant," Ms. Snark blurted out in her best snide tone.

Milt's bushy white eyebrows shot up. "Well, that's big of ya,

Herb, takin' on another man's child."

"No, I'm married," I stammered, which of course made things worse.

His eyebrows had reached the spot where his hairline should be. Herb chuckled. "She's the dog trainer, Milt. Not my girlfriend."

"Oh, so the gal last night, she's your girl?"

"No, no. She's Marcia's assistant. They're both helping me learn how to work with Dolly."

"And that requires they stay the night?" Milt asked, his tone sharp.

Herb didn't say anything. Heck of a time for him to clam up, but I suspected he was embarrassed to admit he was too anxious to stay in the house by himself.

"It's complicated," I finally said.

And none of your business, old man, Ms. Snark said internally.

Tsk, tsk, show some respect for your elders! My inner mom's voice this time.

Herb returned from having ushered Milt to the door. I was grateful for the interruption of the warring voices in my head.

"So, can you stay tonight, Marcia?" he asked, his tone sheepish.

"Tell me again what's been happening here at night."

"Well, except for last night, there's usually odd noises. Moaning. Sometimes it sounds like a woman crying in the distance, or I hear a muffled voice. I'll wake up and there are lights dancing on the ceiling in the dining area." He ducked his head. "And ever since Char… well, there's been a voice that kinda sounds like hers, again muffled."

He shook his head slightly. "But then night before last, it sounded like… like she was talking directly to me, telling me…" He trailed off, looked away.

"She's telling you what?" I tried to keep the impatience out of my voice. I needed to make a decision soon about where I was sleeping. I was exhausted. And it was nine-thirty. I needed to call my mother.

Herb sucked in a deep breath and looked right at me. "She's telling me I should join her." Another gulped breath. "That I should kill myself."

CHAPTER TWELVE

Those words made the choice crystal clear. I was *not* going to lose another client to suicide, not if I could help it.

The very first veteran I'd worked with—the one I'd originally trained Buddy for—had done beautifully with the dog. Then two years later, his wife was murdered and he was arrested for the crime. I'd been trying to find evidence to clear him when...

I stopped that train of thought. Now was not the time to be dwelling on all that.

I briefly considered trying to get Herb hospitalized? That would keep him safe. But being forced to leave his house would set him back to square one, or worse, with the agoraphobia.

I shook my head. He wasn't saying he was feeling suicidal, only that the voices he heard at night were telling him to kill himself.

"That's okay," Herb backpedaled. He must've thought I was saying no. "I know it's just my imagination. That's what Char always said, that the house isn't haunted, I'm only imagining things."

But I had seen the lights on the ceiling. Those, at least, were not his imagination.

"And my doc gave me some new pills, a light sleep aid, he called them–"

"No, no," I interrupted. "I was thinking about something else. I'll stay."

His hunched shoulders and tense face relaxed. "Thank you," he breathed out.

"But the hall door needs to stay unlocked."

"Yeah, of course. You need to be able to get out if there's a fire or something."

"How about I leave Dolly out here with you?"

His face downright brightened, and he even managed a smile. The first I'd seen since that letter from the county had arrived.

⊷───↠

It turned out to be the "or something."

I'd had some trouble falling asleep, thanks to a low rumbling sound I assumed was coming from the industrial park. It seemed like I'd barely drifted off when a sharp bark brought me straight up in bed.

Buddy was standing by the locked bedroom door, alternating between whining and barking.

I grabbed my robe and yanked it on one-handed, while unlocking and easing the door open. The distant rumbling had stopped, but now there were muffled noises coming from the living room.

Heart pounding, I raced down the hall, Buddy on my heels. I froze in the doorway to the living room.

Herb lay on the sofa bed, the sheets twisted around him. He was moaning, his eyes closed.

Dolly was trying to wake him up from his nightmare, as she'd been trained to do, by nudging his arm with her nose.

His eyelids fluttered. He moaned again. Was he having a bad reaction to his new meds?

Then I heard something else—below the moans and Dolly's frustrated whining—a low mumbling sound. A woman's voice.

The voice spoke again, slightly louder. I caught the words *join me*.

Insides quivering, I stepped forward. "Who's there?" I called out, a touch of hysteria in my voice. Buddy leaned against my knee, sensing my anxiety.

Herb jerked awake. He sat up in bed. "Wha'?"

And the mumbling voice was gone. Had I imagined it?

"Okay, girl," Herb said to Dolly, his voice groggy. Then to me, "What's going on?"

"It looked like you were having a nightmare, but Dolly couldn't get you awake. Buddy must've heard either your moaning or her whining from our room. He alerted me."

Herb shook his head as if to clear it. "I was having a bad dream. I think I took too much of that new medicine."

"What's the normal dose?"

"The doc said to take one and see how that worked, but I could take another if needed. The first one didn't seem to be doing much, so I took a second pill."

I walked over and sat down on the edge of the armchair's seat. "Do you remember what you were dreaming about?"

"It's a little foggy. I was in that bombed-out house again, in Syria. Only there were two women there. They were kinda vague. I could see through them. I realized they were ghosts, and one of them looked like Char, a younger Char, from when we were first married. She was saying something I couldn't quite make out." Herb scrubbed a hand over his face. "But the gist of it was that she couldn't 'go on' without me." He made air quotes. "Then something about how I needed to die too, and come join her."

"Is that what she usually says when you've heard her before at night?" I tried to keep my voice calm, but my heart was racing.

"Yeah, words to that effect."

"And do you usually hear her in dreams or when you're awake?"

"Some of both. Often it starts in a dream like that, but the voice usually continues for a few seconds after I wake up." He ducked his head. "I discovered awhile ago that if I made a loud noise, stomped my foot or sat up and yelled, the noises would stopped… Marcia, do you think I'm going crazy?"

I debated for a second. "No, I don't think so. Because I'm pretty sure I heard a voice too, when I first came out here. It was faint. I said, 'Who's there?' and it stopped."

Herb sat up farther and tried to untangle his sheets from his pajama-clad legs. "So maybe this house really is haunted." He gave one hard yank and the sheet came loose. He turned toward me. "And now Char's ghost has joined the other one."

Pish, posh, inner Mom said. *There's no such thing as ghosts.*

Ms. Snark snorted. *Oh yeah? Where were you when we were on that island and that teenage ghost kept popping up?*

Inner Mom was silent.

Herb stood up, grabbed his robe from the foot of his bed. "You want some tea or something?" He marched toward the kitchen without waiting for an answer.

I followed and perched on a barstool.

"That stuff that Char…the ghost was saying in the dream…" Herb put the tea kettle on the stove. "That she can't go on without me. Do you think she was still in love with me and that's why she killed herself?"

"Did she ever give any indication that she still had feelings for you?"

He shook his head slowly. "Not really. Other than continuing to hang around and help me out. But I always thought that was more about guilt."

Or control. I kept that thought to myself. Out loud, I said, "Maybe she means she can't go on from here, as in passing over. You know, going into the light."

He nodded as the tea kettle whistled. He got down two mugs and a box of tea bags—*Lipton Decaf*, the label said.

Phew, not herbal.

We sipped in silence for a few moments. I tentatively said, "Could it be that your imagination has added Char's ghost to the mix? I mean, I thought I heard a voice, and I think the words *join me* were in there. But that could mean a lot of things."

Herb groaned. "So the house is haunted, *and* I'm losing my mind."

"No. It's a natural grief reaction, to think you hear a deceased lov…uh, person's voice. After my dad died, I thought I heard his voice in a crowd at least a half dozen different times."

"Maybe." He downed the rest of his tea and turned to put his mug in the sink. With his back to me, he said, "I still haven't come to terms with the idea that she killed herself."

"I'm still not sure she did," I blurted out.

He turned back to me. "What do you mean?"

"Well, I had begun to investigate, and I'd found out that Char had a lot of enemies."

"Like who?"

"Pretty much everybody who worked for her. But especially the agent who used to be engaged to Frank, Merrilee Brooks."

"Ya know, I think I want you to start up the investigation again. If somebody killed Char, well, that person needs to be brought to justice." He took a deep breath. "Then maybe she can rest easy."

＊━━━＊

To say I didn't sleep well for the rest of the night would be an understatement.

I called Will at seven-thirty, hoping he hadn't been assigned a new case that had kept him out half the night.

"Hey there," he said by way of greeting. "How's Bumpkin?"

"And what am I, chopped liver?" I said in a mock offended tone.

He laughed. "You are the mother of my child. Now, how's Bumpkin?"

"She or he is doing fine. The nausea hasn't been as bad the last few days. And I felt another kick yesterday."

"Really? Awesome."

"I hate to deflate the mood here, but…" I filled him in on the events of the previous day and night. "Herb has rehired us," I concluded.

"Which makes it even less likely that he killed his ex," Will said. "Why stir things up when the death has been ruled a suicide?"

"Exactly."

"You gonna call Elise and tell her to dig deeper with these folks?"

"That's the plan."

"I'd like to come over there later. You said you saw the lights the other day in the kitchen. I want to check out that ceiling."

"Good idea."

"Mar-see-a," he dragged my name out, "don't you be getting up on a ladder before then. You've got Bumpkin to consider."

"Of course not." I tried to sound offended, but that *was* exactly where my mind had gone. I could make myself wait, though, for him to do the physical labor. I wasn't that crazy about ladders anyway.

We signed off as Buddy rose from beside my bed. He looked at me expectantly.

"I know," I said. "Time to go out back."

I did a quick morning toilette in the hall bathroom, then threw on my stretchy denim capris, which were a bit overdue for a washing, and yesterday's tee shirt, plus the red oversized camp shirt which I left open like a jacket.

While the dogs did their business in the yard, I texted Elise, telling her to dig deeper into Merrilee and also run a check on Frank Hawkins.

Herb said he'd slept well enough after we'd gone back to bed, and neither of us had heard any more moaning or voices.

We had a good morning. Not only did Herb manage to cross the street to his mailbox, but he got Milt's mail as well and took it to his front porch.

As we were crossing the street back toward Herb's house, Louise came out on her porch next door. She held a hand up to screen her eyes from the morning sun. "Is that Herbert Wilson I see walkin' about the neighborhood?"

Herb grinned at her. "Yup."

She let out a loud woot and her diminutive figure hopped up and down. "Congratulations!"

He chuckled. "Thanks." His phone rang as we were mounting the porch steps. He checked caller ID. "It's Frank. I should take it."

"Go ahead."

There were two wicker chairs on the porch, covered with twigs, leaves and dust. Herb settled in one, the phone to his ear.

I brushed off the other and sat gingerly on the edge, hiking up my new shirt so it wouldn't get dirty.

Dolly took up the cover position next to Herb's chair.

Herb smiled down at her. "You've got my back, don't you?" Then he laughed and said into the phone, "No, I was talking to my dog. But yeah, you got my back too, Frank, and I appreciate it."

Two smiles and two laughs in less than ten minutes. He was definitely doing better. Staying last night had been the right thing to do.

"Okay, thanks again," Herb said and disconnected. "He's come up empty on the eminent domain issue. Nobody knew what he was talking about. He's recommending a lawyer the community can hire, but he says it's hard to fight eminent domain."

"You can't fight city hall," I muttered.

He nodded glumly. "Only in this case, county hall."

"Did you tell Frank about that strange paragraph toward the end of the letter?" I was a little concerned that Herb and/or Frank would get in trouble if they were violating a judge's gag order.

"Yes. He said he was careful who he talked to and swore them to secrecy."

The reason behind the eminent domain seizures might be a secret, but the fact that it *was* a secret was rapidly becoming the worst kept secret in the county. I rose from the chair and brushed at my butt.

Herb stood and said, "Do you think I could try taking Dolly out back by myself?"

"I think that's a grand idea."

His face brightened.

"You mind if I borrow your washing machine? I didn't get a chance to do any laundry when I was home." What I didn't mention was that my wardrobe was very limited these days. Only a few things still fit—baggy, stretchy things—plus Edna's new camp shirts.

"No problem," Herb said, leading the way back inside, once Dolly had cleared the living room.

I changed into the lounge pants I used as PJ bottoms, took off the tee shirt I was wearing and buttoned the camp shirt instead, then grabbed the semi-dirty tee shirts I'd stuffed in my duffle bag yesterday morning. I'd assumed I'd be staying at Mom's last night and could do laundry there.

I dumped them in the washer and checked the pockets of my capris before adding them.

I fished out the black plastic thingie I'd stepped on the other day. Setting it on the counter next to the washer, I added the pants to the load and some detergent.

Buddy and I went out back to join Herb and Dolly. We sat in the Adirondack chairs for a while, enjoying a light breeze, a rarity in Central Florida this time of year.

Will arrived at four. I introduced the two men, first names only to preserve some semblance of confidentiality. They shook hands.

Herb, with Dolly's assistance, led the way outside and to a door on the back of the house. He unlocked it and stepped back.

Will opened the door. It was a small mechanical room, housing his heat pump, hot water heater, and a storage area.

"Ladder's behind the hot water heater," Herb said.

Back inside the house, Will set up the ladder in one corner of the kitchen/dining area, lifted the ceiling panels of the drop ceiling, and shone a flashlight around. He repeated the process in each corner.

"I'm not seeing anything," he said, his head still stuck up

above ceiling level.

"Why the drop ceiling?" I asked Herb.

"Frank put that up for me because the old ceiling was all stained. Apparently the roof had leaked at one time, but we had a new roof put on."

Ms. Snark wanted me to ask who's idea it was to install a new roof—Char's, Frank's or Herb's. I ignored her.

She had a point, though. Char and Frank acted like over-eager landlords, fixing things that Herb hadn't even asked them to.

"What were you looking for exactly?" I asked Will.

"Not sure. Maybe some kind of projector or light, on a timer maybe. But I didn't even see any signs that anything had been there. Just a few empty screw holes that could've been from something attached there before the new ceiling was put up."

"Yeah," Herb said. "There were these hanging baskets, for fruit, I guess. But I didn't use them, so Frank took them down."

Will nodded.

He walked into the living room and did a slow circuit, visually examining the walls, baseboards and ceiling—no drop ceiling in this room. He stopped near the powder room door and pointed up to the corner.

Squinting, I could barely make out the outline of a small white box. It blended in with the white crown molding.

"What's that?" Will asked.

"It's a motion detector," Herb said. "Part of the alarm system."

Will got the ladder and climbed up to examine it more closely. "Yup, it looks like a motion detector."

"Who installed it?" I asked.

Herb gave me a curious, why-do-you-ask-that look. "The alarm company."

Legitimately part of the alarm system then.

"I don't ever use the motion detector setting though," Herb added. "It's for when you leave the house."

Will had descended the ladder. He closed it up and headed for the back door. I trailed along behind.

I spotted the black plastic thingie from my pocket, still sitting on the counter. I went over to pick it up and throw it away. Then my eyes went wide and my heart rate kicked up, as I realized the implications.

Will had stopped moving. "What's that?"

"I stepped on it the other day. Over there." I pointed to the section of rug next to the small wooden dining table.

"Was that before or after you saw the lights along the ceiling?" Will asked.

"I…I honestly don't remember."

Will took it from me and examined it carefully. "It could be part of a plastic bracket." He glanced up at the ceiling.

"Is there anything else it might be?" He handed the thing to Herb.

"Like what?" Herb looked at the glob of black plastic sitting on his palm.

Will shrugged.

Herb held it up and squinted at it. "I guess it could be off of something I ordered. I get a lot of stuff online, and I usually unpack the boxes here on the table."

"I think we should hang on to it for now," Will said.

I nodded and held out my hand. "I'll put it in my laptop case."

⟵——⟶

I'd decided it was time to leave Dolly with Herb. He was ecstatic and insisted he didn't need me to stay that night. "I've imposed enough."

I didn't argue, but when Will and I were outside, beside our respective vehicles, I told him that I wasn't really up to driving the two hours home tonight. It had been a long day, and except for those few minutes relaxing out back, I hadn't had my afternoon nap.

"I don't have to be in early tomorrow. You wanna go to your mom's?"

"Lemme call her."

Of course, Mom was happy for us to come. "Have you eaten?

I'm making lamb stew. And I've got chocolate cake."

My stomach rumbled loudly. "Bumpkin approves of the menu."

Mom laughed.

Not only was the food delicious but the company was delightful. I hadn't realized how tense I was from dealing with Herb's situation, until I felt my muscles relaxing at my mom's kitchen table.

Will and Clint got into a can-you-beat-this contest, telling stories about stupid criminals.

"There was this one guy," Clint said with a chuckle, "who asked me for directions. I wasn't in uniform, but I still can't believe he didn't recognize me. I was runnin' for re-election at the time, and my face was all over billboards around the county. The address the guy gave me was a vacant house where drug deals went down on a regular basis. I told him I'd show him where it was. And when we got there, I arrested him and the guy waiting to sell him drugs."

We all laughed.

"Instead of gettin' high, the poor sap spent the night in jail." Clint gave a mock mournful shake of his head. "A couple years later, the county took that house and the one next to it, which was also known for nefarious activities, to put in a new road."

"Oh," I said, "speaking of the county taking property. My client got an eminent domain notice yesterday…" I trailed off, remembering the confidentiality thing. Although no one at this table was a blabbermouth, except maybe me.

"Oh, that poor man," Mom said. "He can't catch a break."

I nodded agreement, then said, "The letter had some mumbo jumbo at the end about the reason being confidential, and that a judge had authorized a gag order."

Clint's brow furrowed. "That's strange."

"I thought so. Um, do you know anything about it? Nine households got them in Palmetto Springs. They're trying to get organized to fight it. It would help if they knew what the county planned to do with the properties."

"I don't recall anything happenin' regarding that community."

Clint rubbed the stubble on his chin. "Lemme do some discreet askin' around. See what I can find out."

I thanked him, silently hoping that his asking around would get better results than Frank's had.

⋆—⋆

The next day, Herb, the dogs, and I got some more good training in. Buddy got to do his bit where he pretends to be somebody's out-of-control playful pet and tries to distract Dolly, but Herb kept her on task just fine.

We were winding down around four when my phone vibrated in my pocket. In the midst of a training session I would normally ignore it, but since we were basically done, I pulled it out, thinking it might be Will.

It was my mother.

"Thank God I got you, Marcia."

Mom does not take the Lord's name in vain, so her words were a legit prayer of thanksgiving. That and her urgent tone made my insides tense up.

"What's the matter?"

"It's Clint. He went to the golf course this afternoon, to practice by himself. Another golfer found him in a sandpit, out cold. They've taken him to the hospital."

"Oh my G–" I caught myself before *I* took the Lord's name in vain. Mom would not appreciate that. Although in her current state, she might not notice.

"Is he okay?"

"I don't know. They said the doctor was in with him now. I need to get there." A pause. Rustling sounds. "Where are my keys?" Her voice was on the edge of hysteria.

"Mom, no! Don't try to drive! I'm on my way."

CHAPTER THIRTEEN

I'd left the dogs with Herb and driven as fast as I dared to Mom's, calling Will from the car.

I was in luck there. Not only was he finishing up for the day, but a witness interview had brought him toward this side of the state. He was only a half hour away. My gut had untwisted some.

Now I held my mother's hand in the ER waiting room. Her eyes were glazed over as she mumbled a prayer under her breath.

I wouldn't admit it to her, but I was praying too. *Please God, don't take him from her now!*

She had been so happy since meeting Clint.

The ER's automatic doors swished open and Will strode in. He looked around, spotted us, and was next to me in a heartbeat. A few of my tight muscles relaxed as he wrapped an arm around my shoulders. I leaned into him.

"What's happening?" he asked in a low voice.

"Don't know." I was trying hard not to break down. "He's still unconscious. He was hit over the head by something hard. Lots of blood." I sucked in air. "But that's kinda how head wounds are."

"Hard, as in?" Will's tone was all detective now.

"Narrow and hard, the doc said. Probably the shaft of a golf club." Another deep breath. "More than once."

"Holy sh…crap." Will glanced sideways at my mom, who was still mumbling under her breath, her eyes closed now.

My face heated and my chest suddenly felt like it might explode. *Okay, God, you took my dad away from her out of the blue. Don't you dare let this man die!*

Another shoulder squeeze from Will.

A young doctor in blue scrubs and a white jacket wandered into the waiting area. "Mrs. Burns?"

It didn't register for a second that this was Mom, until she jumped up. "Yes?" she said in a choked voice.

The doc held out a reassuring hand. "Your husband's in stable condition now. He's conscious but woozy."

He glanced at me and Will. "*You* can go in to see him now, Mrs. Burns. But we need to admit him, for tonight at least."

Ignoring the implication that we should stay in the waiting area, Will and I rose and followed on Mom's heels.

The doc scowled at us. We kept going, crowding into the curtained-off cubicle.

Clint lay on a gurney, almost as white as the sheets. His face was battered. A bandage encircled the top of his head.

Mom leaned down to give him an awkward hug and a kiss on the cheek. "Sweetie, how are you doing?"

He produced a feeble smile. "Been better."

She laid her cheek against his. "Love you," she whispered.

His smile was a little less feeble this time.

He looked past her cheek at Will and his face clouded. "Weren't no robbery," he said, his words a bit garbled.

Mom straightened, still clinging to his hand.

Will stepped in closer. "Is that what they're assuming?"

"Don't know, but…" Clint paused to pull in air, "…not."

Will laid a hand on the older man's shoulder. "Take it easy. Slow and easy. Just hold up fingers. How many?"

With the hand Mom wasn't clutching, Clint held up two fingers.

Crapola! My heart started pounding as I imagined him out on a deserted golf course, being attacked by two people.

"Did you recognize either of them?" Will asked. "One finger for yes, two for no."

Two fingers went up.

"One finger if they were white, two if they weren't," Will said.

A slight hesitation, then one finger came up. "Tanned," Clint whispered.

A nurse pushed back the curtain. "A room's ready for you, Sheriff." Her expression as she looked us all over, was half curious, half displeased. She gestured, and a beefy orderly entered and grabbed the end of Clint's gurney.

We trailed along behind the gurney as it progressed down the hall, a small parade of the Burns/Banks/Haines family. My throat tightened, even as my chest filled with warmth.

By the time we got to his room and the nurse and orderly had transferred him to the bed, Clint was more alert. He gestured for Will to come closer.

"Two guys, in a golf cart. I thought they were course maintenance people." His voice was hoarse. "Baseball caps, sunglasses…Didn't think anything of it until they got closer."

He paused, seemed to gather his strength. "Light-colored bandannas over their faces… wasn't alarmed. Some folks still wearin' masks, 'cause of Covid."

Clint tensed. "Then they jumped me…" One hand fidgeted with the edge of his blanket. "It's kinda fuzzy after that." He squinted as if that would help him visualize the scene better.

"It would be," I said, "with a concussion."

My mother, the retired nurse, nodded. She'd taken the only chair, next to the bed.

"I fought 'em, as best I could, and I got my hand on my gun."

"Where was your gun?" Will asked.

"Middle-a-back holster." Clint said, almost all one word.

But I knew what he was talking about. Will used one for his backup pistol—a holster attached to one's belt that tucks inside the waistband, at the small of the back.

I shuddered, the reality of the dangers of a cop's life hitting home—even a *retired* cop. Will couldn't get out of the field fast enough to suit me.

He was patting Clint's shoulder. "You chased 'em away. They probably didn't expect you to be armed."

"Force a habit." Clint said, barely above a whisper. He was getting tired.

Mom's face crumpled. She was fighting tears. "I've been trying to get him to break that habit." She choked up, stopped, cleared her throat. "Now I'm glad I didn't succeed."

"What happened to the gun?" I asked, wondering if Clint had fired it.

"The other golfer who found him," Mom answered, "he said it was still in Clint's hand. I guess the sheriff's department has it."

"Have they been here yet?" Will asked.

Mom nodded. "Earlier, when he was still out cold. Rick said he'd come back later."

Clint's eyelids were drifting closed.

Mom made a shooing motion and stood up. She kissed Clint on the forehead.

He smiled slightly but didn't open his eyes.

⊷———⊶

Sheriff Rick was at the nurses' station, and he did not seem happy to see us.

"Now, can I interview my victim?" he said to the young nurse behind the counter.

She looked nervous, apparently intimidated by this red-faced man in a uniform with a big fat sheriff's badge on his chest.

She opened her mouth, but Mom beat her to it. "No. He just drifted off. He needs to rest."

"He told us the gist of what happened," Will said.

The sheriff threw his hands in the air. "Great. Now my victim's story has been contaminated by civilians."

Will's eyes narrowed but he didn't otherwise react.

I did, however. "My husband is not a *civilian*. He's a detective with the Marion County department. He *knows* how to interview a witness without leading them."

The sheriff glared at me, then sucked in a big breath.

I was braced for him to blast me, but instead he shook himself slightly and his body relaxed some. "Sorry. I guess I'm more rattled than I thought by having one of our own attacked like this."

Startled, I warmed a little toward Sheriff Rick. It hadn't occurred to me that he and his department would still think of Clint as one of their own, but of course they would.

Will nodded by way of acceptance of the apology. "So, do you want to know what he said?"

Sheriff Rick shook his head. "I should hear it first from the victim, without any preconcep–"

"Stop calling him that!" Mom said, in the voice she used to use with my brother and me when we were in trouble.

We all turned toward her, and she burst into tears. "Stop calling him a *victim*!"

"Aww, Mom." I gathered her into my arms and walked her away from the men. But not too far. I wanted to hear what they were saying.

Half my attention on her, half trying to eavesdrop, I missed the first few words. But I caught "…robbery gone wrong." This from Sheriff Rick.

That sure sounds like a preconception to me, Ms. Snark commented internally.

Yes, and exactly the one Clint assumed they would jump on.

But why was Clint so sure it wasn't that? Two guys, disguised, riding around a golf course on a cart. Why wouldn't their intention be to jump an old man who was likely to have a fat wallet on him?

An icy tingle ran down my spine. I shuddered.

⊱——⊰

After a barely palatable dinner in the hospital's cafeteria, Will said he needed to make a couple of phone calls.

Mom and I went to check on Clint again. He'd been asleep now for a couple of hours.

"Shouldn't we be waking him up periodically?" I asked.

Mom shook her head. "That's no longer the protocol. The nurses will be checking his vitals regularly. They're watching for signs of him slipping into a coma. But he seems to be sleeping naturally so far."

My cell phone pinged with an incoming text message, from Herb. *How's your stepdad doing?*

Hmm, I didn't really think of Clint as my stepfather, but I guess that's what he was.

Definitely family, Ms. Snark said, without her usual snide tone.

My chest warmed again, as I sent Herb a reply that he seemed to be recuperating.

Clint stirred. "He's waking up," Mom said.

I dutifully called the sheriff, as we'd promised.

When he arrived, the three of us were with Clint, trying to chitchat like it was normal to have a family gathering in a hospital room. The nurse had found us an extra chair. Will was perched on the edge of the windowsill.

Sheriff Rick asked us to leave him alone with his former boss.

Mom stiffened in her chair, but Will put a hand on her shoulder and nodded.

We trooped out. Mom settled in the waiting area, but Will took me aside. "We should try to get your mom to go home soon."

I glanced over. She had leaned her head back against the wall, eyes closed. The normal imprints of aging for a sixty-something woman—crow's feet around her eyes, worry lines on her forehead—had deepened into full-blown wrinkles.

"She does look exhausted. But she's not going to leave him in the hospital alone."

"I'll stay with him. I need to ask him about a couple of things."

"Such as?"

"He said last night he was going to make some discreet inquiries this morning, about the eminent domain issue. I want to find out who he talked to."

I grimaced. "You think this is related?"

"Don't know, but I'd like to follow up with those folks. See how they react to the news he was attacked, and also ask if they told anybody else about their conversations with him."

I shook my head. It seemed like a stretch. "This is crazy. I mean the letter said the whole thing was confidential and hinted at legal repercussions if people talked about it. But attacking a person for asking questions? Governments don't work that way, at least not in this country."

Will shrugged. "We need to rule out that there's a connection."

My stomach—already unhappy about the cafeteria food—roiled. Had my attempt to help Herb and his neighbors put Clint in someone's cross hairs?

CHAPTER FOURTEEN

Will took a half day of personal leave. I already had the morning free because Herb's counselor had scheduled an online session with him, at ten.

I'd touched base with him by phone and told him I would be there by noon.

"Char's funeral is tomorrow," he'd said. "Do you think we could get me to the point where I could at least go to the graveside service?"

"Yes," I replied, around the small lump that had suddenly formed in my throat. "I think that's doable."

We'd said our goodbyes and I'd disconnected—then said a silent prayer that his counseling session would be productive, that his counselor would be able to...

Do what? Help him cope with the death of his ex-wife, who might have committed suicide or might have been murdered? Figure out if he's losing his mind or if his house really is haunted? Help him sort out what to do if he lost his house to the county?

Seemed like a very tall order for a one-hour tele-med session.

I shook my head to clear it of Herb's woes. Right now, Will and I needed to sort out why Clint was attacked.

He'd told Will that he'd talked to three people the previous morning—two county council members and the current sheriff. Will suggested I take the older of the council members.

"I'll take the sheriff, since you two don't seem to get along all that well." He had a slight smirk on his face.

I resisted the urge to stick my tongue out at him. Since I was going to be a mother, I needed to practice more mature behavior, be a good role model and all that jazz.

"Whoever finishes first," he continued, "can move on to Councilwoman Hersh."

I left Buddy at Mom and Clint's house, promising him I wouldn't be long.

My assignment—the chair of the county council, Robert Graham—was the owner of the local feed store. A clerk pointed me toward the loading dock in the rear where sacks of feed were being unloaded from a tractor-trailer.

I assumed the thin older man with the weathered face was my target, since he was supervising the two teenagers doing the unloading. He wore jeans, a tee shirt with the feed store's logo on it, and a straw cowboy hat. I approached, my hand out, introducing myself.

He shook my hand with a well-practiced grip, firm but not bone-crushing. "Call me Bobby, little lady. What can I do for you?"

"Sheriff Burns, I mean, the former sheriff–"

"After all his years in office, he'll always be 'Sheriff,'" he made air quotes, "to folks around here."

I nodded. "Did you know he was attacked while golfing yesterday?"

"Yeah, I heard 'bout that." Councilman Call-Me-Bobby shook his head. "Scary what this world is comin' to when a man ain't even safe on the golf course. He's all right, though? That's what I'd heard."

"Yes, he's recovering okay. He's my…stepfather actually." I

only stumbled a little over the title. "He talked to you yesterday morning?"

"Yes." Bobby's eyes grew wary. He took my elbow and led me farther away from the boys and truck driver.

"Was anybody nearby," I asked, "when you and the sheriff talked?"

"Nope. We were in my office."

"Is it soundproof?"

"Not completely, but nobody was around. My clerk was up front and there weren't any customers right then."

That you know of, I thought but didn't say. *Someone could've come in after you all went into the office.*

"Did you tell anyone about the conversation?"

"No reason to. Clint said he was lookin' into it, that he'd keep me posted. You thinkin' our talk was somehow related to him bein' attacked?"

"We don't know. We're mostly trying to eliminate that possibility at this point."

"The thing he was askin' me about, you know what it is?" Bobby was squinting at me, as if the sun were in his eyes, except we were standing in the shade.

I hesitated, then nodded. Will and I had debated whether to admit to that, considering the judge's gag order. But I couldn't resist the opportunity to find out what this man might know about the eminent domain seizures.

Bobby had bumped his cowboy hat back slightly, exposing a tan line across the top of his forehead. "I told Clint I had no idea what that was about."

Crapola. "Don't you think that's strange? I mean, wouldn't the council have to approve any new construction or whatever?"

Bobby scrubbed a hand over his rugged face. "Most of the time. But it could've been a project voted on a while back that got postponed, maybe because of the pandemic."

"Then why the confidentiality order?" I blurted out.

Bobby's eyebrows shot up. "Where'd you hear about all this anyway? From Clint?"

"No."

"Then where?"

"That's confidential."

He tilted his head, his hat almost slipping off. "How so?"

"The person who told me is a client." Which was true on two levels.

"Client how so?"

I struggled not to visibly gulp. I was digging myself in farther and farther here. "Um, my husband and I own a private investigating agency."

I held my breath, waiting for the next question. When had I lost control of this interview?

Bobby took a step back and looked me up and down. Straightening his hat, he grinned at me. "Bet you'll be real good at undercover work. Nobody'd ever guess you was a gumshoe."

Gumshoe, now there was a word I hadn't heard in years.

I grinned back, thanked the man for his time, and skedaddled.

⋆────⋆

I texted Will. *Finished with my guy.*

Me too. Meet you at the councilwoman's office.

OK.

Barbara Hersh was an independent real estate agent, a competitor of Char's agency. Will and I met outside the small cement-block building that housed her office.

I gave him a brief synopsis of my conversation with Call-Me-Bobby Graham. "What did the sheriff have to say for himself?"

"Yes, he and Clint talked. No, no one overheard, nor did he tell anyone."

"And he has no clue why the county's taking my client's neighborhood?"

"Nope. But he said he wouldn't necessarily be privy to that information." Will pulled the building's door open. A jolly little bell announced our entry.

A slightly plump, fortyish woman—well dressed, with

carefully coifed dark hair and flawless makeup—sat behind a desk. She lifted her head. "Well, hello. Are you two looking for a new home?" She gave my baby bump a meaningful glance.

Aha, it was finally big enough that she immediately thought *pregnant,* instead of *letting herself go.*

Will introduced us and pointed out that we were here to talk to her in her role as councilwoman. She grew wary much faster than Bobby Graham had.

Will asked her about her conversation with Clint.

"As I told him," she said, "I'm not very familiar with that community."

Seriously? Ms Snark sneered internally. *She's a real estate agent!*

"And I'm fairly new to the council," Ms. Hersh continued. "I'm not sure what projects already approved in the past might be involved there." She suggested we consult with the county planning officer.

Officer or Office? Ms. Snark asked.

I think she said officer.

An internal giggle from Ms. Snark. *As in, this county is too small to have a full-blown planning* office*!*

I tried to keep a straight face.

"We're more concerned," Will was saying, "about whether anyone could have overheard the conversation you had with the sheriff. Or did you tell anyone about it?"

"No?" Her voice rose slightly, turning it into a why-do-you-ask question.

I spoke for the first time. "Didn't you hear that Sheriff Burns was attacked yesterday afternoon?"

Ms. Hersh turned to me. "No, I didn't." Her expression shifted to concerned, about two seconds later than it should've.

"The sheriff…the current one," Will clarified, "thinks it was an attempted robbery. But the perps took off when Clint fought back."

"That's terrible. But what does all that have to do with my conversation with him?" The woman rose to put a file away in a cabinet.

"We're not sure that it does," I said, realizing that she wasn't all that plump, only well-padded—in all the right places.

"Gotta cover the bases," Will added.

"But why are you investigating the attack?"

Will glanced sideways at me.

"Clint Burns is my stepfather." This time I didn't stumble at all.

Barbara Hersh nodded. She looked at Will. "And you're a former cop."

It wasn't a question, and Will didn't correct her. He was *still* a cop, albeit out of his jurisdiction.

But why did she assume he was a *former* cop?

"We're only trying to figure out," Will said, "whether or not Clint is still at risk. Or was it, indeed, just a random robbery attempt."

She nodded again but offered nothing else.

"And investigating is what we do," I said. Might as well advertise a bit. "We recently opened a PI agency."

"That's nice," Hersh said. No signs of surprise though.

Will thanked her for her time, and we left.

"Well, that was amazingly informative," I said.

Will's eyebrows went up slightly. "Are you being sarcastic?"

We walked toward my car. "Yes and no. The fact that she was so on-guard tells us something."

"True," Will said, "but *what* it tells us is the question. I'd like to know how she knew I was a cop."

"I'd like to know why she assumed you're a *former* cop."

"I guess because I'm now presenting myself as a private investigator."

"Except we didn't mention that until the end of the conversation."

"Maybe she heard it on the grapevine," Will said.

"The only two people around here that I've told our plans to are my client—and he doesn't get out much—and Councilman Graham, less than fifteen minutes ago."

We'd reached my car. I leaned against the front fender. "*And* he seemed much more surprised than she did."

Will stood facing me. "Maybe Clint or your mom has mentioned it to folks?"

"I doubt it. Neither of them are the type who brags on their kids' accomplishments. But we can ask them."

I took Will's hand, smiling up at him. "And as for how she knew you were a cop. If you don't want folks to know that, you might want to stop calling the bad guys *perps*."

He opened his mouth, then shut it again. "Good point," he said with a chuckle.

A gracious answer, considering he was supposed to be the experienced investigator who was training *me*.

Will used his phone to search for the Crystal County government's offices. He found a number for "planning" and punched it in. After a few seconds, he put the phone on speaker and held it out so we could both hear the canned message. "…am on maternity leave until September thirtieth. For urgent matters that cannot wait for my return, please contact the county council's offices at…" The young woman's voice rattled off a phone number.

"It really is only one person." I snickered a little, despite the frustrations of the moment.

"And not even a specified back-up person for when she's on maternity leave."

"Well, since we've already talked to the chair of the council, who knows nothing about it, seems like we just went around in the proverbial circle."

Will blew out air. "Yup, like a dog chasing his tail."

⟵—⟶

The next morning, Herb and I stood next to each other at the back of the crowd around the grave site. The dogs, on either side of us, were both in the cover position, watching our backs.

This was the best Herb could manage, but considering how far he'd come in less than two weeks, I thought it was pretty darn good. And especially with all the other stuff going on.

He wore a navy polo shirt and dress slacks. Fortunately, I had packed Edna's black camp shirt. The only bottoms I had, however, were my denim capris.

I'd asked Herb how he'd slept last night. He'd said fine, but there were circles under his eyes. I had a strong suspicion there had been nightmares and/or another visit from the ghost or ghosts.

The service ended and people started moving across the grass, toward the cars lined up on the cemetery's roadway. Frank was striding toward us.

He stuck out his hand, giving Herb a wan smile. "Thanks for coming, man. I'm really glad to see you getting out of the house."

Herb shook the proffered hand. "You and me both."

A man I didn't recognize came up to Frank to offer his condolences, and the two of them wandered away.

"I think it's great how you two get along," I said to Herb.

"Frank's a nice guy," Herb said.

Movement in my peripheral vision had me glancing over my shoulder, even though the dogs hadn't indicated that anyone was approaching us.

Fifty feet away, a man gesticulated rather emphatically as he spoke to Frank out by the road. It was not the same man he'd wandered off with—he'd had blond hair and wore a suit. This guy was dark-haired and dressed in Florida business casual—khakis and a polo shirt. And he was slightly huskier than the other fellow.

He and Frank were standing next to a low-slung, red sports car, and they were obviously arguing.

Who picks a fight with a man on the day he's burying his fiancée?

I stepped around in front of Herb. "Let me get a picture of you and Dolly." I backed up a few feet, holding my phone up, until I could snap a shot of the two men over Herb's shoulder. Then I took one of him and the dog as well.

I wasn't quite sure why I wanted a photo of Frank's angry companion, but it seemed like the right thing to do at the time.

CHAPTER FIFTEEN

Herb perked up some as we drove back to his house in my car. As we passed a section of undeveloped land, he heaved a sigh. "It feels good to be out in the fresh air and sunshine."

I agreed and turned a corner onto the main road that eventually led to his development. We passed the industrial park, with its ugly rectangular buildings.

Herb's phone chirped in his pocket. He pulled it out and squinted at the screen.

"It's a text from Louise," he said in a defeated voice. "The lawyer called her back. He doesn't think we'd get far fighting the eminent domain. Said we'd be wasting our money."

I didn't know what to say so I kept my mouth shut, for a change. It had taken until my mid-thirties, but I'd finally gotten it that silence is preferable to saying the wrong thing.

Herb sat back in the passenger seat and blew out air. *Not* a contented sigh this time. "Maybe it's for the best, considering how poorly I'm sleeping these days."

A roundabout way of saying, *considering my house is haunted.*

I wondered what happens to ghosts when the places they haunt are bulldozed under.

He glanced over his shoulder at the dogs in the backseat. They were curled together, napping on the seat. "With Dolly, I'll probably be able to handle having to move."

He sighed again. "You know, it's not like I'm attached to that house. We picked it for its layout, and the nice high fence around the backyard. Plus it was convenient for Char to stop by to help me with things."

I nodded. So all the reasons he'd picked the house were related to his PTSD and agoraphobia. If Dolly helped ease those symptoms, why not move on?

"You know," I said, "going through some houses when there are no people there would be a good next step in the training."

"Are you saying you'd go with me to shop for a new house?" A hint of excitement in his voice.

"I can't think of a better way to ease you into going more places with Dolly. We could see some this afternoon, if you like."

Herb sat up straighter and grinned. He poked at his phone, then put it to his ear.

"Ask for Merrilee," I suggested, thinking it might give me a chance to pump her for more info.

"Isn't she the one who hated Char, because of Frank?"

"Yeah, but she's a good agent. She found my mom and stepdad a house in record time."

He did ask for her and, when she came on the line, explained what he was looking for. "And, uh, I need for there to be nobody home, because–" He went silent, listening.

"Oh, okay. We'll meet you at the office at one." He disconnected and turned to me. "Apparently, everybody at the agency knows about my 'mental disability.'" He made air quotes, his face turning red. From embarrassment or anger? Maybe some of both.

I winced. Seems discretion was not Char's strong suit.

Merrilee looked at me funny as we exited my car in front of the real estate agency.

I could almost hear the words going through her mind… *You*

sure are turning up everywhere.

But she plastered on a smile and turned to Herb. "I've got three great properties to show you. I know at least one of them will be your next true love."

I suspected it was a canned speech, but it seemed a bit crass in light of the fact that Herb had watched his ex-wife—his last true love—go into the ground this morning.

"My car's over here," she chirped.

"We have the dogs," I said. "We'll follow you."

Her smile became even more plastic. But she nodded and walked to her car.

At the first house, all went smoothly. Buddy and I hung back. Dolly cleared each room, and Herb was relatively relaxed as we toured the house.

But his reaction was one of underwhelm. Obviously this 1970s rancher was not his next true love.

While he checked out the kitchen appliances, I sidled up to Merrilee. "I guess things are more pleasant now at the agency, without Char looking over everyone's shoulders."

She caught herself in mid eye roll. After a beat, she said, "We've always gotten along well there, but everyone is quite sad today, what with the funeral and all."

I decided on a more direct approach. "You know, I'm still not convinced that Char's death was a suicide. Did she have any other enemies at the agency?"

Merrilee bristled. "What do you mean by *other* enemies?"

Ms. Snark snickered. *Open mouth, insert foot.*

I ignored her. "Well, I know a few of the agents didn't like Char, but did anybody truly hate her?"

Merrilee gave me a glare that said loud and clear, *you mean besides me?*

Crapola! The direct approach didn't work either. *Note to self, ask Will about subtle interview approaches.*

Merrilee stomped across the kitchen. "Let me show you the lovely pantry," she said to Herb.

A few minutes later, we moved on to the second house—which

turned out to be the first house Mom and I had looked at a few days ago.

By the light in Herb's eye, I'd say this was closer to a true love moment. This house had a semi-open floor plan, with an over-sized opening between the living room and the dining area, which was separated from the galley kitchen by a short breakfast bar.

"Two owners ago," Merrilee said, "the husband was in a wheelchair. They widened most of the doorways."

I was impressed that she'd researched the house's background. She might be a pill, and a potential murder suspect, but she was a good real estate agent.

We moved on to the smaller bedrooms that Mom hadn't both-ered to check out. Herb gestured for Dolly to clear the first one we came to. When she didn't return to the doorway, I stuck my head around the doorjamb.

The room was set up as a sewing room, and the dog was standing in front of a headless mannequin with a work-in-prog-ress dress pinned to it.

Herb leaned around the other side of the doorway just as Dolly sat and let out a hesitant woof. We both burst out laughing.

Dolly looked over her shoulder and tilted her head, as if to say, *Did I get it right?*

I wiped laughter tears from my eyes, as Herb praised her and gave her a treat.

Merrilee's expression was confused but we didn't bother to enlighten her.

After checking out the other bedrooms, Herb and his dog explored the backyard. Dolly truly was becoming his dog now, which tugged at my heart strings that I'd have to let her go soon.

Merrilee and I looked on from the deck running across the back of the house. Grabbing the opportunity, I sidled up to the agent again. I'd decided to try an even more direct approach—the truth.

"Seriously, Merrilee, I need to know if Char had any enemies at the agency, or elsewhere. It's more than idle curiosity. In addi-tion to training dogs, I'm a private investigator." I crossed my fingers behind my back to negate the partial fib. I wasn't a PI *yet*.

"My agency has been hired to investigate her death."

She turned to me, her eyes blazing. "Char was not always a nice person. She had enemies. But ones who hated her enough to kill her…" She made a scoffing noise.

"Why should I believe that *you* didn't kill her? You told me yourself that you hated her."

She glared at me so intensely, I expected daggers to start shooting from her eyes. "Because Char Mathers wasn't that important to me. She certainly wasn't worth going to jail over."

She snapped her fingers. "Hey Herb," she called out, "I forgot to show you some of the details of the main bath." She turned abruptly and headed back inside.

We dutifully followed her, slowed a little by the need to have Dolly clear each space.

In the bathroom, Merrilee leaned over the modern jacuzzi tub, pointing out various knobs that controlled certain jets.

The silver chain around her neck fell forward, dangling over the tub. The overhead light glinted off a diamond ring hanging from the chain.

Merrilee must have sensed my scrutiny. She glanced my way, then down, and quickly stuffed the ring back into her cleavage.

Hmm, apparently she had gotten over Frank and had moved on. But why hide her engagement ring from the world?

━━━

Herb was animated on the drive back to his place. The third house hadn't been all that impressive, but we'd politely let Merrilee show us around.

House number two had definitely struck his fancy, however. "I think I'm going to make an offer on it."

"Um, not that it's any of my business," I said, "but how's this going to work timing-wise? Won't you need the money from the eminent domain buyout or from your inheritance in order to settle on the new house?" The wheels of government turn slowly. It might be months before he got his money. And wills took time to go through probate.

"Merrilee said she could probably arrange some kind of temporary financing. And if I can move out within thirty days, maybe I can get that bonus from the county." His voice was excited. "Then when Char's will is probated, I can pay it off."

But wait, the title of Herb's current house wouldn't be free and clear until after the will was probated. He wouldn't be able to sign it over within the thirty days. And something else was niggling at the back of my brain about that eminent domain letter.

"You know," Herb said, "there might be a hitch with the title on my house." Apparently, his mind had been on the same track as mine. He pulled out his phone and called Frank.

I couldn't glean much from his side of the conversation. It was mostly noncommittal uh-huhs, but he was smiling as he disconnected. "He says he'll lend me the money for the down payment, until we can get everything straightened out."

"That's very generous of him."

"Oh, and Frank talked to the lawyer himself earlier today. He agrees that eminent domain cases are rarely won by the homeowners."

Then it hit me, what the niggling feeling was about. The eminent domain letter had looked official enough, but there'd been no address or phone number for the Planning Office. And no name typed under the signature. Was it even legit?

I opened my mouth, but closed it again. Maybe best to wait to bring up my concerns until after I'd talked to Will about them.

"I may be recalled to active duty," Herb said a few minutes later.

I almost drove off the road. "What?"

"I'm on the temporary disabled list. I have to be re-examined every six months. The board may decide that, with Dolly, I can go back to limited duty."

I digested all that. The veterans I'd worked with before had been medically discharged, but many of them had also had physical disabilities.

"You sound happy about the prospect," I said.

"Oh, I am. I love the Marines. I mean, I won't be able to go into combat, but I can work behind the scenes and do my part."

"What if you're stationed somewhere else? What about the house then?"

"I'll rent it out. But I like the idea of having a home base, and eventually I'll retire."

I nodded. "Well, if you want that house, you should tell Merrilee to write up a contract. I hear the market's pretty hot right now."

"You think I should do it?" Herb said, now a slight doubt in his voice.

"Hey, it's totally up to you. But to my thinking, taking control of the situation and finding yourself a house you love sure beats wasting time and money trying to fight the county."

But what if the whole eminent domain thing turns out to be bogus? Ms. Snark asked internally.

It's not a bad idea for him to get out of that house anyway, I pointed out.

True. And he'll still be getting money from Char's estate.

Herb had taken out his phone and was talking to Merrilee. After he disconnected, he grinned at me. "Guess I'd better start cleaning out closets if I'm moving soon."

⟻——⟼

I left Herb to his closets, and Buddy and I went back to Mom's. And found her doing exactly the same thing. She was leaning over, the top half of her body swallowed by the clothes hanging in the closet in the guest room. A box slid out into the room.

"Hey, Mom," I said from the doorway.

A grunt from the closet. "You're back early."

"A little bit." I didn't feel like giving an explanation to her derriere.

"How's Clint doing?" He'd been released yesterday afternoon.

She pulled her head out of the closet long enough to say, "He's getting grouchy, which tells me he's feeling better. Right now, he's taking a nap, so I figured I'd get some packing done." She dove back in and another box slid out onto the carpet.

"Can I help?"

"Yes," her muffled voice from the closet, "get me some paper grocery bags from the kitchen."

When I came back with the bags, Clint was standing in the doorway of my temporary abode. "What are you doin', woman?" he demanded.

"Sorting books," came Mom's reply, in the super sweet voice she uses whenever someone is sick. I think of it as her nurse-mode voice.

"Those are my books!" he growled.

I tapped his shoulder, and he stepped aside to let me and Bumpkin past.

"I know, dear," Mom was saying. "Come sit on the bed and tell me which ones you want to keep. Some of these are over thirty years old."

Clint stepped into the room. Mom opened two of the bags and sat them upright. "One's for trash, the other for the county library."

Clint sat on the bed, grumbling.

"And those you want to keep go back in the box."

While Mom held up one book at a time and Clint pointed to where it should go, I filled them in on the events of the afternoon.

"Well, seems everybody's moving house at once," Mom said cheerfully when I'd finished.

"How's your client gonna handle the down payment while he's waitin' for his money from the county?" Clint asked.

I blew out air, not up for trying to explain Herb's complicated finances. "He thinks he'll be able to work it out. And there's a bonus for vacating within thirty days."

Clint's bushy eyebrows came together in a frown and he shook his head. "It don't work that way. Usually it's all tied up in court for months, then another two to three months are allowed for people to relocate."

"Their lawyer is telling them it's not worth fighting, that they'll lose."

"Yeah, they probably will, but that doesn't usually keep folks from tryin'. If there's even one holdout, it'll tie up the whole thing."

"I hope not, but he's got a backup plan. He really has his heart set on that particular house. It was the first one you and I looked at, Mom."

"That was a cute house, just too small for us." She dropped a book into the library bag.

"And I can't imagine where they're gettin' the money for bonuses," Clint said. "The county council's usually stingier than Scrooge."

Hmmm, another reason to question the legitimacy of those letters.

Clint's phone rang. He fished it out of his back pocket. "Burns," he snapped into it. He listened for a few seconds. "Okay. I'll be there soon."

"Be where?" Mom asked, as he disconnected.

"That was Rick. They found an abandoned golf cart, about a mile from the course. He wants me to come over there, see if I recognize it." Clint rose carefully from the foot of the bed, not completely steady on his feet.

"You are not driving," Mom said from the floor. "Doctor's orders," she added, when he scowled down at her.

"I can take you," I said. "And Mom can sort books so you can look through them quickly later."

I had an ulterior motive, maybe more than one.

We followed Rick's directions to a country road that dead-ended at a stand of pines and live oaks. Several official-looking cars lined one side of the road.

Sheriff Rick stood at the edge of the trees. He nodded to Clint and scowled at me. But he let me follow them into the woods.

I kept Buddy close by my side, out of people's way. A couple of technicians were going over the cart, which had been driven into the woods along a trail more suited to ATVs.

"No prints, Sheriff," one of them called over.

"None?" Rick said in an incredulous voice.

"Nada," the tech said.

The sheriff turned to Clint. "Well?"

Clint shrugged. "You seen one golf cart, you've seen 'em all, but I'd say it's the same one. Why else would it be wiped clean?"

He raised a hand to the bandage taped to one side of his shaved head. "And I wasn't lookin' all that closely at it. Too busy dodgin' the guy who was tryin' to clobber me with my own golf club."

Rick's eyes widened. "You didn't tell me that before, about the golf club."

"Just now remembered it, I guess."

It's not unusual for details to come back later, after a concussion, but Rick was now scowling at Clint.

"Can we get his gun back?" I asked.

Rick turned his scowl toward me. "Ballistics still has it."

"Why? Was it fired?"

"No, it hadn't been fired recently. I'll check into it."

"Any leads on who attacked Clint?" I asked.

"No." His expression neutral now, he gestured toward the golf cart. "Only this, which isn't telling us anything." He turned to Clint. "Sorry for dragging you out here for nothing."

"It was good to get out of the house and…" Clint glanced my way. "Get some fresh air."

Yeah, not what you meant to say, Ms. Snark commented, but with a chuckle.

I hid a smile. I couldn't really fault him for wanting to get away from Mom when she was in sorting and tossing mode.

Back in my car, Clint asked, "Why were you pushin' him about my gun?"

I shrugged. "I like to yank his chain." I wasn't sure how to tell him that I thought he and Mom were vulnerable.

But he was no dummy. "I've got another gun," he said, his voice grim, "in case I need it." A pause. "Haven't used it in a while. But I can't do any target practice, not 'til my head stops spinnin'."

"Your head's spinning?" I asked, alarmed.

"Only a little." He shot me a sideways glance. "Do *not* tell your mother that."

I hesitated, then made a zipping gesture across my lips.

Back at their house, I was unhooking Buddy from his safety strap in the backseat, when my phone rang. The screen read *Herb.*

"Hey, what's up?"

"Uh, I think you better come over here." His voice was funny.

"What? Why?"

"Is your husband around? He should see this too." Yes, he was definitely sounding shaky.

"See what?"

"I think I, uh, found some evidence that Char was murdered."

CHAPTER SIXTEEN

Herb was sitting on the front porch, his face as white as a sheet. Dolly sat in the cover position beside him.

"What's the matter?" I said as Buddy and I approached. "Did you see a ghost?"

He shook his head, giving me a wan smile.

But I hadn't been joking. I was now more than half convinced that the house was truly haunted.

Herb rose, turned and opened the door. Dolly ran inside and did her spin around the living room.

"Maybe you can think of another explanation for this," Herb said, as he led the way to his study, barely waiting for Dolly to clear the hallway first. Once there, he pointed toward the open door of the closet. "I was pulling boxes out of there to go through and happened to lean a hand on the back wall…"

I stepped over in front of the closet. A section of the back wall was exposed. And there was a half-inch gap between the end of that wall and the side of the closet. I touched the wall and it moved slightly.

I nudged harder, but something was now stopping it from moving. "What's on the other side of this?"

"The back of the master bedroom's walk-in closet."

I jogged out into the hall and down to the master bedroom door.

Herb came up behind me. "I haven't been in there yet."

The door was splintered where the inside slide bolt had been torn off. A small, new slide bolt was now on the outside. Herb slid it open, and I pushed the door wide. To my right was a small bathroom. To the left, the closet. Both doorways were open.

"I took the doors off the hinges at one point," Herb said from behind me, "so I could see in there at a glance."

I nodded and flipped a switch on the inside of the closet. The light revealed clothes rods with garments scattered along them—a suit, some slacks and casual shirts on the left, a dress Marine uniform and camouflage fatigues on the right. On the back wall, was a section of empty shelves and, beside them, two boxes stacked in the corner.

The end of the back wall that had moved would be behind those boxes.

I started to reach for the top box, then caught myself. "You got any gloves?"

"I'll be right back."

While he was gone, I examined the closet with my hands in my pockets. The section with the uniforms was shorter, stopping several feet before the back wall and creating the space where the boxes were stacked.

"I don't remember what's in those boxes."

I startled, whirled around, my heart pounding.

Herb face was flushed. "Sorry. But it's good to know I'm not the only one who's jumpy." He handed me blue latex gloves.

I put them on and hefted the boxes out of the way. They weren't all that heavy. I was curious about their contents, but more curious about the wall.

I slipped two fingers in the gap at the end and tugged. The section of the back wall between the end of the shelving unit and the side wall swung silently toward me.

And we were staring through it into Herb's study.

"Locked room mystery solved," I said under my breath.

"Should we call the sheriff's office?" Herb said from behind me.

I shook my head, pulling out my phone. "Not just yet. You were right. Will needs to see this."

I called Mom to let her know I wouldn't be back for a while. Then Herb and I decided on the backyard as the best place to wait until Will could get there.

We sat in the Adirondack chairs, and I was probably as anxious as Herb. The idea that his house had secret passages in it… My stomach roiled.

The dogs in the cover position on either side of us, we sat in silence for a while. Herb said, "Is this as creepy as I think it is?"

"It's very creepy," I said.

He nodded and we fell silent again.

Finally, a text from Will. *I'm out front.*

At the front door, Will took one look at my face and enveloped me in a hug. I clung to him for a few seconds, then let go and took his hand.

Herb actually led the way into the hallway, after Dolly quickly cleared it. But he stood back from the entrance to the master bedroom.

We'd left the door open. Will strode in ahead of us and turned into the closet. He whistled softly when he saw the opening.

He walked through the closet, keeping his arms down by his sides.

"Those boxes," I said, "were in front of the door." I called it that for lack of a better term.

Escape hatch? Ms. Snark offered.

I ignored her. "How did they get them there after they'd gone through the opening?"

Will had stopped a few feet shy of the opening. He pointed to the floor. "See how the carpet's flattened some here. It's a wider path than the bottom of the boxes. They–"

"Put something down," I said, "with the boxes on top and used it to drag them into place after pulling the door thingie closed."

"Yeah." Will crouched down, a position I could no longer accomplish, thanks to Bumpkin. "Thin cardboard most likely. The area is pretty consistently flattened. When the door was closed and the boxes in place, they pulled a little harder to get the cardboard out from under them." He gestured toward the opening. "What's on the other side?"

"Herb's study." We both backed out of the closet and headed for that room, Herb and the dogs following behind.

Will scanned that closet. He pointed to a large sheet of poster board tucked behind some hanging jackets. Donning latex gloves from his pocket, he reached up to the shelf above the clothes rod. His hand came down with fine white powder on the fingertips.

"Herb, I need your ladder."

"I'll get it." My client didn't even hesitate, nor did he bother to have Dolly clear the hallway before he left the room. Apparently, real invaders had finally supplanted the imaginary ones in his psyche.

He and Dolly returned after a couple of minutes with the ladder.

Will set it up and climbed a few steps to examine the closet shelf. "There's an access panel to the attic here, and some drywall dust on the shelf. Looks like someone has made the opening bigger. Where else is there an attic access?"

Herb, standing beside the ladder, paled. "In the storage room out back."

I felt the blood drain from my own face. Someone had used the attic access to sneak in and out of the house.

⊷——⊶

No one was staying in Herb's house tonight. After several

hours of dealing with Sheriff Rick and his people, we were all dragging. Me especially, with Bumpkin draining my energy.

I'd called Mom earlier and asked if she had another spare bed somewhere.

After I'd explained what we'd found, she said, "There's a daybed in Clint's study. I'll make it up." Her voice was matter of fact, but there was a tremor under the surface.

My chest tightened. She'd only gotten this close once before to the investigations I'd been involved in. I suddenly had second thoughts about our new endeavor. Would we give Mom a heart attack if we got into hot water as PIs?

Insurance fraud and adulterous spouses, that's what Will had said were the bread and butter of private investigators. *Not* murders!

Insurance fraud and adultery, I repeated in my head like a mantra, as we turned into Mom and Clint's driveway at ten p.m.

Mom heated up leftovers and fed us, then we all scattered to our beds, emotionally as well as physically exhausted.

I checked on Herb and Dolly in the study off the kitchen. Dolly lay beside the day bed. Herb was yawning. I wished him a good night.

Will and I snuggled under the covers of the guest room bed. He kissed my neck.

The tingle of the kiss traveled southward. I squirmed a little. "Behave," I whispered. "I am *not* making love in my mother's house!"

Will chuckled and snuggled closer.

I quickly drifted off.

◄———►

I woke up coughing, a wet nose nudging my arm.

It took a second to register that the room was full of smoke. I jerked fully awake and shoved Will's shoulder.

"Fire!" I bolted out of the bed, heart pounding, and hesitated only long enough to make sure Will was awake.

He was leaping from his side of the bed.

Buddy and I ran out into the hall. Will was on my heels. Somehow he'd managed to pull on his jeans.

The smoke was thicker out here. "Get out, Marcia!" he yelled.

I shook my head. "Get Herb and Dolly!"

Buddy and I ran for Mom's bedroom.

CHAPTER SEVENTEEN

Violently shaking Mom awake, I shouted, "The house is on fire!" A crackling noise said the flames were getting closer.

She and I struggled to get a groggy Clint upright. We were all coughing.

Clint shook his head to clear it and grabbed his phone from the nightstand, I guessed to call 911.

"We gotta get out first," I bellowed. "Down on the floor!"

On hands and knees, we made it to the doorway. I could feel Buddy's hot breath on the back of my knee, through the fabric of my lounge pants.

Will met us there, crouched down, an elbow crooked over his mouth and nose.

"Herb and Dolly are out. He's calling—" Will's report was cut short by a violent coughing spell.

Up to that point, my brain had been insulated from panic by the convincing message of denial that we would be okay. Now, reality broke through. I opened my mouth to scream Will's name, and went into a coughing fit of my own.

He grabbed me and dragged me down the hallway. "Buddy!" I called over my shoulder, unable to see anything in the swirling smoke.

And then we were outside and I was gasping for air—sweet, non-smoke-tainted air! I flashed back to a fire several years ago, at Edna's old motel, and shuddered violently.

A sneeze beside me. I looked down. Buddy gave me his *what's-up* look. I dropped to my knees and hugged him.

Will knelt and wrapped his arms around both of us.

I succumbed to the comfort of those arms for a moment, then scanned the yard.

I spotted my mother and Clint, huddled together, by an ambulance. A paramedic was asking them questions.

How did the fire department get here so fast? I spotted a stocky middle-aged couple in bathrobes, hovering nearby. Clint's neighbors. They must've called 911.

My head swiveled, searching for Herb and Dolly. My eyes were watering, making it hard to focus. And lights were flashing everywhere, with fire trucks and an ambulance parked on the grass. Static from radios and the crackling of the fire filled the air.

Finally, I spotted Herb. He was waving his arms around, then pointing to the ground, yelling something.

I looked down to where he was pointing. Dolly lay, unmoving, on the ground. My heart missed a beat.

I jumped up, almost knocking Will over backward. Racing over, I yelled, "Help her! She's a valuable service dog."

A paramedic sprang into action, awkwardly holding an oxygen mask over Dolly's nose. After a few seconds that felt like decades, Dolly roused, her legs moving. She pulled back from the unfamiliar feel of the mask, let out a low woof.

Herb fell to his knees and gathered her into his arms. She licked his face. He let out a chuckle that morphed into a choked-off sob.

Satisfied they were okay, I turned back to Mom and Clint, who were now sitting on the back bumper of the ambulance. Sheriff Rick was standing over them.

I pulled toward them, yanking Will in my wake. Buddy followed.

The sheriff was peppering Clint with questions, even though it was obvious he was struggling some to take in air.

I'd opened my mouth to give Rick a piece of my mind, when one of the paramedics stepped up. "We really need to take you to the hospital, Sheriff."

A moment of confusion since there were two sheriffs present. But the paramedic was looking at Clint. "I just learned," he said, "that you're still recovering from a concussion due to a recent attack."

"How could those two things possibly be related?" Clint said, a distinct wheeze in his voice.

The paramedic opened his mouth, but Sheriff Rick said, "That's what I'd like to know."

At the same time, Mom said, "You don't need to stay if the doctors say you're okay."

Clint scowled at Sheriff Rick. "I meant, medically."

"They aren't necessarily," Mom said, "but please, let them take you to get checked out."

Clint threw his hands up in the air. "Okay, I'll go to the hospital, but they're not keepin' me this time."

"Mom and I will follow in my car." I turned to Will.

He put a hand on my shoulder. Gave it a squeeze. "I'll take Herb and the dogs and find a pet-friendly motel."

"Only one motel around here," Clint wheezed out. "And they're a little too friendly with pretty much anybody, so lock your doors good."

"I'll be right back." I jogged over to where Herb was standing at the periphery of the chaos, Dolly beside him in the *cover* position.

Buddy was sticking to my side like glue.

I told Herb the plan. "Will you be okay in a motel room?"

"Guess I gotta be." He shook himself slightly. "Yeah, I'll be fine."

I gave him a wan smile. "You're getting the *in vivo* part of the training thrust on you fast and furious here."

He returned the smile with a lopsided one of his own.

I told him Clint's warning about the motel not being the safest of places, hoping that wouldn't make things worse for him.

"I know the place." He let out a wry chuckle. "You know, I'm realizing that real threats, like the house I'm staying in catching fire, they aren't the problem. I'm a Marine, trained to deal with real threats. Only the boogeymen my brain pulls out of thin air make me nervous."

I patted his shoulder as Will approached.

Then it hit me. How *did* the house catch fire? Had it been intentional? Had someone just tried to kill me—and the people and dogs I loved most in the world?

Despite the humid summer night and the added heat from the fire, an icy shiver ran through me.

⊷——⊶

I checked on Herb first thing the next day—although first thing wasn't all that early.

By the time the ER doc had checked Clint over and we had all answered Sheriff Rick's questions to the best of our ability, it had been after five in the morning. I'd had roughly three hours of sleep.

A change in light indicating movement behind the peephole, and Herb opened his motel room door. He didn't seem to be particularly anxious, a good sign.

"Good morning." He sounded far more cheerful than I felt.

"Morning," I mumbled. "We're going to that diner across the street for breakfast. You want me to bring something back for you?"

His stomach growled by way of a response. "Does it have outside tables?"

I turned and squinted across the street. "Looks like there are some picnic tables."

"I'll go with you then, if that's okay?"

"Sure. Tell Dolly to lead."

He did so, and after Dolly had checked out the sidewalk, he came out of his room. Clint, Mom, and Will joined us, and the five humans and two dogs paraded across the country road.

Herb and I settled at one of the tables, Dolly in the cover position beside him and Buddy lying at my feet.

"Egg and cheese sandwich on a biscuit?" Will asked me.

"Of course." I smiled up at him.

"I'll have the same." Herb started to pull out his wallet.

Will held up a hand. "My treat."

Herb shook his head slightly. "How about my treat? You two are doing enough for me already."

I gave Will a meaningful look, and he took the bills Herb held out.

Will, Clint and Mom went into the diner. I took a deep breath of the fresh air. It was still relatively pleasant, in the low eighties with a light breeze. Later, the temperature would climb into the nineties and people would huddle inside in the air-conditioning.

I took another deep breath and wrinkled my nose. My hair still smelled of smoke, even though I'd washed it. At least I had fresh clothes—too-big sweatpants and an oversized tee shirt—lent to me last night by Mom and Clint's neighbors.

I looked over at Herb, whose face had sobered. "How are you holding up?" I asked.

"Fine." He paused, thought for a moment. "Surprisingly well, to be honest. I never was comfortable with the idea that Char committed suicide. Then we found that opening in the closet…" He trailed off, shook his head. "And now the fire. Do you think it was intentional?"

"We'll have to see what the fire department concludes. But it's an awful big coincidence, along with everything else that's been happening."

His face clouded. "I brought this down on your family. I'm so sorry."

"It's not your fault. But we really need to figure out who's behind all this."

Will approached with a grease-stained paper bag in one hand and a metal bowl of water in the other. "One does not get plates if you eat outside." He plopped the bag on the table and leaned down to set the water on the ground. "But the dogs get a real bowl," he added with a chuckle, then swung a leg over the bench on my side.

"Not a problem." I grabbed the bag and passed out sandwiches and napkins.

Clint and Mom came out and settled at the other table. Their expressions were grim as they ate. They too wore borrowed clothing.

My heart squeezed in my chest. I prayed they hadn't lost everything in the fire.

At least they don't have to worry now about selling the house, Ms. Snark commented internally.

That's horrible!

Sorry, only trying to lighten the mood.

"First," Will said, once the worst of his hunger was appeased, "we need to figure out who's going where. Your mom and Clint," he tilted his head in their direction, "are going to stay at the motel for now. They need to get their insurance company out to the house to assess the damage."

He took another bite of his sandwich and chewed quickly. "I suggest that the three of us go back to your house, Herb. I'd like to take a closer look in your attic."

"Didn't the sheriff's people search it yesterday evening?" I asked.

"Yeah, but they wouldn't let me go up there." He made a face, apparently annoyed that he was being treated as a civilian.

"I should call Frank," Herb said. "See if he can somehow board up those access panels–"

I held up my hand. "Maybe you *shouldn't* call him. Frank's a major suspect at this point."

Herb's face sagged.

Will swallowed the last bite of his sandwich. "No, go ahead and call him. See if he can come over. I'd love to have a little chat with him. But don't tell him what you found."

Now Herb looked confused, and a bit wary, but he pulled out his phone.

I narrowed my eyes at him. "You had time to grab your phone last night?" It registered that he was dressed in yesterday's clothes. Had he set the fire to stop us from investigating? Had he actually killed Char?

No, that was crazy. He'd asked us to investigate in the first place. And if he'd been the one to use that tunnel to drag Char's body into that bedroom, then used the hidden door to make his exit, why would he tell us about the door?

"I was so tired last night," Herb was saying, "I didn't bother to get undressed, just flopped down on the bed."

Still uneasy, I whispered to Will as Herb made the call, "What about your work?"

"I already called in," he whispered back. "And I caught the look you gave Herb, so before you ask, I grabbed my jeans last night because my pistol was still on the belt. A fire and ammunition are not a good combination. My phone was in the pocket."

My insides settled down some.

"When my captain heard about the fire," Will continued, "he said to take as much time as I need."

Worry and guilt tightened my chest. We'd planned on cashing in his accumulated leave, when it was time for him to separate from the sheriff's department. That was to be the nest egg to see us through until we got the PI agency firmly established.

But then again, if we found Char's killer, we'd get a good-sized payout from Herb. And with two successful cases under our belts, we'd be off to a good start.

"What the…" Will's voice broke into my reverie.

At the same time, Herb disconnected from his call. "Frank will be there around three-thirty."

"What?" I followed Will's line of vision to the motel across the street. Two sheriff's department cruisers had pulled into the parking lot, their lights flashing but no sirens.

Several men in uniform piled out of the cars. And they were headed for our rooms!

After a minute, one of them turned from Herb's door—where, of course, there had been no answer to their knock. He spotted us by the diner, pointed our way.

"This is not good," Will muttered, rising from the bench. "Stand up, Herb, and keep your hands where they can see them."

I stood as well, and Clint stepped over next to me. "Go sit with your mother."

I opened my mouth to protest, then thought better of it. The dogs and I moved over to the other table.

The cruisers turned around in the motel's lot and shot across the road, screeching to a halt in front of us. Sheriff Rick and a deputy climbed out of the lead car and approached Herb.

"Herbert Wilson," Rick said, "you are under arrest for the murder of Charlene Mathers."

Will's head jerked up and he stared my way, eyes wide, his mouth hanging open.

What the heck was that about? We all knew this was going to happen, as soon as we'd seen the cruisers across the street.

Clint stepped forward. "What's going on?"

"There's an insurance policy," one of the deputies answered. "Half a million, set up a couple of months ago. The ex-husband," he nodded toward Herb, "is the beneficiary.

CHAPTER EIGHTEEN

If Sheriff Rick's glare had been a thunderbolt, the deputy who'd spoken up would've been toast.

Herb, now handcuffed, was staring at them, his mouth gaping open. "First I've heard of it."

The sheriff nodded slightly, and another, younger deputy moved Herb toward a cruiser.

Dolly whined and tugged against her leash, but she was too well-behaved to pull hard. "We'll be right behind you," I called over to Herb.

"No you won't," Rick said emphatically. "This is none of your business."

Seriously, Ms. Snark said inside my head, *we're going to do that dance,* again*!*

We'd had a similar debate a few years ago, over my other client. But today, I didn't have the energy for it. I gave him the Cliff-Notes version. "He's my client. So yeah, he is my business!"

Rick grumbled and turned away.

The cruiser that now contained said client pulled out onto the street. Egg-flavored bile rose in the back of my throat at the mental image of Herb being dragged into the sheriff's department, through multiple doorways... I swallowed hard. "I need to get to the jail with Dolly."

I turned toward the motel, dogs in tow—and found Will and Clint jogging beside me. My heart missed a beat. Was it a good idea for Clint to be jogging?

"Gimme your keys," he said, as we neared the vehicles. "And get the dogs loaded."

I hesitated.

"I'm okay," he growled. "Head's stopped spinnin'. Now, gimme your keys."

I tossed him my car key—the spare one I'd retrieved last night from the little magnetic box inside my front tire well. Then I quickly strapped the dogs into the backseat.

"We'll follow in my truck," Will called after us.

Clint already had the engine running and had shoved the seat back to accommodate his bigger frame.

I jumped into the passenger seat, and he floored it, gravel spewing. He glanced at the rearview mirror, frowned and adjusted it. "Sorry for the rough ride, pups," he said to the dogs, once he could see them.

Then he scowled at the mirror.

"What's wrong?"

"There's a cruiser right behind us," Clint said. "But no worries. No deputy in this county is going to give *me* a speeding ticket."

"Unless it's Sheriff Rick," I said.

He shot me a sideways glance, then chuckled at the nickname. "Yes, unless it's Sheriff Rick."

But apparently it wasn't. The cruiser followed us to the sheriff's department, where the older deputy climbed out. I noted the sergeant chevrons on his uniform sleeves.

We'd caught up with the car carrying Herb. The younger deputy from that car was taking Herb's arm to help him out of the backseat.

"Wait up," Clint called out.

When we reached them, my wonderful stepfather said, "Hang on for a sec while this service dog does his job for Sergeant Wilson, who happens to be a decorated Marine."

Herb's cheeks pinked. The young deputy hesitated, nodded.

I took Dolly to the department's entrance, opened the door and told her to clear the room.

Two barks, a third, then a fourth. Meanwhile, I'd sidled up closer to Herb. "You okay?"

"Yeah," he said, but there were beads of sweat on his forehead, and he'd just exited an air-conditioned car.

The deputy led him into the sheriff department's lobby. Clint, Buddy, and I followed. There were two women sitting off to the left, and a middle-aged man to our right, impatiently tapping his foot. Those three and the deputy behind the duty desk accounted for Dolly's four barks.

Herb and I both let out pent-up air as Dolly trotted over to us.

The young deputy led Herb toward a door—the one I knew from past experience led to the back part of the building, where the jail was located.

I opened my mouth, but Clint beat me to it. "Hang on, son." He hustled over and whispered in the deputy's ear.

Again, the young man looked hesitant, and a little bewildered. My guess was he wasn't sure if he should be taking orders from the former sheriff.

But the sergeant, who'd entered the lobby, wasn't at all conflicted. He reached for Dolly's leash.

I let him have it and he stepped up beside Herb on the other side. More whispered conversation.

The dog, Herb, and the two deputies stepped forward. The desk deputy buzzed the door unlocked. The sergeant opened the door and let go of Dolly's leash.

"Clear," Herb said.

She was back in a few seconds, sitting in the open doorway.

Herb's tense shoulders relaxed some. He and the two deputies followed Dolly into the hallway behind the door.

Clint was suddenly beside me. His hand dropped onto my shoulder. "Joe'll take care of things until Herb's in a cell. He should be okay then, right?"

"Yeah." The word came out on a choked exhale.

He'd be able to see beyond the bars, know that no enemy lurked unseen. "Yes," I said more confidently. "He'll be okay in a cell, as long as he's by himself."

"Joe'll make sure of that, then he'll bring the dog back to us."

I turned to Clint to thank him, and felt my face crumbling. A sob erupted from my throat.

Crapola. I couldn't wait to get all these cry-baby hormones out of my system!

Clint wrapped his arms around me.

I expected the hug to be awkward, but I'd forgotten that he was an experienced father and stepfather. His hug was gentle, accompanied by a rhythmic patting on the back.

I sobbed on his shoulder. Out of the corner of my eye, I saw Buddy looking up at me, concern in his eyes.

"It's been an intense morning," Clint said, as I finally stepped back, sniffing loudly. He offered me a clean white handkerchief.

How quaint, Ms. Snark commented.

Aw, shut up, I replied internally.

Harrumph.

Will and Mom had entered the lobby while I'd been boo-hooing on Clint's shoulder. Will came over and put his arm around my shoulders. "We need to talk," he whispered in my ear. He glanced at Mom and Clint. "Later."

I nodded, even though I had no idea what he wanted to talk about.

We all shuffled over to some empty chairs and sat down. A few minutes later Will's phone buzzed. He answered it, then held it out to me. "It's Elise, says she's been trying to reach you."

"Thanks." I took the phone. "Hey, Elise."

"Hey yourself. What's going on with your phone?"

I sighed. "It's a long story." Said phone was no doubt a clump of melted plastic somewhere in Clint and Mom's charred house.

"Okay, well, I only wanted to make sure you got my last report. My email's been acting up lately."

"Lemme check." I awkwardly poked at Will's phone until I'd managed to open a browser and call up my email. Sure enough, there was an unopened message from her. Leaving it unopened, I clicked back. "Yup, it's in my inbox."

"Good. Let me know if you want me to dig any deeper on any of these folks."

"Okay. Um, wait…" I was trying to think. There was someone I'd intended to have her check out. Oh, yeah, the councilwoman.

"Hang on a sec," I said to Elise, then to the others, "I'll be right back." Buddy and I escaped out into the sunshine.

I walked a little bit away from the front of the sheriff's department. "Can you do a background check on Barbara Hersh, please? I don't have a home address but she's on the county council of Crystal County, and she's a local real estate agent."

"That should be enough info to narrow things down," Elise said.

"Hey, did I ever ask you to do a background check on Frank Hawkins?"

"Uh, that's the one I just sent you."

I shook my head. "Don't mind me. I'm sleep deprived at the moment." Not up to explaining why that was, I quickly changed the subject. "I found a dog that might work for you. His name is Cinnamon." I described him.

"Er," she said, "his name…is it okay to change it?"

We were hoping you would, Ms. Snark commented internally.

"Sure. It's the one the shelter staff gave him. He's probably not used to it yet."

"Since his coat is reddish-brown, how about Rusty? It needs to begin–"

"With an R," I said, chuckling. "As in E and R Electronic Investigations." My tense stomach loosened up some. Talking about the dog was a good distraction.

She chuckled. "Exactly. Hey, by the way, did everything work out okay with Will's case?"

"Yes. We've even gotten the client's payment already."

"Okay. Glad to hear it. It seemed so weird to me, that's all, when all their addresses were in the same area, and they were supposed to be employment checks but..."

I started to zone out—too little sleep last night, too much excitement this morning.

"...in his eighties and another was a disabled veteran."

A jolt went through me. "What did you say?"

"Um, they were all addresses near each other?"

"No, about the old guy and the veteran."

"This one guy was like eighty. Maybe he ran through his retirement savings and–"

Heart racing, I cut her off. "Was his first name Milt, by any chance?"

"Yeah, Milton."

The proverbial lightbulb clicked on inside my head. "And was he the one who was using a fake name?"

"Yes. How'd you know about that?"

"Will told me that much, without mentioning any names. Was the veteran Herbert Wilson?"

"Yes! There is something fishy going on, isn't there?"

"I would say so. I'll call you back in a little while." I disconnected and stared down at Buddy, lying at my feet.

"And now I know what Will wants to talk about, boy."

CHAPTER NINETEEN

As if on cue, Will came through the sheriff department's door, with Dolly in tow. Mom and Clint followed. "Your boy's all tucked in," Clint said.

I opened my mouth, but before I could say anything, an expensive-looking white car pulled into the lot. A fifty-something man in a business suit quickly climbed out.

Clint waved at him. "Henry, thanks for coming out on short notice."

The man shrugged as he walked toward us. "Nature of the biz. But it's kinda ironic, ain't it? That you're now referrin' cases to me." He chuckled and without further ado entered the sheriff's department.

"Who was that?" I asked.

"Best criminal lawyer in the county. He'll have your veteran friend out of there by suppertime."

Will drove Mom and Clint back to their house to meet the insurance adjuster and get their vehicles.

I headed for Herb's place with the dogs.

When Will arrived, I was standing in the front yard, staring at the house as if my glare could make the front door open.

"What's the matter?" Will asked.

"I don't have my key." This not having my own things—my purse, my keys, my phone—was getting old.

"He gave you a key?" Will's tone was incredulous.

"Yeah, he doesn't like answering the door. He gives keys out like candy. And he said there's a key hidden outside. I'm trying to recall where."

Was it taped under a windowsill? I ran my fingers below each window and eventually found it.

Opening the door and stepping back for the dogs to go in first, I said, "Char had a key too, as does Frank, and at least two of the neighbors."

Even though I hadn't asked her to, Dolly cleared the room, coming back to sit in front of me, a doggie smile on her face.

"Good girl." I patted her head.

"So Frank's not the only one with easy access," Will said. "Lend me that key for a moment."

I handed it to him and he headed out the kitchen door. I gestured to the dogs to lie down.

A couple of minutes later, Will returned. "As I suspected, the lock on the storage room uses the same key."

"Great." I threw my hands up in the air. "That widens the list of suspects considerably."

"Unfortunately." Will's face was grim. He gestured toward Herb's small wooden table. "I need to tell you something that you absolutely have to keep confidential."

I nodded as we sat down. "One of the people your mystery client had you checking on was Herb."

Will's mouth fell open. "How'd you know?"

"Elise let something slip earlier that I put together with what you had told me. Plus, I noticed your shock when you heard

Herb's full name. You hadn't seen it in the newspapers?"

"We've been rather busy lately, in case you hadn't noticed. I haven't been paying attention to the news." He shook his head slowly. "I knew Elise was right, that there was something fishy about that whole deal, but I figured I hadn't been hired to be nosy about my client's business. My job was to do the background checks."

"Which the client could have easily ordered directly from a company like Elise's. So why go through you and add an extra layer of expense?"

"Now we know why—to provide an extra layer of anonymity."

"There's more," I said. "The guy who's operating under an assumed name, did you report him?"

Will shook his head again. "I'd decided that too was none of my business."

"He's one of Herb's neighbors who also got an eminent domain notice. Milt something."

Will's eyes went wide.

"Yeah," I said. "The plot thickens. Elise said all the addresses of the people on your list were near each other. I think they were all in Herb's community. Somehow those background checks are related to what's going on."

Will pinched the bridge of his nose between thumb and index finger. "I can't believe I didn't even look at their addresses. I was focused on criminal activity or anything else that looked suspicious in their backgrounds."

I reached over and took his hand, gave it a squeeze.

"Elise did find one thing on that Milt guy," he said. "He bought a house, eighteen years ago, for cash. But she couldn't find anything on him before or after that."

He paused, staring into space. "But how does all this tie into Char's murder?"

"Maybe it doesn't." I shrugged. "But it would be a bit of a coincidence, and I know how you law enforcement types feel about them."

He gave me a feeble smile, then pushed himself to a stand.

"Well, first let me take a look at that attic. See if it yields any answers."

He went back out the kitchen door, and a minute later, I heard thumping sounds above my head.

It dawned on me that I might have some spare clothes here. Had I taken all of my things out of the dryer the other day? Sure enough, a couple of my tee shirts were still in there. They were a little wrinkled, but they were clean, smoke-free, and mine!

I hurried to the guest room to put one of them on, the dogs trailing along.

A thud from Herb's study next door. I trotted around the corner.

Will stood in front of the closet, brushing his hands along his arms, where flecks of off-white foam clung to the hairs. Little pieces of it also dotted his tee shirt—which smelled a tad ripe and smoky since it was on its second day and he'd slept in it last night.

"I wonder where Char's clothes are," I said, "that she was wearing the day she died."

"Good question." He made eye contact. "You're thinking her clothes had some insulation on them."

"Exactly." I pointed to the ceiling. "What's up there?"

"The insulation is the spray foam type that expands and then solidifies when it dries. It fills the whole attic, which isn't that big. Someone carved a fair-sized tunnel down the middle of it, tall enough for a man to walk crouched over. They also laid down a plywood floor."

"How in the heck could anyone do all that work," I said, "without Herb noticing the noise?" Then I answered my own question. "Wait, there are rumbling sounds sometimes, coming from the industrial park next door. Herb said they're often worse at night."

Will nodded. "If whoever did all that…" he gestured toward the ceiling, "if they timed it right, the noises they made might be masked by the rumbling. The plywood isn't nailed down, just laid across the joists."

"And any stray noises that weren't covered up," I said. "Herb might have incorporated them into his dreams, or thought they were related to his ghost. Now I'm thinking the ghost is fake."

Will nodded again. "Somebody went to a lot of trouble to try to freak Herb out and then frame him for Char's death."

"Even with all the keys out there, Frank is still high on my list. Speaking of whom, let me see what Elise found out about him." I held out my hand for Will's phone, opened my email and found her message.

It was a little hard to read the attached report on the phone but I waded through it. "He's squeaky clean as far as the law's concerned," I told Will. "No arrests, no lawsuits. But financially he's somewhat over extended. He's cosigned on several real estate deals with various other companies, probably investments."

"Real estate's usually a pretty safe bet as an investment."

"He's got a lot of personal debt as well, but Elise doesn't have the details. She wants to know if she should dig deeper." I looked up. "Which means we're paying, or should I say bartering, for an advanced search."

"And if Herb is convicted of killing his ex," Will said, "he won't inherit and can't pay us."

"What should I tell her?"

His forehead furrowed. "Is Frank inheriting anything from the will?"

"I got the impression that Char left the real estate agency to him. And…" I pointed up toward the attic, "he has the skills to do all that."

"Then yes, tell her to dig deeper."

I tapped in the email message, hit *send*, and handed the phone back to him.

"I'm going to go to the hardware store and get some wood and new locks," Will said. "Do you wanna come?"

I opened my mouth, and promptly yawned. "I think Bumpkin wants a nap."

He frowned. "It isn't safe—"

"I've got the dogs," I cut him off. "They'll sound the alarm. And whoever's doing this has what they want at the moment.

Herb has been arrested."

My husband didn't look happy, but he handed his phone back to me. "You keep this for now. If you're still asleep when I get back, I'll install the storage room lock first, before I start boarding things up."

I locked the front door behind him, made sure the back door was also locked, and headed for the guest room. But before settling in for my nap, I called Clint.

I got his voicemail. "Hey, how are things going? Um, I know you're pretty busy with the house stuff, but is there a way we can find out what happened to Char's clothes, from the day she died?"

I was about to crawl into the bed when Clint called back.

"The adjuster's lookin' over the house now," he said, his voice grim. "As far as the lady's clothes are concerned, the ME would've bundled them up as evidence and sent them to the FDLE lab."

FDLE—Florida Department of Law Enforcement—the state's equivalent to the FBI.

"Would they have processed them?"

"Maybe, maybe not. Depends on whether they got to them before Rick decided her death was a suicide."

"Would they still have them?"

"Most likely. I can discreetly find out."

My stomach churned. The last time he'd discreetly tried to find something out, it didn't go so well.

"No—"

"It's okay, Marcia. I have a good friend at the lab. He will keep it under his hat. And the insurance guy says the fire was likely arson. So your mom and I now have some skin in this game."

That did *not* settle my stomach down one bit.

"Clint, you've gotta stay out of this then. I don't want—"

"Girl, this is still my county!" His tone was emphatic, almost angry. "I'm not lettin' somebody get away with murder and with tryin' to burn my house down with my family in it. You tell Will to let me know if there's anything else I can do."

"Okay." My voice sounded a little feeble to my own ears.

"Thanks."

I disconnected and looked around the guest room. What was I thinking, trying to take a nap in this creepy house?

But my body felt like lead, and I yawned so wide my jaw cracked.

I went over and locked the bedroom door. "Protect," I told Buddy.

He laid down in front of the door. Dolly curled up next to him.

And I laid on the bed, now wide awake, anxious butterflies dancing the rumba in my chest and stomach.

The word *arson* echoed inside my head.

CHAPTER TWENTY

"Mar-see-a." Someone was calling my name, but I couldn't find them. I was in Clint and Mom's house, wandering around. The air was thick and gray.

"Mar-see-a." A male voice, but not Will's or Clint's.

The grayness was smoke! I coughed.

And jolted upright. It took me a moment to remember where I was…in Herb's guest room.

And it was Herb's voice calling, "Mar-see-a. Can you open the front door, please?"

I jumped up, unlocked the bedroom door, and trotted to the living room, the dogs on my heels. When I reached for the deadbolt on the front door, it was already unlocked.

"Herb?" I called through the door.

"I unlocked it, but then couldn't bring myself to open it, without Dolly to clear for me."

I threw the door open. "How'd you get out so quick? And who brought you home?"

"A deputy, and that lawyer is one smooth talker."

"Clint said he'd have you out by suppertime. It's…" I pulled out my, uh, Will's phone to check the time. One-forty. Later than I'd thought, but still. "It's barely past lunchtime." I stood back to let him in.

He hesitated.

Duh! "Dolly, clear." She did a circuit of the room, coming back to me and sitting.

Herb crossed the threshold with only a couple of nervous glances to his right and left.

Dolly let out a low woof and went to him, leaned her weight against his leg, responding to his anxiety.

Herb rubbed her head. "I missed you too, girl."

"How did you arrange bail so fast?"

"No bail. Released on my own… What's it called?"

"Own recognizance."

"Yeah. The lawyer convinced them I wasn't likely to take off since I'm officially diagnosed with agoraphobia. For once, it's paying off."

"How'd you deal with going through the doorways at the jail?"

His chuckle had a nervous undertone. "It wasn't easy. I just kept focusing on the fact that I was getting out of there."

The back door opened and Will came through it.

Herb startled, but recovered quickly.

Will walked into the living room. "I've changed the lock on the storage room and boarded up that attic access." He handed Herb two keys, then pulled two more out of his pocket. "These, I'd suggest you only give one to Marcia, but nobody else. They're for the front door lock that I am about to change."

He stepped past us and started working on that lock.

Herb and I settled on the sofa bed and armchair respectively.

"I'm gonna wait until after we talk to Frank this afternoon," Will said, his eyes on his work, "before closing up the attic access in that bedroom. I want to see his reaction to it."

"In the meantime," I said, "Herb, can I leave the dogs with you for a few minutes?"

"Sure."

Will glanced my way, turning the last screw in the new lock.

"You know, that other case," I said to him. "I think we need to talk to the man who wasn't who he seemed."

Will nodded.

Outside, we walked to Milt's house across the street.

"What if Herb happens to look out his window?" Will asked.

I shrugged. "I'm gonna tell him about Milt, when we know more."

Will took the wooden porch steps two at a time and stood off to one side of the door, so I would be the only one visible to someone peering through the peephole.

I rang the bell, keeping my eye on that peephole. Light shifted behind it. Someone had looked out, but the door remained stubbornly closed.

I punched the bell again. The door cracked open and a watery gray eye peeked out, over rimless reading glasses.

"Whatever you're sellin', I don't want any." Milt tried to close the door.

But Will had deftly stuck his foot between it and the jamb.

"It's me, the dog trainer, Marcia. We met at the meeting at Herb's house the other night."

"Oh." Bushy gray eyebrows furrowed, then recognition dawned in the watery eyes. "The girl who ate most of the brownies."

Will was wearing his cop face, but I knew he was smirking inside.

"I only had two," I said, slightly indignant.

"Whaddaya want?" The door still remained more closed than not.

"We need to talk to you, um, about Herb selling his place. Can we come in?"

"Who's this guy?"

"My husband."

Milt's expression relaxed some. "Okay, I guess." He stepped back and opened the door for us.

He shuffled to an overstuffed armchair, next to a small table covered with pill bottles, an empty coffee cup and a folded newspaper.

Will and I perched on the edge of the sofa. "So, did you hear that Herb's selling?" I said.

"Yeah. Good decision. That house is full of bad memories now."

I nodded. "Any holdouts left?"

Milt made a face. "Only a couple. Louise is the most determined. But she may cave now that Herb is sellin'."

"Herb's already made an offer on another house, based on the assumption he'll get the money from the eminent domain seizure quickly."

The old man's face brightened. "Good for him!"

I leaned forward. "Sir, how–"

He held up a hand. "If we're gonna sit here jawin', you might as well call me Milt."

I smiled, while trying to identify his accent—Southern or West Virginian? It seemed to come and go.

"Milt, how likely do you think it is that the whole thing will fall apart because of holdouts?" I was pretending that the holdouts had a snowball's chance in Hades of fighting the county.

"I hope not. I'm really looking forward to moving into a retirement community."

The words were right, but the tone lacked enthusiasm.

I glanced at Will, wishing we'd thought to discuss strategy ahead of time.

He was watching me. Why did I have the feeling this was some kind of test?

You can chime in here anytime now, Bub, Ms. Snark commented internally.

I discreetly sucked in some extra air and plunged onward. "Milt, there's something else we need to ask you about. You see, we've been checking into Char Mathers's death–"

"Why are you all lookin' into that? I thought it was ruled a suicide."

You all, *not* y'all. *Interesting.* People from states like Maryland, on the cusp between the North and South, sometimes said *you all*.

I glanced at Will again. He gave a slight nod.

"We're private investigators," I said.

Milt's face paled. His lips pressed together in a thin line. "So you're just pretending to be a dog trainer?" he demanded.

"No, I really train service dogs as well."

He threw his hands up in the air. "You young people with your multitasking." His tone was disgusted.

And the accent was gone. *Very interesting.*

"Do one thing at a time, I always told my kids, and do it right. *Then* move to the next thing."

"How old are your kids?" Will asked, his voice low and calm.

Milt looked startled. After a beat, he answered, "They're in their forties now, got kids of their own."

"How many kids do you have?" I asked, following Will's lead with a calm tone.

"Two…a boy and a girl…and five grandchildren." Hesitation gave way to pride in his voice. "Three boys and two girls."

I nodded. "That's the kind of thing we wanted to ask you about. You see, when we did a cursory check on the folks around here, we couldn't find out much about you."

I thought I'd phrased that in a non-threatening way, but the old man blanched again and jerked back in his chair.

Then his face shifted from pale to red. "What gives you the right to be checking on me?" he growled.

"It's all public information, sir," Will said.

Milt lumbered to his feet. "I think you all need to leave now."

My eyes met Will's. He shrugged. We rose and trooped to the door.

The old man slammed it behind us.

We waited to say anything until we were down the porch steps. "What did you think of that?" Will gestured with his head back toward the house.

Instead of answering him, I pulled out my phone, rather Will's phone. "Siri, in what states do people say *you all* rather than *y'all?*"

A half beat, then Siri's voice saying, "Here's what I found on the web for in what states do people say *you all* rather than *y'all.*"

I was staring at a color-coded map comparing regions where people said, *you all*, *y'all*, *you guys* or plain old *you*. Will had stopped beside me.

"Apparently, Kentucky or Oklahoma are where people are most likely to say *you all.*" I was a little surprised by that. I'd thought it was a Maryland thing, but only part of Maryland was the pale yellow color that represented that phrase.

Will shook his head. "He didn't sound like he's from either of those states."

"It's said in parts of Maryland, northern Virginia, and West Virginia as well." I looked up at him. "And his accent kept changing. He sounded northern half the time. I think the southern accent is fake."

Will's baby blues sparkled as he grinned down at me. "Dang, you're gonna make a good PI."

"Why, thank you, kind sir." I batted my eyelashes at him.

He chuckled, then his face sobered. "This guy has a fake name and a fake accent. Definitely hiding something."

"And he was pushing for the neighbors to go along with the property seizures, to take the money and run. I have a funny feeling that your mystery client was searching for dirt on the people in this community to use to pressure them to not fight the eminent domain."

The curtain on Milt's front window fluttered. We started moving away from the house.

"But," Will raised a finger in the air, "said client didn't ask for more info on this Milton guy."

My brain chewed on that as we walked back toward Herb's house. "He didn't want *you* to find out what old Milt is hiding. You might have felt compelled to tell the authorities. It was enough leverage just to know that he's hiding *something.*"

Will gave me a half smirk. "Dang good PI. Next step?"

Okay, this was obviously a test. "We need to talk to Milt again, but maybe let him stew a bit first."

Will nodded as we reached the front of Herb's house.

Still basking in the *dang good PI* compliment, given not once but twice, I kind of floated up the steps and onto the porch.

CHAPTER TWENTY-ONE

"We've got way too many puzzles here," Will said, as he paced across Herb's living room.

Herb and I sat at the table in the dining area. We were trying to outline what we knew, what we needed to find out, and how the heck it all interacted. Herb was taking notes on a legal pad he'd retrieved from his study.

"Okay, one," Will raised an index finger, "we have secret passages in this house that point toward Char's death being murder, not a suicide."

"The question is who created the tunnel in the attic and the hidden door between the closets." Personally, I was voting for Frank, but Will had said we shouldn't jump to conclusions.

Herb leaned forward and scribbled on his pad.

"Two," I said, and Herb flipped over to a fresh page. "We have the eminent domain notifications, and the fact that two county council members have no idea what they're about."

"And," Will added, "when Clint made inquiries about that, he was attacked and then his house was torched."

He and I had discussed, while lingering on the front porch earlier, how much to tell Herb. I'd contended that he was an innocent victim, who'd also been in the house that had been set on fire.

"What if he set the fire?" Will had said. "And only pretended to be escaping from his room when I went to get him?"

"I won't say that thought hasn't crossed my mind. But it would be pretty risky, since his escape would be delayed by needing to have Dolly clear each doorway."

Will grimaced. "I had to literally haul him out of his room. There wasn't time to have Dolly do her thing… Unless he was faking that resistance."

"Then he would've been faking his phobia of doorways all this time. Why would he do that, and do you really think Herb is that good an actor?"

Will had shaken his head, and the decision was made. We would include Herb in our brainstorming. He knew many of the people involved and his insights might be valuable.

"Three," Will was saying now, "we had a secretive client recently who hired us to check out the residents of this community."

We'd already filled Herb in on that. "He didn't give you any name at all?" he asked.

"Yeah, and a business name." Will glanced at me. "I texted Elise earlier to run both names. Guess what, they're–"

"Bogus," I finished for him.

At least the cashier's check had already cleared the bank! *Note to self: always run a background check on the clients, to make sure they're on the up and up.*

"The company name he gave me," Will said, "was MNF Enterprises."

Hmm, did the F stand for Frank?

Herb was scribbling on a fresh page.

"Which brings us to number four." I took a deep breath. "We talked to your neighbor, Milt. He has a secret. We don't know what it is yet, but we think whoever's behind the eminent domain seizures used it to get him to pressure everybody to accept the offers."

I was braced for Herb to be upset, but he only nodded. "I wondered about his reaction. He's said several times in the past that he loves his house." He started writing on a fresh page. "So what is Milt's secret? And how is that related to everything else that's been going down?"

Then he tore the four pages off the pad and lined them up on the table. "Should the fire be on a separate page? It could be a coincidence that it happened right now. Clint, no doubt, has enemies around here. Lowlifes he's put in jail."

Will shrugged. "Wouldn't hurt to separate it out for now. But I suspect all this is related."

Herb labeled a new page *2A–House Fire* and placed it between two and three. He stared down at the papers for a beat. "The suicide note. Char said something about 'what you've set in motion.' What if the thing that was set in motion was the eminent domain seizures?"

"Good question," Will said. "Write that on page one."

Herb jotted down the note and then tapped page two. "One of the council members y'all talked to was Barbara Hersh, right?"

We both nodded.

"I saw something about her in the local paper recently." He stood up and headed for the kitchen. "It should still be in the recycle bin."

"You were right," Will whispered. "His knowledge of the locals is coming in handy."

More compliments! My heart warmed in my chest.

Herb came back with the newspaper. "It's in the gossip section. *What county council member was seen at BubbaQue's in Williston with someone other than their spouse?*"

Will's eyebrows went up. "What's a Bubbaque's?"

"Barbeque place," I said.

"*A certain council member,*" Herb continued reading, "*was spotted in a corner booth with someone who was obviously not her spouse…oops, I mean their spouse. The companion was facing away from yours truly and quickly got up and left out the back.*"

When this intrepid reporter went out the front, there were three men walking toward or getting into vehicles at various spots in the parking lot. It was impossible to tell which may have been the council member's companion."

Herb snorted. "Intrepid reporter. Phyllis is just plain nosy."

"How do you know that was Barbara Hersh?" I asked.

"She's the only woman on the council," Herb said.

Will pointed to our page two on the table. "Write down re-interview the councilwoman and also the reporter's full name."

"Getting back to the suicide note," I said. "She said something in it about loving the person she was directing it toward. That makes me think it's Frank who set something in motion she didn't like."

Herb grimaced. "She kinda overused the word *love*. She was always saying 'love ya, darlin'' to female friends as they parted."

"Okay," I nodded toward the pad, "can you make us a list of the people she might have been directing 'I love you dearly' toward?"

"Sure." He sat back down and began writing again.

Meanwhile, I was attempting to reconcile the image of a woman running around telling everyone she loved them with my impressions of Char. Mom had called her a narcissist. I tried to recall what my abnormal psychology prof in grad school had said about that personality disorder. Something about them seeming to be confident, even arrogant, but they were overcompensating. They were actually riddled with self-doubt inside and had usually been starved for attention as kids.

Both Herb and Frank had mentioned that Char tended to be insecure. I felt a little guilty that I'd judged her so harshly.

Will was running a hand through his hair. "The list of people we need to talk to is getting pretty long."

"We'll need to split up," I said. "I can take on Milt again, see if I can get him talking about his kids and then segue into what is he hiding?"

Will shook his head. "You're not talking to him alone."

I bristled.

But Herb interrupted our budding argument. "Milt's got kids?" His eyes were wide. "He's never mentioned them."

"Really?" I said. "He seemed kind of proud of them, and he's got a bunch of grandchildren."

"That's fishy," Will said. "What grandparent isn't eager to talk about his grandkids?"

Herb nodded slowly, handing over a list of seven names—four friends and three coworkers, including Merrilee.

"I can go with Marcia," he said, "and use taking Milt his mail as an excuse."

"And showing off your new-found ability to be out and about." I turned to Will. "Problem solved. I think two people in their thirties can handle one old man."

Will was still frowning but he gave in. "Just be careful, okay? There's two of you that you need to keep safe now." He gave my baby bump a meaningful glance.

"I know." I conjured up a smile. I didn't like his tendency to be overprotective, but with Bumpkin along for the ride right now, he had a point.

Herb looked at his watch. "We can't talk to him now though. Frank'll be here soon."

"Okay," Will said, "let's discuss strategy, before he gets here."

⊷───⊷

Figuring it wouldn't hurt to have Frank somewhat off kilter from the get-go, we let him try to unlock the front door with his key.

When it didn't work, he rattled the knob. After a beat, the doorbell rang.

Will, who'd been standing near the door, unlocked it and threw it open.

Frank jumped back and almost fell off the edge of the porch. "Who are you?"

"Marcia's husband. She asked me to come over and help Herb with a couple of things."

"What things?" His tone was irritated.

Good. He's definitely off kilter.

I took a step forward. "It's kinda hard to explain, easier if we show you." I beckoned for him to follow and led the way to the hallway.

Will brought up the rear, intentionally, ready to stop the guy if he tried to take off.

Herb and the dogs were already in the master bedroom. I stepped aside so the two men were facing each other.

Herb looked genuinely relieved. "Frank, you're here. Thank goodness. This has really got me spooked." He gestured toward the walk-in closet.

He's a better actor than I thought.

Frank shook his head slightly. "What's going on?"

"See for yourself," Herb said.

"Wait." Frank's body visibly relaxed. "You found the opening, didn't you?" He stepped into the doorway of the closet, where he could see the secret door, sitting ajar. "I *told* Char we should show it to you, but she was afraid the whole story would freak you out."

"What whole story?" Will said from behind him.

Frank turned slightly toward me. "Remember, I told you a young woman had committed suicide in the house, back in the 90s. She left a note. Turns out her stepfather had been using this secret passage to go into her room at night. It had been going on for years."

Beside me, Herb let out an expletive.

"Yeah," Frank said, his expression grim. "We didn't know about any of that until you'd moved in here. Herb, I'm sorry. Like I said, I wanted to tell you, but…" He trailed off.

"You didn't think this was relevant to Char's death?" I asked. "Why didn't you tell the sheriff about it?"

"I, uh," Frank stammered. "I was pretty shook the day…*that* day. It didn't occur to me."

Ms.Snark scoffed internally. *And he didn't think of it all this time between then and now?*

"There's something else," Will said. He stepped aside and I

maneuvered quickly past Frank to once again lead the way. Will followed him, with Herb and the dogs now bringing up the rear.

We'd intentionally put Buddy behind Frank. He was our secret weapon. Will had trained him to do certain tasks that police dogs do, such as grabbing a culprit's arm, again hoping Buddy could protect me when I "poked around" in things.

I led the way down the hall and into the guest bedroom. That closet door was also sitting open.

I pointed up at the oversized opening in the ceiling.

Frank stared at it, blinking, as his cheeks paled.

Will gestured toward the stepladder and handed Frank a flashlight. "Climb up and take a look. It's quite a set-up."

Frank climbed the ladder, stuck his head and the light up through the opening. "Where does it lead to?" His voice was muffled, but it sounded shaky to me.

"The storage room out back," Herb said.

Frank climbed down the ladder. His face was even paler than a minute ago. His hand shook as he gave the flashlight back to Will. "What does this mean?"

"What do *you* think it means?" I asked.

Frank turned wide eyes in my direction. "Char…she was murdered, wasn't she?" He looked like he was about to faint.

CHAPTER TWENTY-TWO

Will had finished closing off the access to the attic and securing the opening between the bedrooms. Then he'd announced he was going to try to catch the gossip column reporter before she left her office.

After he left, Herb and I made an attempt to do some training, but our hearts weren't in it. Twenty minutes later, we gave up.

"Do you believe him?" Herb asked, as he packed some fresh clothes into a backpack.

"Who...Frank?" I said from the armchair.

He nodded.

"I don't know. He seemed sincere and his reactions were appropriate."

Or he could be a darn good actor.

Herb sighed. "I was happy for Char when they got together. She needs an easygoing man like him. She's a tad high maintenance." I doubted he realized he'd slipped into the present tense.

"I've known Frank for almost two years now," he continued. "I guess we've become friends in our own right."

He sat down on the edge of his bed. "I can't believe some-body did all that up there," he looked up at the ceiling, "and I never even knew they were up there."

"Our guess is they timed things to when there were noises coming from the industrial park."

"I did hear some thumping noises one night," Herb said, "quite a few months ago now. I mentioned it to Frank and that's when he told me the house might be haunted. I guess anything I heard after that, I assumed it was the ghost."

How convenient, Ms. Snark said internally, sarcasm dripping from her words. *Do you think Frank had the lie ready or did he make it up on the spot?*

"And that *doesn't* make you suspect him?" I asked out loud, gesturing toward the ceiling. "He had ready access."

Herb seemed lost in thought for a moment. "Yes, he did, but others did too." He shuddered and dropped his gaze to the floor. "I was so worried about imaginary attackers… I guess I should have been more careful about giving out keys."

Dolly, who'd been lying near the bed, sat up and whined, watching him intently.

He chuckled. "I'm okay, girl, but thanks for noticing."

I'd seen the dynamic he was describing before. Some trauma survivors were paranoid about threats in the here and now. But others, as a defense mechanism, numbed out to the possibility of current threats.

Herb picked up our notes from the table, stuffed them in his backpack, then handed one sheet to me.

It was the list of people Char had said she loved. "Are you willing to pay for background checks on all of them?" I asked.

He nodded. "Even if I don't get any money from Char's will, I'll pay what it takes. After this morning, I know I wouldn't last long in prison."

"What about that insurance policy the deputy mentioned?"

He shrugged. "That's the first I'd heard of it. Char must've taken it out without telling me. I meant to ask Frank about that."

Or someone took it out in Char's name," Ms. Snark said, *to strengthen the frame-up.*

I silently agreed.

Will returned, frustration written on his face. "That gossip columnist was no help at all. She wouldn't even confirm that she had been talking about Barbara Hersh in that article."

I commiserated with him, then said, "Guys, I'm exhausted. It's been a long day."

"One of the longest of my life," Herb said with fervor, hefting his backpack onto one shoulder.

We went out to our vehicles. Herb helped me strap the dogs in. He climbed into my passenger seat, as I opened the driver's side door.

"Marcia, you've got something stuck under your windshield wiper." He gestured toward it.

I snatched the paper out from under the wiper. Assuming it was an advertising flyer, I was about to crumple it up, when I noticed the dog.

It was a picture of a dog—a black dog. Printed on a plain sheet of paper.

My heart raced as I looked more closely. It was Buddy. And the background was Herb's backyard. The picture was round. Faint lines crossed in the middle of the circle.

Cross hairs! My stomach heaved.

Someone had taken Buddy's picture through a rifle sight.

◆———◆

I couldn't stop shaking.

Will had one arm wrapped around my shoulders and held the picture in the other. "I think this was photo-shopped," he said. "The cross hairs were added."

That was only mildly reassuring. Without my knowledge, someone had taken a photo of Buddy, sniffing around Herb's backyard for the perfect spot to do his business. And the cross hairs, added or not, were a threat.

Will coaxed me into the driver's seat of my car, told me to

sit tight. Then he did a circuit around Herb's privacy fence in the back.

He found footprints near one of the posts, where there was a gap in between it and the fence slats. He took pictures and called the sheriff's department.

"I'm not holding my breath about them making a cast of the prints," he said, back at my car. "The shoes are flats, smooth soles. Not sneakers. Medium size. Could be a woman with slightly large feet, or a smaller man."

My mind flashed to Milt. He was heavy now, but his was not a big frame. Was he capable of violence against a dog, in order to keep whatever secret he was hiding?

Belatedly, Will noticed I was shaking again. "Herb, do you have a current driver's license?"

"Yeah, but I haven't driven in almost two years."

Will was looking down at me, his forehead furrowed, but he spoke to Herb, "Have you ever driven a pickup?"

"Sure, lots of times." Herb got the hint. He jumped out of my car.

Will tossed him his keys and gestured for me to move over.

My gratitude knew no bounds. No way was I fit to drive. Again, I realized I was overreacting because of pregnancy hormones, but that knowledge did nothing to stop the shakes.

While Will released Dolly and transferred her safety strap to the small backseat of his extended cab, I gratefully slid over to the passenger seat of my own car.

I felt like such a wimp, but nothing unnerves me quite like a threat to my animals, especially Buddy.

At the motel, we encountered another shock. The management had disabled the electronic key to Herb's room.

He was trying to get it to work, when Mom stuck her head out of her room. "I'm so sorry. We argued with the staff, but they insisted that getting arrested negated their obligation to keep the room available."

A little shell-shocked at this point, we all, dogs included, trooped into Mom and Clint's room.

Mom turned to Will and me. "The good news is, we were able to retrieve your things. The bedroom side of the house is still relatively intact, mostly water damage."

She gestured toward the bed and I practically pounced on my stuff—my phone, purse, laptop case and my small duffel bag. The latter smelled of smoke, but I was grateful for the changes of clothes inside, including Edna's shirts.

But I was even more grateful to have my phone back. I was tempted to kiss it.

Mom was talking to Herb. "We couldn't get to your things. The fire apparently started on that side of the house."

"That's okay." He held up his backpack. "I brought more stuff from home."

"Any word on the cause of the fire yet?" Will asked.

Clint frowned. "County fire marshal wouldn't say officially, but he's a friend of mine. He told me unofficially that he thinks it was arson. Some signs of accelerant on the outside of the house."

Will looked at me, as if judging how stable I was now.

I nodded.

He gave a slight nod back. "Do you think they were targeting Herb, or just happened to pick that side of the house?"

Clint shrugged. "No way of knowin' that."

"So we're down one motel room," Mom said.

I had a solution to that percolating in my brain, plus the solution to another problem. "We might be able to give our room to Herb."

I checked the time on my phone—my precious phone! It was only a little after six. I hit the speed dial number for Becky.

She answered with her usual cheerful, about-to-laugh voice. "Hey, Marcia. How ya doin'?"

She'd sobered a good bit by the time I explained everything to her. "Sure. Come on over. I'll check that there are fresh sheets on the spare bedroom's bed."

I turned to Will. "Can you get us to Becky's without anyone following us?"

He gave me a mock offended look. "Of course I can."

"We'll be there in twenty minutes," I said into the phone.

⟵———⟶

Have you ever argued with your spouse in whispers? It's challenging!

Becky and her husband, Andy had greeted us graciously. We'd gulped down vegan stew, left over from their dinner, and visited for a while. Then we'd retired to the guest room, next door to the nursery.

Where I had presented my plan to Will that we leave Buddy with Becky in the morning, when we returned to the task of tracking down Char Mather's killer.

"No way," Will hissed quietly. "The only reason I'm semi-okay with you investigating is that Buddy is there to help protect you."

I had no counter-argument for that. Honestly, I was somewhat uncomfortable about not having Buddy with me. Okay, make that a fair amount uncomfortable.

But nevertheless, I was going to keep my dog safe! I hissed that message back at Will.

He put his hands on my shoulders. "Sweetheart, let's put it aside for now and go to bed. Nobody followed us here. We can relax and get some quality sleep. I'm worried about all this stress, its impact on you and Bumpkin."

I glared up at him. "You know, I really hate it when you're reasonable."

He chuckled. "Tomorrow, our heads will be clearer. We'll figure out then where to go from here."

We brainstormed with Becky and Andy the next morning over breakfast. With the usually rambunctious twins confined to their highchairs and preoccupied with their breakfast, we could focus on what to do next.

"We're happy to keep Buddy here," Becky said, her heart-shaped face sagging with worry. "But I kinda agree with Will that it might be better for you to have him with you."

"We'll still have Dolly with us," I said.

Will made a scoffing noise, and Becky said, "Is that the cute border collie I met last time I was at your house?"

"Um, yes," I admitted reluctantly. Dolly wasn't what anyone would consider a scary dog.

Becky shook her head, her dark curls bouncing. "Again, I've got to agree with Will."

Her husband shook his head as well, although his own more closely cropped curls did not bounce. "Where's the Crystal County sheriff on all this?"

Andy was an officer in the Williston Police Department, so of course, he wanted to know the official law enforcement stance.

"I guess he considers the case closed," Will said, "now that he's made an arrest."

"This is Clint Burns's successor, right?" Andy said to me. "That hotshot detective you had a run-in with a couple years ago?"

I nodded, and Andy started to roll his eyes, then caught himself.

"Look," I said, wanting to get back to the decision about Buddy, "I'm only going to be interviewing agents at the real estate office today. Surely I'll be safe enough doing that. We can regroup later and decide whether or not Buddy should go with me after that."

I was trying to sound reasonable, but I was just as determined in the light of day as I'd been last night to keep Buddy safe. Yeah, maybe the picture was photo-shopped, but I couldn't get the imagined scenario out of my head, of a shot ringing out and Buddy dropping dead on the ground.

It dawned on me that I was much braver in a direct confrontation. The thought of a sneak attack terrified me.

Which helped me to better understand the mixture of anxiety and bravery that Herb had been exhibiting. It really did depend on which "bogeymen" happened to push your psyche's buttons.

I finally wore Will down and he gave in. On Becky and Andy's front porch, I told Buddy to stay, and we walked to Will's truck.

Buddy tilted his head in his *what's-up* look, as I climbed in and closed the passenger door. That was the image frozen in my mind—him looking confused and a little forlorn—as we drove away.

It made my throat ache, but it was a distinct improvement over the image of him falling to the ground dead.

CHAPTER TWENTY-THREE

Herb had called Frank and asked for the use of a conference room at the agency's office, to interview "some people." On my instructions, he hadn't gotten any more specific than that.

After dropping me at the motel, where we'd left my car, Will took off to track down the friends from Herb's list.

Herb and I reviewed Elise's preliminary reports for Char's coworkers. She hadn't had time to get much more than the basics on them. Armed only with that sketchy info, we headed over to the agency.

Entering the real estate office was a new challenge for Herb and Dolly. I told myself that this was still "training," even though I knew darn well that training had taken a backseat to solving Char's murder.

It took Dolly several minutes to make the circuit of the agency's bullpen. She stopped in front of Merrilee's chair and sat. The woman reached out to pet her, bracelets jangling, but the dog took off again, stopping to sit and bark at several other agents' cubicles. She also sniffed at closed office doors, sitting momentarily in front of one of them, to indicate the room was occupied by someone she knew.

I glanced sideways at Herb. He was wearing a small grin. "She sure takes her job seriously."

I smiled back. "As she should."

Finally, Dolly came back to the agency's front door and sat in front of Herb, panting a little.

As we entered, Frank came out of the office where Dolly had stopped and sat. He gestured for us to follow him and led the way to a small conference room. Dolly cleared that space in a couple of seconds.

The first woman we interviewed was fairly relaxed. She'd been with the agency for years, long before Char had taken over. Also a protégé of Char's mentor, she seemed genuinely fond of him and of her.

But that could be an act. Perhaps she had resented Char's moving so quickly into the position of the owner's assistant. I asked that question, as diplomatically as possible.

She laughed. "I was offered that assistant's job before Char was. I turned it down. I like working more independently. It's one of the main reasons I got into real estate."

The second agent on the list, Jennifer Peters, sat stiffly in her chair, her mouth a thin straight line. She mostly nodded or shook her head in response to our initial questions.

I leaned forward in my chair. "Ms. Peters, why might Char have said to you, 'I love you dearly, but…'"

The woman scowled. "I hated all that fake lovey-dovey stuff. Air kisses and 'darling this' and 'darling that.' It made me sick."

Tell us how you really feel, Ms. Snark commented internally.

"You didn't consider her a close friend?" Herb asked.

"I didn't consider her a friend, period. She was my employer. I've never liked mixing business with friendship." She opened her mouth to say more, glanced at Herb, then clamped it shut again.

The words, *Even if I had liked her,* hung in the air.

I made a mental note to have Elise dig deeper into this woman's background.

We had planned to talk to Merrilee as well, but when I went looking for her, I was told she had left. Nobody seemed to know where she'd gone. "She's probably meeting a client," the male receptionist said.

Crapola. We'd have to track her down later. I returned to the conference room to collect Herb and Dolly.

Leaving also involved Dolly clearing the larger bull pen area first, although there were fewer people at the desks this time.

Frank came out of his office. "Did you get everything you needed?"

"Yes, thank you." *Except for Merrilee.*

"Where's your dog?" Frank asked.

"Um, at the vet's. Annual checkup." I gave him a fake smile. "Well, thanks again for the use of your conference room."

⊷——⊷

We headed back to Herb's neighborhood, to interview Milt again.

"You still suspect Frank?" Herb said from my passenger seat.

"He's not off the list."

"Buddy's not really at the vet, is he?"

I gave him a sideways glance. "No, and I'm not telling anybody where he is."

Herb let out a noise that was half snort, half laugh. "Don't worry, if asked, 'I know nuthink, nuthink.'" He did a credible imitation of Sergeant Schultz on the old sitcom, *Hogan's Heroes.*

I glanced his way again.

He was grinning. "One watches a lot of old TV shows when housebound."

I returned his smile.

On Paradise Court, Herb went to Milt's mailbox. "Good he hasn't gotten his mail yet."

A minute later, we were on Milt's porch, Herb's face in front of the peephole, envelopes in his hand. Dolly sat in the cover position next to him.

I hung back and off to the side.

Milt opened the door, a big grin on his face. But it disappeared when he spotted me.

"Hey, Milt," Herb said. "Here's your mail, but I also wanted you to be the first to see me enter someone else's house!"

The old man glanced nervously at me, but he really didn't have much choice, not unless he was willing to be incredibly rude to Herb. He stepped back and made a come-in gesture.

"Dolly, clear," Herb said.

The dog ran inside, made a quick circuit of the small living room, then stopped and sat in front of Milt by the door.

Herb took a deep breath and stepped over the threshold.

"Have a seat." Milt gestured toward the sofa that sat several feet away from the wall—a room divider that defined a library of sorts behind it, maybe five by ten feet and lined with bookcases.

Herb eyed the space, his body language tense.

"Dolly, clear." I pointed to the area behind the sofa. She whizzed around it and came back to us.

Herb gingerly lowered himself onto the sofa.

"Cover." I pointed to the spot next to Herb's end. Dolly sat there in the *cover* position.

Herb gave me a grateful smile as I sat down on the opposite end of the sofa.

Milt looked impressed. "Can I get you all somethin' to drink?" he asked.

"No, I'm fine," Herb said. I shook my head.

The old man settled in the armchair. He and Herb made small talk for a few minutes. During a lull, Herb asked, "Why didn't you ever mention your kids to me?"

Milt jerked a little in his chair. "Well, I just kinda assumed that, because you didn't have no kids, you wouldn't be interested."

"Of course I'm interested. You got any pictures of them?"

Milt froze for a half beat. "Not recent ones."

When neither of us said anything, he pulled out his wallet and held it open. Two kids, about eight and six, looked out at us, innocent grins on their faces. The younger, the girl, was missing a front tooth.

"They're adorable," I said.

Milt snapped the wallet closed. "They were. That was a lot of years ago. They're grown now."

"I've never seen your kids come to visit," Herb said.

Milt shook his head slightly. "Their lives are more complicated than mine, so I go to them."

Herb shot me a quick sideways glance that I interpreted to mean Milt was lying. Since the old man had brought him his mail daily, he would've noticed any absences. There hadn't been any such trips.

"I bet you love playing with your grandkids," Herb said.

Suddenly, the old man's eyes were shiny with unshed tears.

And I felt like a heel. I wasn't sure what had gone down between this man and his grown children, but we were obviously yanking the scab off an old wound.

"I've never met any but the oldest one in person," Milt said. "My boy's eldest. The kids don't come to visit, and I can't go to them."

"Why not?" Herb asked.

Milt pushed himself to a stand, his face grim, his lips clamped in a tight line. For a second, I thought he was going to throw us out.

But he walked to a bookcase behind us and pulled something off the shelf. Herb turned in his seat, following his progress.

As Milt came back around Herb's end of the sofa, Dolly's tail thumped against the hardwood floor, distracting me.

When I looked up, the old man was standing in front of me, holding something behind his back.

He's got a gun! Ms. Snark yelled inside my head.

I froze, my heart racing.

Milt stood still, staring in my direction, his eyes glassy with a far-away look.

I held my breath. *What was I thinking, coming here without Buddy or Will?*

I glanced at Herb. He was watching *me*, a concerned expression on his face.

I felt lightheaded.

Now would be a really bad time to faint! Ms. Snark pointed out.

CHAPTER TWENTY-FOUR

"Are you okay, Marcia?"

Herb's words seemed to pull Milt out of his reverie. He turned to his chair and sat down, placing a thick photo album on his lap.

I blew out pent-up air, willing my galloping heart to settle down.

Sheez Louise, Ms. Snark said inside my head.

You! You're the one who panicked!

No response.

"It's all gonna come out now anyway," Milt said with a sigh. He handed the album to me.

I slowly pulled in air and let it out, then opened the album on my lap, so Herb could see it too. On the first two pages were eight-by-tens of the two kids we'd just seen in the old man's wallet.

Milt gestured toward the album. "I keep copies of those two shots in my wallet to remind me of why I did it all. The kids don't come to me because they're afraid my ex will have them followed, and I can't go to them because she's bound to find out they're still in touch and try to force them to tell where I am."

"What?" Herb said. "Are you hiding from her? Why?"

I turned a few pages in the album. The kids grew into teenagers.

Milt sighed again. "My ex is an alcoholic. She beat the children when they were little. I didn't realize what was going on at first 'cause she did it during the day, when I was at work. Then one day, she broke my son's arm, and it all came out. The kids told me what had been happening."

I turned another page. The son's graduation from high school, then the daughter's on the next few pages.

"I took them and left. The next day I filed for divorce and custody. But my ex is a good liar. She cleaned herself up for court and tearfully convinced the judge that she was the innocent one and I was the child abuser, now depriving her of her kids."

"Didn't the judge talk to the kids, or have a social worker interview them?" I asked, horrified by the story he was telling.

Milt snorted. "This was in the 1960s, before anyone thought to do either of those things. The kids were put in a foster home while the case was pending. They told me later they were terrified they'd never see either of their parents again. My ex ended up getting full custody and I got supervised visitation."

The next page of the album was a full-page wedding shot, the son and a lovely young bride.

"She behaved at first, but after a while, I was seeing bruises on them again." Milt leaned forward in his chair. "One day, I decided to take things into my own hands. I went to their school at recess time and waved them over to me. I grabbed their little hands and we took off through some woods to where I'd left my van, with all my worldly possessions crammed into the back. We came here to Florida. I'd bought fake IDs for each of us." He sat back again. "So you see, if my ex finds me, I'll go to jail for kidnapping."

"Surely by now," I said, "the statute of limitations has run out on a parental abduction."

Milt shrugged. "They didn't have separate laws about parents taking their own kids back then. It was a kidnapping, a felony—and a federal crime, since I crossed state lines with them. I supported us by starting a handyman service, all off the books.

Never paid income tax either. I couldn't afford to leave a paper trail anywhere."

He shook his head slightly. "After the kids were grown I took the risk and bought this house. I was tired of throwing money away on rent, and I'd saved enough over the years to pay cash for a modest place. Nobody questions your ID if you're not applying for a mortgage."

He paused, took a deep breath. "And it was good that I'd taken all those precautions. My ex was as vindictive as I'd thought she would be. She'd hired a private detective to try to find us, and apparently kept paying him for years. He tracked my son down shortly after my oldest grandchild was born. Of course, my boy wouldn't tell her where I was. She even threatened to call the police on him, for harboring a fugitive. He called her bluff, and she didn't do it."

Either that or the police laughed at her, Ms. Snark commented internally, her voice a bit tentative.

Milt had paused again, was staring at the floor. "Now the grandkids are in their teens. We talk on Zoom some, but even that worries my kids. They don't want me goin' to jail."

I leafed farther through the album, watched the grandchildren growing up.

After Milt had been silent for a moment, I said, "Someone found out about your past and threatened to expose you, if you didn't pressure your neighbors to sell out."

Milt's head came up, eyes wide. Then he nodded. "I got an anonymous note, tucked inside my screen door the day we got the letters. It said if I didn't want my secret revealed, I'd better make sure everybody accepted the eminent domain offers without a fight."

"It only said your secret?" I asked. "Nothing more?"

"Yeah, no details, but I couldn't take the chance. I really don't want to spend my final years behind bars."

I seriously doubted that anyone would pursue the kidnapping charge, but the IRS would likely want their pound of flesh for all those years of back taxes.

"You have no idea who's behind the threat?" I asked.

He started to shake his head, then stopped. "We all got a letter awhile back, with offers for our houses. Some developer wanted the land. But enough of us refused that they couldn't do whatever they had planned."

"First I've heard of that," Herb said. "But Char probably wouldn't have told me, if the letter went to her. She'd know it would've freaked me out."

"How long ago was that?" I asked.

Milt stared at the ceiling for a few seconds. "I'd say about a year ago."

"Do you happen to remember the name of the developer?" I said.

"No, but I have the letter around here someplace." Milt shoved himself up out of the chair again and rounded the sofa to rummage through the drawers of an old-fashioned file cabinet, lodged between two bookcases.

"Here it is." He brought the sheet of paper to us.

I glanced over it. "Can we take this? I'll make a copy and get the original back to you."

He waved a hand in the air. "Keep it. If you can find out who's behind this, I'll be grateful. I really didn't like the idea of trying to pressure Louise into selling. And I don't want to go into some retirement community if I don't have to."

I nodded. "I'll try to keep your name out of things if I can."

"I'd appreciate that," Milt said.

As he walked us to the door, I couldn't help wondering what the ex-wife's side of the story would be, but it wasn't my business. I already had plenty of mysteries on my plate.

As soon as we were back in my car, I texted Elise with the name and address of the development company on the letter. I asked her to rush the background check.

Then I remembered the I-hate-the-lovey-dovey-stuff real

estate agent. I sent another text asking for a check on her as well.

"Lemme call Frank," Herb said.

"Why?"

He didn't answer, but a faint ringing sound told me he'd put his phone on speaker.

"Hey, Herb. What's up?"

"Hey, Frank. Do you know anything about J and B Development Company?"

What's with all the blinkin' initials? Ms. Snark asked internally. I ignored her.

"Not much," Frank said. "I've negotiated a couple of deals for them. Why?"

"One of my neighbors just told me they made offers to all the residents of my community last year." Herb sounded so calm and casual. "Did they make an offer on my house? The letter might have gone to Char."

"If it did, I didn't hear anything about it. Of course, Char wouldn't have considered it. She wouldn't have been willing to uproot you, no matter how good their offer was."

"How good was the offer?" I asked, hoping to trip him up.

A beat of silence. "Hi, Marcia. I misspoke. I meant, no matter how good the offer *might've* been."

Herb made small talk with Frank for a few moments, then signed off. He didn't say anything, only cocked an eyebrow at me.

I drove us back to the motel. Will's truck was there, and he was waiting outside Herb's door.

Dolly cleared the room, darting into the bathroom as well, without being told.

Border collies were considered the smartest dog breed, and for good reason. Dolly was adapting to Herb's needs, anticipating his commands.

Herb and I sat down at the small table by the motel room's window.

Will perched on the end of the bed. "None of the friends I talked to had much to say. They all claimed to be devastated by Char's death, but no tears were shed. No subtle reactions to the line, 'what you've set in motion is intolerable.' And they had no idea what it might be referring to."

I told him about the one employee whom Char supposedly "loved dearly" but who was less than enthusiastic about her boss's affections.

Then I gave a short synopsis of Milt's secret, leaving out the unpaid taxes.

Will was shaking his head sadly by the time I finished. "I doubt he'd be in all that much trouble at this point."

"That's what I was thinking too, but he didn't want to take the chance, so he did what the anonymous note told him to—tried to get his neighbors to let their houses go without a fight."

My phone pinged. A text from Elise. *Check your email.*

She had sent a preliminary report on J and B Development Company. *Wow, that was super fast.*

Herb and Will watched as I skimmed the report on my phone. It was very basic. Not surprising. She would send more later, no doubt.

I clicked on the second attachment, labeled *photo of CEO.* And my mouth fell open.

Will stepped up behind me and looked over my shoulder. "Do you know that guy?"

"No, but Frank does."

CHAPTER TWENTY-FIVE

The CEO in the headshot was the dark-haired, slightly husky man Frank had been arguing with the day of Char's funeral. His name was Frederick Jacobs.

I scrolled through the photos on my phone and showed Will and Herb the one of the guy angrily gesturing at Frank after the graveside service.

Then Herb told Will about our phone conversation with Frank. Will didn't say much. Most people would say his expression was neutral, his cop face. But I caught the flash of anger in his eyes.

Herb spread out the five sheets of notes on the motel room bed, along with the letter Milt had given us. He and Will stared down at them.

"We need to talk to Frank again, don't we?" Herb said, a mournful undercurrent in his voice.

"Yes." Will glanced my way and his expression softened. He gave me a lopsided smile. "But we'll let him stew awhile."

I had booted up my laptop on the table and was reading Elise's report more carefully.

The development company owned two-thirds of the houses in Herb's community. They were currently rented out, with month-to-month leases. And…

"Guess who owns that ugly industrial park next to your house, Herb?"

Both men turned my way, but Will answered, "J and B Development Company."

"Yup, give that man a prize."

I got up and went over to look over the sheets of notes myself. I pointed to page four. "The mystery of Milt's secret has been solved."

Herb scribbled a note on that sheet.

I stared at the letter Milt had given us, from the development company. It reminded me that I'd never talked to Will about the eminent domain notices.

I asked Herb if he still had his letter.

He grimaced. "It was in the duffle bag I took to your folks' house."

I mirrored his grimace. "In other words, it's ashes now."

Will pointed to page two of the notes. "We still need to talk to the councilwoman again."

I tapped the addendum page about the fire. "Should we stop by the house, see if there's anything helpful there?" Maybe we'd discover that the letter had miraculously survived the fire.

Will nodded. "We'll go by there first. Then corner the councilwoman at her home later. She might be more forthcoming, if she thinks we're going to tell her husband what we know."

"What do you mean?" I said. "We only know what was in the gossip column."

Elise's report on Barbara Hersh hadn't offered much besides her address and standard background info—where she'd grown up, gone to school, etc.

Will gave me a wicked grin. "Yeah, but Hersh doesn't know that. I can pretend the reporter told me more."

We stood in front of the house where Clint had lived for over thirty years, where he had raised his children and stepchildren and had nursed his dying wife. A lump formed in my throat.

One third of the house, the kitchen and den side, was in ruins. The roof and one whole wall were gone, only a few charred studs silhouetted against the sky. I gave up any hope of finding the eminent domain letter in that rubble.

The other side of the house—where the bedrooms were—was relatively intact, although Mom had said there was a lot of water damage from the fire hoses. The insurance adjuster had declared the house totaled.

The lump grew.

"If they were trying to kill us," I pushed the words out, "why start the fire on the opposite side from the bedrooms?"

"They wouldn't have necessarily known the layout of the house," Will said. "Or they might have been afraid that the dogs would hear them poking around outside and sound the alarm."

"They wouldn't have known that Herb and Dolly were in Clint's study." My throat closed completely and my stomach churned. If Buddy hadn't woken me up…

Will shook his head, as if to clear it of similar what-ifs. "Let's look around."

We began to walk the perimeter of the house. "Do you really think we'll discover anything useful?" I asked.

He shrugged. "Don't know, but a good detective checks out everything. You never assume that something is unimportant. Some little detail here might click with some other detail we saw elsewhere, and the pieces start coming together."

I nodded. I'd been an unofficial participant in enough investigations to know how that worked. And the feeling, when the puzzle came together, was exhilarating.

We circled the house twice, but saw nothing helpful from the outside.

"I should go in," Will said.

"Not without me, you don't."

"Your mom said the south side was relatively safe."

"Okay, I'm going with you." I was bluffing. I didn't want either one of us going into that unstable building. The arsonist hadn't gone inside—the Fire Marshall had told Clint that the accelerant was on the outside of the house—so one of us going in there wouldn't accomplish a thing.

Will was shaking his head. "We've got to consider Bumpkin."

"Exactly! Obviously, I have to survive in order for him or her to be born, but once that happens, both parents are needed."

Will opened his mouth.

I cut him off. I'd just thought of the perfect argument. "If it's too dangerous for me, it's too dangerous for you!"

Will froze, lowered his gaze to the ground. After a beat, he nodded slowly.

"We make a pact," I said, "if either of us is going into a dangerous situation, we take a nanosecond to ask ourselves whether we would try to stop the other from doing it. If the answer is yes, we don't do it."

Will stood perfectly still for another second, then nodded again. "But," he said, "if we assess that we have the skills to deal with the situation, even though the other one might not have those skills, we can do it."

I shook my head. "Only if those skills are unique to us, not the other."

He looked at me with a confused expression.

"Okay, you have certain skills as a trained police officer, so maybe you can handle some situations that I can't. But I have other skills with my psychology background and as a dog handler…" I trailed off realizing I'd painted myself into a corner.

Will grinned at me. "Only if you have your dog with you."

Touché, Ms. Snark quipped.

◄────►

The home of Barbara Hersh, full-time real estate agent and part-time councilwoman, was in what passed for a posh neighborhood in Crystal County. It was a sprawling rancher, at least four-thousand square feet, on several acres of manicured lawn.

When we arrived, the sun was setting, casting a golden glow across that lawn. And Barbara and her hubby were settling into their living room for some after-dinner TV.

Will politely suggested that the councilwoman might want to discuss certain things elsewhere. She led the way to a study on the opposite end of the house.

Will began by asking whether or not she'd heard anything more about the purpose behind the eminent domain notices.

She hemmed and hawed some, but basically said nothing concrete.

Will furrowed his brow. "We also heard a rumor about some male companion at a restaurant…" He trailed off, as if he wasn't sure if that was relevant of not.

Ms. Hersh's face turned pink and she dropped her gaze. Then pink morphed to red. "That was a spurious lie!" she spit out while keeping her voice low.

She glanced nervously at the closed study door. "I was having lunch with a female friend who happens to have broad shoulders and short hair. She went into the back to use the ladies' room, *not* the rear exit."

Will nodded, his expression sympathetic. "I'm still a little confused though. How could the county send out eminent domain notices without the county council knowing what they were for?"

A slight hesitation. "I don't know."

"Hmm." Will pulled out his notepad. "Could we get the name and contact info for your female friend? To be thorough, ya know…"

She froze for a second. "Why? What the heck does that have to do with whatever it is you're investigating? What *are* you investigating anyway?"

"Well," Will said, "we were looking into Charlene Mathers's supposed suicide, before the sheriff reopened that case. Now we're investigating why the county is trying to take people's homes away from them, for no apparent reason."

"Who's your client then? Not that guy, the victim's ex?"

"We're not at liberty to say," I replied, "but there are several people involved." True enough. Several people had received the seizure letters, although only one was our client.

"So what does my lunch date with a friend have to do with that?"

"We don't know that it does, ma'am," I said. "But we have to follow all leads."

The councilwoman's eyes went wide and she snapped her fingers, acting as if she had just now thought of something—but she wasn't a great actor. "I did hear a rumor, that the land is being seized for some new county buildings, including an expanded sheriff's department and jail. I guess so everything is on one campus. It's all hush-hush though, for some reason. Apparently, all that was approved before I came into office."

Will nodded, scribbling on his pad. "Thanks. That helps a lot. Do you remember where you heard the rumor?"

She paused as if considering the question. "No. I think it may have been an overheard conversation."

Will and I exchanged a look. "Can you think of anything else, ma'am?" I asked.

She shook her head.

We thanked her for her time and left.

Back in Will's truck, I asked, "Do you believe her about the lunch date?"

"Nope."

"Me neither. Do you think it's relevant?"

"Maybe, but probably not. Pursuing that, however, got the result I was hoping for, that she would distract us with the information that we really wanted to know."

"That's what I figured you were doing." I grinned at him, then sobered. "Only she lied. First of all, the council chair, Call-Me-Bobby Graham, would've known about the project."

"Your stepfather would've too."

I noted my lack of reaction to the word *stepfather*. I was getting used to thinking of Clint in that role. My chest warmed. My child would have a grandfather.

Will put his truck in gear and pulled away from the curb. "No way would they plan a new sheriff's department and jail without consulting the sheriff, which would have been him. Projects like that take months to plan, if not years."

I nodded. "I was already beginning to suspect the eminent domain letters were phony."

He glanced my way. "What do you mean?"

"The letter Herb got, I don't think it had an address or phone number on it, only the county logo and the words, *Planning Office*. The signature was a scrawl. I don't remember anything typed under it."

Will was looking thoughtful, his eyes on the road. "We could get a copy of the letter from one of his neighbors."

"Yeah… But doesn't all that seem sloppy to you? Why send out phony eminent domain notices, knowing that some residents would object and were going to ask awkward questions?"

"Unless they're not completely phony and someone in the county government is in on the deal, whatever the heck the deal is."

Will took one hand off the steering wheel to scratch the five-o'clock shadow on his chin. "Handy coincidence that the sole person in the planning office is on maternity leave."

"With no one designated to fill in for her."

"And it's not all that sloppy," Will said. "Yes, it's a long shot that it would work. But with no contact info on the letters, how would anyone trace them back to the sender?"

"True. The sender covered his tracks well." I stared at Will's profile. "Are you thinking what I'm thinking?"

Will glanced over again, then looked back at the road. "They covered their tracks, just like our mystery client. And I've got a hunch they're both this Jacobs guy."

We were headed back to the motel, to pick up my car. Our route took us past the industrial park, but on the opposite side from Herb's community.

The security lights were coming on, as dusk settled into semi-dark. The starkly-lit, ugly metal buildings and asphalt parking lots were mostly deserted.

Except… I did a double-take. "Speak of the devil."

Two buildings were *not* well lit, and they were the only ones that still had activity around them—trucks backing up to loading docks, dim figures of workers moving about.

That's strange. Why are they working in the dark?

Off to one side, a man leaned against the front fender of a flashy red sports car. I only caught a glimpse before we'd gone on by, but I'd bet good money he was the guy who'd argued with Frank at the cemetery.

Frederick Jacobs, the owner of the industrial park and two-thirds of the houses in Palmetto Springs.

CHAPTER TWENTY-SIX

Back at the motel, we checked in on Herb. He and Dolly were fine. "What's your next move?" he asked.

"We need to find out more about this Jacobs guy," Will said.

I nodded.

But once we were outside again, standing by my car, I said, "Yes, we need to check out Jacobs, but I think we need to talk to Frank again. I didn't want to say anything in front of Herb. He gets a little freaked out every time he's reminded that Frank's a suspect. I think he's not quite ready to let go of the man as a friend and lifeline to the world. I wish we'd had more training time in, before all this hit the fan."

"Maybe you can get some training in tomorrow," Will said. "I really should go into the office in the morning."

"It's Saturday." I winced at the slight whine in my voice.

"Yeah, but there's a ton of paperwork on my desk, and if I go in tomorrow, it makes up for some of the time I took off this week."

I couldn't really argue with that. And I did need to get back to training Herb, so that when all this was resolved, I'd be able to go home.

I fantasized for a moment of sleeping in, and then spending my time setting up the nursery. It seemed like heaven.

Will broke into my reverie. "Do you still have that hunk of plastic you found on Herb's floor?"

"It's in my laptop case." I reached into my car for the case, fished out the plastic thing and handed it to him. "Shall we roll by the real estate office? Frank might still be there."

He was, along with a couple of agents out in the bullpen area, doing paperwork and making phone calls.

Frank ushered us into his office. It was large and decorated with rather stark chrome and black furniture. I had a funny feeling it had been Char's office.

I took one of the black leather and chrome visitors' chairs, but Will remained standing long enough to pull the plastic piece out of his pocket. He tossed it on Frank's desk, then sat.

The man stared at it for a moment, his face pale. He licked his lips and looked up with a fake smile. "I wondered where that went. It was part of the packaging from those hinges I replaced the other day."

Will narrowed his eyes, his expression saying he didn't believe that for a New York minute.

But I wasn't up for playing the game. It was getting late and my back hurt. "We don't believe that, Frank. Try again?"

His eyes went wide, and the smile evaporated.

"You rigged the house to make it seem like it's haunted," I said. "You've got the skills and the ready access, plus you were the one who supposedly found out about that old suicide there, which we haven't been able to verify, I should add."

Elise had tried but had found no references to any young woman dying while living there. Which didn't mean it hadn't happened, but I found it hard to believe this guy was a better researcher than Elise.

Frank stared at me, his Adam's apple bobbing as he swallowed hard.

Will held out his hand, palm up. I looked at it in confusion for a nanosecond, before realizing he wanted my phone.

I pulled up the photo from the cemetery and handed it to him.

"You know this guy?" Will turned the phone toward Frank.

"Yeah." Frank looked at me. "That's the developer we were talking about earlier."

"Yes," I said, "but you acted like you didn't know him all that well."

Will said, "You apparently know him well enough to argue with him at your fiancée's funeral."

Frank blanched even paler. "He's kind of a jerk."

"We get that," I said, "but what were you two arguing about?"

"Just business."

"Crapola, Frank!" I raised my voice. "Char's dead. Don't you want to know who did it, and why?"

"Settle down." Will made a calming gesture toward me with his hands. Then an aside to Frank, "You'd better tell her what she wants to know. If she loses it…" He shook his head. "It ain't pretty."

Our bad cop-good cop routine needed work, but it seemed to be doing the trick. Frank was nervously glancing back and forth between us.

"We were arguing about Palmetto Springs. He's wanted to buy those properties for a while, to expand the industrial park."

"But now he can't because the county's taking them," I said.

Frank's face went blank for a second. "Yeah, but before that, he was trying to get me to pressure Herb into selling. He'd tried to get Char to do that last year, back when he bought up a whole lot of the houses and then rented them out. But she wasn't about to disrupt Herb's life."

"But you've been trying to get Herb to want to move for some time, haven't you?" I said. "By spooking him with scary noises and random lights."

Will picked up the piece of black plastic. "This looks a lot like part of a bracket for something, like a light or a projector. I found several places above that drop ceiling where things had been screwed into the walls in the past."

"Okay, okay. Jacobs…" Frank gestured toward my phone, still in Will's hand. "He offered me a lot of money if I could get Herb to move out. So I rigged a speaker and some lights above the ceiling that I could control remotely." He leaned forward, his palms flat on the desktop. "But I didn't do anything illegal. I had permission to be on the property from the owner."

No wonder we hadn't seen any lights lately. Frank hadn't only been replacing cabinet hinges that day. He'd been dismantling his ceiling light show, to keep me from discovering it. And Carla hadn't heard the ghosts because Frank knew she would be there that night, but he hadn't known I would stay over the next night.

My chest tightened. "It might not have been illegal," I spat out, "but it sure was unethical as all get out. Something tells me you'd lose–"

"No!" Frank cried out, his eyes shiny.

Crapola, is he tearing up?

"Please don't tell…" His voice caught.

I expected him to say the real estate board. That's where I'd been going with my previous sentence, that he'd lose his real estate license for such behavior.

But that wasn't it.

"Herb would be so hurt if he knew I'd done that. Please don't tell him, not for my sake, but for his. He's a good guy, and he deserves better than what life…what Char and I…" He trailed off and looked away.

A long pause, during which I worked on calming myself down.

"What you did," I said, in a more neutral voice, "you and Char, was help him out when he needed it. But you also kept him dependent."

Frank still avoided eye contact. "I knew what was going on wasn't totally healthy for him, but I wasn't sure what to do about it. Any time I said something to Char about helping him be more independent, she'd turn it around somehow and accuse me of being jealous of him."

I arranged my face into a sympathetic expression. "That's partly why you did it, wasn't it? Because you thought he'd be better off if he did move."

Frank nodded, his expression relieved.

"And because this Jacobs guy has something on you," Will said, in a hard voice, "doesn't he?"

You realize, I hope, that you've switched roles, Ms. Snark pointed out. *You really do need to work on this act.*

I ignored her internal commentary and carefully watched Frank's face. He was trying hard not to let on that Will had struck a nerve.

My earlier assessment that he was a good actor required adjustment. Apparently, that was only when he could anticipate what was coming. He must have realized, when Herb asked him to come over to the house, that we might have found the secret door between the closets. But now, when he had to ad-lib...

"You knew the door was there," I said, "between those two bedrooms."

"Yeah, that's what I told you."

"No, I mean you knew about it because you either built it yourself, or had used it before, to move around the house without Herb knowing you were there. You built that tunnel in the attic as well, so you could get in from the outside."

He started to shake his head.

"No more lying, Frank." My voice was firm.

He sighed. "Initially, I was gonna rig speakers in the master bedroom and the study, but Herb kept all the inside doors locked, day and night, and he had the only key. So one night, I tunneled through between the storage room and that closet. It wasn't that hard to do. The insulation is open foam, not closed, so I was able to scoop out the tunnel with hand tools–"

I was making a get-on-with-it gesture. "We don't need the construction details."

Frank nodded. "I discovered the opening between the bedrooms when I was rigging the speaker in the study. It gave me the idea for the back story behind the girl's suicide." There was a touch of excitement in his voice, as if he was enjoying finally being able to share how clever he was. "And it solved the problem of how to get into the master bedroom during the day to rig a speaker in there. I had planned to cut through that wall between the closets."

This time, Will made the get-on-with-it gesture.

"Yeah, so, before I could rig that second speaker, Herb started sleeping in the living room. He asked me to put up that door between there and the hallway, and he put a slide bolt on it."

"So you put a speaker in the living room instead," I said, "and added the light show for good measure."

He nodded again. "I didn't use the tunnel after that, and it was only big enough to crawl through. Somebody else expanded it and made the openings wider. That's why I was surprised when I saw it."

"Somebody who wanted to bring a dead body into the house," Will said.

"But that wasn't me, I swear!" Frank's face crumpled. "I'd never hurt Char. I loved her." He covered his face with his hands. A choked sob escaped.

Will leaned forward in his chair. "You had a lot to gain from her death." He waved a hand in a circle to encompass the office, the agency.

And Frank had a lot to lose if Char had found out about the fake haunting. Was that what she was referring to in her note, that he'd set that in motion? So she was breaking up with him and he would lose it all.

"Char found out, didn't she?" I said.

"That's why you killed her," Will added.

Franks' head jerked up. "No, no! I didn't. You've got to believe me. And she didn't find out about the ghost. That's not it at all."

"Anybody else know about the tunnel in the attic?" Will asked. "And the opening between those two closets?"

Frank's eyes went wide again, but this time it looked genuine. "Jacobs! Fred Jacobs knew what I was doing, that whole set-up.

That's what we were arguing about at the cemetery. I told him I needed more time, that I could definitely get Herb to move if I convinced him Char's ghost was now haunting the house as well."

◆———◆

We'd brought both vehicles, planning to go our separate ways from here, me to Williston and Will home so that he could go to work tomorrow morning. But in the parking lot, I climbed into Will's truck first, to discuss what we'd just learned.

"Do you believe him?" Will asked me.

"I think I do. He probably fudged a few details, but I don't think he killed Char. I don't think he has it in him. Maybe strangle her in a fit of rage, but methodically plan a fake suicide?" I shook my head.

Will shrugged. "You never know what people are capable of, when backed into a corner, but I'm inclined to agree with you."

"Time to go back to our home away from home?" I asked hopefully.

"You can, but I want to do one more thing tonight."

"What's that?"

"Before we confront Jacobs with all this, I want to check out that industrial pa–"

"I'm going too," I said.

"I only want to take a look around. I'll go in from the back, from Herb's street."

"Not without me, you won't."

"Aren't you tired?"

"I was, but that lively little interrogation…" I gestured toward the front of the agency. "It gave me a second wind."

"It won't be dangerous," Will said. "I'll keep to the shadows. I want to check out those two buildings where we saw activity earlier."

"Which *could* be dangerous, but if I'm along, you won't take any major risks."

He sighed. "Okay, we'll come back for your car." He held

out his hand, palm up.

I took it and he squeezed gently. "All for one and one for all."

"Wasn't that the three musketeers' mantra?"

He looked meaningfully at my stomach. "Yup. You, me, and Bumpkin."

We parked in Herb's driveway and waited for full dark.

Will brought a flashlight from his truck. We crossed Herb's side yard to the thin strip of land separating the cul-de-sac from the industrial park.

Will shone the light into the weeds, making sure no critters were going to be surprised by our passage, and perhaps would deliver a surprising bite of their own.

Then he turned off the flashlight and led the way, staying in the shadows. This part of the park was peppered with tall street-lights, plus almost every building had floodlights on each corner.

Will expertly ducked between the lighted areas until we were hugging the wall of one of the buildings that had activity around it earlier. We edged along it to a window.

Will cupped his hands around his face to shut out the ambi-ent light from the floods. "Hmm, interesting." He stepped aside so I could look in.

It was mostly dark inside the building now, only one security light shining from a corner of the ceiling. It was enough to make out several pieces of earth-moving equipment—a front loader and two backhoes.

"Why interesting? It's a heavy equipment manufacturer's warehouse."

"Look again. How are they parked?"

Dutifully, I looked again. They were scattered around the cement floor, with some large gaps.

"A manufacturer or shipper of such equipment," Will said quietly from behind me, "would have them lined up, to make the best use of the space."

I nodded, but Will was already slipping along the side of the building. I caught up with him at the corner.

He turned to me, put his hands on my shoulders. I could barely make out his face in the dark. "Sweetheart," he whispered, "I need you to stay here."

I opened my mouth, but he put a finger on my lips. "There's some kind of curtains over the windows in the next building." He pointed behind him. "With moving shadows silhouetted against the cloth. People are in there, doing something."

He paused, took a deep breath. "This is one of those times when my training makes it safer for me to go alone. I can move quickly, stay out of sight. I'll be careful. I only want to see if I can get a look at what's going on in there."

I didn't like it, but I swallowed hard and nodded. "Just be careful, *Dad*," I hissed softly.

He kissed my forehead and was gone, darting across to the next building. It did not have outside floodlights.

A noise from inside the building—a muffled shout, maybe? I held my breath. Had someone spotted Will?

Then a rumbling and the earth began to shake beneath my feet.

My stomach flipped and my heart missed a beat. *Crapola! What's that?* The rumbling was no surprise. It was the sound I'd heard in Herb's study, only louder here.

But what was making the earth shake?

Earthquake! Ms. Snark yelled inside my head.

Ignoring her and my pounding heart, I tried to rationally figure this out. I'd never heard of an earthquake in Florida, but sinkholes happened. What did they feel and sound like when they opened up?

Will was suddenly beside me, shouting, "What the h–"

But whatever expletive he'd let slip was drowned out by a deafening roar.

CHAPTER TWENTY-SEVEN

The rumbling and ground-shaking abruptly stopped. Heart still racing and my insides quivering, I looked around for the source of the roar.

Twenty feet away, a dark-haired, husky man stood under one of the streetlights. When my eyes focused on what was in one of his hands, my stomach bottomed out.

A shotgun—aimed at us.

"Ya know, I could shoot y'all where you stand for trespassin'," Frederick Jacobs called over, in a conversational tone. He shone a flashlight at us.

"I wouldn't advise that." Will's voice from beside me, amazingly calm. "I'm law enforcement."

I shielded my eyes.

Jacobs was squinting at him. "I make a point of knowin' all the local deputies and you ain't one of them. So, seems like you're out of your jurisdiction. And this is a stand-your-ground state."

"Won't change the fact that every LEO in this county and my own will do everything they can to see you fry for killing one of their own." He gestured toward me. "Plus a pregnant *unarmed* civilian."

"She's pregnant?" Jacobs said, his tone surprised. "I thought she was just fat."

Grrr. Anger surged, displacing fear—and I let my guard down.

Ms. Snark slipped out. "Yeah, well, you're stupid."

"Marcia!" Will growled.

But Ms. Snark wasn't done. "And I'll only be fat for a while. You'll always be stupid."

The whole tableau froze. Then a raspy sound, coming from Jacobs.

Was he chuckling?

"You got moxie, gal. I'll give ya that. Go on, get out of here, both of ya. And stop stickin' your nose in my business."

We stayed frozen for another second.

Jacobs swung the shotgun up straight in the air and fired it.

I jumped at the roar. Will grabbed my hand, and we ran for the weedy patch at the end of Herb's street.

⊷——⊷

"He didn't let us go because of your crazy comments, you know," Will said in a low, angry voice once we'd reached Herb's driveway. "He laughed at what you said in order to save face."

I shrugged, not wanting to let on that I was more than a little shook by our close encounter with the industrial park owner. "I figured if he was going to shoot us anyway, I might as well say what I was thinking."

"Well, it could've pissed him off and made him shoot us in anger."

See, I said internally to Ms. Snark, *you almost got us killed.*

She didn't answer.

Will sighed. "I doubt he was going to shoot anyway. Stand your ground doesn't allow you to shoot unarmed trespassers."

"You have your pistol, don't you?"

"Yeah, but he didn't know that."

"You're assuming he understands the stand-your-ground law," I said. "He really could be stupid."

Will chuckled. "Come on, let's get your car. I'll follow you to Becky and Andy's before I head home, make sure you get there safely."

I opened my mouth to protest again about him going to work tomorrow, then thought better of it. He wasn't angry with me anymore—best to leave it that way.

At their house, Will came in for a cup of coffee before setting out on the two-hour drive back to Mayfair. We sat around their kitchen table, steaming mugs in front of us. Mine was herbal tea, the kind that tastes like old socks. But Becky swore it would calm my nerves and was safe for Bumpkin. Buddy lay under the table, his head on my foot.

Will described our short-lived reconnaissance mission.

"Hope that was bird shot in his shotgun," Andy said, "and not a slug."

"Why?" Becky and I asked in unison.

"Because what goes up must come down," Will said. "Only on TV do cops and soldiers fire into the air. Real ones know better."

"But apparently Jacobs doesn't," I said.

Becky leaned forward. "So the question is, what's going on in those buildings. Maybe that first one was a heavy equipment distributor. And things were arranged that way like a showroom… maybe?" She didn't sound all that convinced herself.

Will shrugged. "Could be."

"I'm sure," Andy said, "that there are all kinds of manufacturing machines that make loud rumbling noises, but shake the earth?" He shook his head slowly.

Will drained his cup. "Well, I'd better hit the road, before it gets any later." He stood, leaned down and kissed my forehead. "Call you in the morning." To Becky and Andy, "Thanks, guys."

Andy showed him out, and I stumbled off to the guest room, Buddy in tow.

He was practically glued to my knee. I suspected he was a

little freaked by the fact that I'd been gone all day. Normally we were close to inseparable.

Becky's tea might have tasted awful, but it did the trick. I was asleep almost before my head hit the pillow.

A ringing sound dragged me out of a deep sleep. It took a moment to register that it was my phone. I groped around on the bedside table.

I checked the time first, before answering the call. Seven-ten. I groaned.

On the rug next to the bed, Buddy tilted his head in his classic *what's-up* look.

Will! That's who's up. His name was on the phone's screen.

I quickly answered before it went to voicemail. "Helro," I mumbled, then cleared my throat.

"Did you see Elise's latest report?"

"No, I…" I was trying to work up the energy to get mad at him for waking me up, but the excitement in his voice had me intrigued. "What's in the report?"

"That expensive house that agent bought–"

"Which agent?"

"Merrilee Brooks. Guess how she could afford it."

It was way too early for guessing games. "How?"

"Frank co-signed the loan, six months after he and the woman supposedly broke up and he and Char had started dating."

"Maybe he was just trying to be nice."

"Nah, nice is you lend your ex fifty bucks until next payday. You don't co-sign a $700,000 mortgage."

"So what do you think it means?" My brain wasn't fully engaged yet. My stomach rumbled, demanding breakfast.

"It means Frank goes back up to the top of our suspect list."

That's what I'd thought it meant. My stomach shifted toward queasy. It could've been morning sickness, although that had been much better lately.

But I was pretty sure it was about having bought into Frank's grief, which had seemed so sincere. I'd even felt a bit sorry for him.

"I've got a hunch," Will was saying, "that he and Merrilee only pretended to break up, so he could romance Char and get his hands on her money."

A metallic flash in my mind's eye. "Merrilee's wearing an engagement ring, on a chain around her neck." I paused for effect. "Hidden inside her top. And she's not the type of girl who has bling and hides it."

Will chuckled gleefully.

"This means we talk to Frank again?" I said.

"Yes, but it may have to wait until tomorrow. I'm on my way to a crime scene. A marital fight that went south, in a really bad way."

I winced. "Has the guy been arrested?"

"No, he's in the wind at the moment, but the neighbors heard a lot of shouting and a gunshot. Should be an open and shut case, once we find him."

"Okay."

"Mar-see-a," he emphasized each syllable of my name, "don't you even think about going to see Frank on your own."

"I wasn't thinking that at all." But only because the thought hadn't fully formed yet in my still groggy brain. "I'll behave and wait for you. I really do need to get in some training today with Herb."

"Okay, call ya later."

"Stay safe! Love you."

"Always. Love you too."

I called Herb while heading toward the motel, Buddy in the backseat this time. Since Will was tied up today anyway, I'd decided to take a break. I was tired of all the drama. Besides, my limited wardrobe was again more dirty than clean. My navy tee and Edna's turquoise camp shirt were both on their second day.

I would put in a morning of training, then go home this afternoon. And I didn't want to have to swing north to Becky's house first to pick up Buddy, before beginning that long trek.

Who are you kidding? Ms. Snark said. *Not knowing what old Milt had in his hand yesterday spooked you.*

You were the one who panicked.

Was not.

I rolled my eyes and refused to further engage with her.

I glanced up in the rearview mirror at Buddy, as the ringing sound continued through the Bluetooth speaker. "I missed you, boy."

"Uh… Marcia?" Herb's voice from the speaker.

"Oops, sorry. I was talking to Buddy. Are you up for some training today?"

"Sure. What did you have in mind?"

"Is there a park anywhere nearby?"

"There is, a couple of blocks from my house. I used to walk there, before things got worse."

"Then that's this morning's agenda. I'll be at the motel in about fifteen minutes."

He was standing in the parking lot, backpack in hand, Dolly in the cover position next to him, when I pulled in. I lowered my window.

"I think I'm ready to move back into my house," he said, "what with Will securing the openings to the attic and changing the locks. I need to thank him again for all that."

"Okay," I said, a little surprised. "That's good. And he was happy to help out." Especially since Herb was supposedly going to pay us for this investigation, eventually.

I said a quick silent prayer for that outcome, as Herb secured Dolly in the backseat next to Buddy, then climbed into my car.

Since we were going to his house anyway, I decided to check on something.

The house was as we'd left it. I got the storage room key from Herb and fetched the stepladder.

When I set it up in the living room and put a foot on the bottom rung, he thrust out a hand to stop me. "What are you doing?"

I pointed to the small white box in the corner of the ceiling.

"The motion detector," Herb said. "Why do you…" he trailed off, staring up at the object for a beat. "I'll get it." He climbed up and removed the box from its bracket. At the bottom of the ladder, he handed it to me.

I examined it. It did, indeed, look like a motion detector, but I suspected it was something else as well.

Frank had said something about controlling the voices remotely. There was an on-off switch on one side of the box. It was in the on position, which was probably necessary for the remote to work.

I turned the switch off and on again, hoping I could get it to play. Sure enough, the box began to moan.

Herb jumped back a step. "Whoa!"

The moaning stopped.

I flipped the switch back and forth and it started again, then weeping sounds followed by faint words…Char's voice encouraging Herb to "come join me."

A chill ran down my spine. Frank had lied. He didn't care about Herb.

CHAPTER TWENTY-EIGHT

Yeah, Frank deserved to be back at the top of our suspect list.

He'd been hoping Herb would move out, but he would have been content with another suicide—which would've definitely closed Char's murder case and cleared the way for Jacobs to buy the house.

Herb raised a hand, scrubbed it across his face.

The sounds emanating from the white box stopped.

"This is your ghost," I stated the obvious. "I suspect it's remotely activated but set to turn off when motion is detected. So when you woke up fully and began to move around, the sounds would stop, leaving you wondering if they'd been real or not."

I chose not to rat Frank out. Because he'd been right about one thing, it would hurt Herb.

"What should we do with it?" Herb asked. "Take it to the sheriff?"

"Let Will and me keep it for now, until we sort out exactly who's behind all this." We knew Frank was behind the fake haunting, but who was behind the rest of it? He kept swearing he hadn't played a part in Char's death. But was he in on the eminent domain notices and the attempts to stop us from investigating? Frank had sworn he'd had nothing to do with those either, but I wasn't particularly inclined to believe that now.

Herb dropped his backpack on the sofa bed. "Well, that's one mystery solved, at least. Let's go to the park." His eyes flashed with excitement.

Dolly cleared the front porch and we walked back out into the sunshine.

Herb paused at the top of the porch steps and took a deep breath. The smile on his face didn't waiver as we walked out to the street and turned our backs on the ugly industrial park.

Shoulders back, Herb marched down the sidewalk, Dolly trotting beside him. I lengthened my stride to keep up.

The park was two blocks away, maybe a couple of acres, with scattered trees and park benches. We settled on one under a live oak tree, the dogs in the cover position on either end of the bench.

Herb took another deep breath and let it out slowly. "It feels so good to be outside."

We sat in silence for a few moments, then he said, "Lemme see if I can handle using the park's restroom."

"Sure."

He got up and went over to the small clapboard building with two stick-figure signs indicating men's and women's facilities. Dolly entered the men's side, came back a moment later, and Herb followed her in.

"Yay," I cheered under my breath.

A phone rang, but not my ring. I glanced down. Herb had left his phone on the bench. It rang again.

I debated whether to answer, decided to let it go to voicemail. When Herb returned, looking quite pleased with himself, I told him he'd gotten a call.

He grabbed the phone and tapped the screen a couple of times.

"Herb, great news." Merrilee's excited voice came from the speaker. "The Hancocks accepted your offer. There's just one thing, though. They're moving in a few days, retiring to South

America, so they wanted to know if you could do your walk-through today. That way, if there are any problems, they can take care of them before they leave."

Herb was grinning from ear to ear.

"Oh, one other thing." She sounded a little breathless. "They want to settle as soon as possible, so they can use the proceeds to buy something in…Argentina, I think they said." She let out a fake laugh.

"I've arranged for a bridge loan, that temporary loan we talked about. Once you get your house sold or get the money from Char's estate, we'll process a regular mortgage with whatever down payment you want to make. Can you come over to the house, say around noon? I'll have the paperwork for the loan with me, and when that goes through, you'll have your house!" Another short laugh that sounded off. "Let me know if that works for you."

"Could you take me over there later?" Herb asked me.

"Sure."

He tapped out a text message to Merrilee, then said, "Do you mind if I take a circuit of the park on my own with Dolly?"

"Not at all. Go for it."

They headed off, Herb practically dancing along the path.

I was delighted to see him so happy, but something didn't feel quite right about this whole deal. First of all… I took out my phone and tapped out a text of my own, to Clint. *Is Herb still under arrest?*

A few seconds later, my phone pinged. *Far as I know. I will check.*

Clint might not know the answer to my second question, but it didn't hurt to ask. *Thx. Do you know if he would be able to get a bridge loan for a house if he's under arrest?*

I will check on that too.

I frowned. What was Merrilee up to? Some scam to get her commission and leave Herb in the lurch?

Then again, maybe I was being too hard on her. It was possible—unlikely, but possible—that she didn't know Herb had been arrested. We hadn't been hounded by reporters recently, so maybe

Sheriff Rick had kept news of the arrest under wraps.

But then again, the motel manager had known about it, and the patrons of the diner had witnessed it. Surely, the local grapevine had spread the word.

I shook my head as Herb and Dolly turned the corner of the walkway, coming back toward me and Buddy. Herb was still grinning.

My throat ached. I didn't have the heart to tell him the house might not be a done deal.

<hr>

Back at his place, Herb managed to take a shower in the hall bathroom, with Dolly keeping him company on the bath mat, waiting to clear the way back out to the living room for him.

He came out in fresh clothes, still towel-drying his hair. "Boy, that felt good. No more washing up in that little sink." He gestured toward the powder room.

A warmth spread through my chest. When our veterans had little victories like these, that made all the hard work worth it.

And a decision was made in that moment. I wasn't giving up this feeling. I would continue training dogs, even if it was only a couple a year.

And I'd take on a new assistant, so I could train him or her to be a trainer, and produce even more dogs for these deserving veterans. Somehow, I'd manage to juggle it all.

We ate an early lunch, then set out for what Herb assumed would soon be his new home.

I was still skeptical, but I kept my thoughts to myself.

As we pulled up in front of the house, my phone rang and Clint's name appeared on the dashboard screen.

"Um, I need to take this call," I said to Herb. "Can you get the dogs out of the back?"

I jumped out of the car and placed the phone to my ear, hoping the call hadn't been lost when I'd turned off the engine. "Clint?"

"Got some answers for you." His voice was gruff. "The boy's

still under arrest, ROR."

ROR? Oh yeah, released on his own recognizance. I walked farther away from the car.

"And I called Barbara Hersh…"

Herb was now standing next to the car, a dog on either side of him, watching me. I held up a finger to indicate *one minute*.

"Without namin' names," Clint was saying, "I asked the hypothetical question about a bridge loan."

Herb gave a slight nod, but he turned toward the house, leaving Buddy next to the car. Had he thought I'd meant I'd be inside in a minute? He and Dolly walked toward the porch.

"She said someone could apply for it," Clint continued, "and the loan company might or might not find out about the arrest before initial approval, but when they did find out, if he hadn't disclosed it up front, they'd likely call the loan."

"Meaning he'd have to pay it all off or lose the house." I started jogging to catch up with Herb, signaling Buddy to heel. "And if he discloses it up front?"

"Then he won't get the loan," Clint said.

Herb was now standing next to the open front door, waiting for Dolly to clear the front room.

Dolly returned and sat, and Herb stepped inside the house with her.

Crapola!

"What's going on?" Clint asked.

"We're at the house Herb wants to buy." I lowered my voice as I climbed the porch steps. "I think this agent's pulling a fast one to get her commission before his case goes to trial."

I was on the porch now, looking through the open doorway. Herb was by the wide opening that led into the dining room.

Dolly ran in there as I moved toward Herb. She stopped and sat in front of someone who was outside my line of vision. A manicured hand, attached to a gold-bangled arm, reached out to pet her.

Merrilee.

But Dolly darted out from under her hand. She ran to a closed doorway, sniffed under it, then sat, without barking.

My heart rate kicked up a notch. *Someone's behind that door.*

"Clint," I whispered, "hang on for a sec."

Dolly took off again, out of sight. A sharp yip.

A stranger's in that room!

Blood pounding in my ears, I dropped the phone, line still open, into my shirt pocket. I frantically gestured for Herb to move away from the doorway.

"It's a trap!" I hissed, then called out, "Dolly, come!" Despite my best efforts, my voice sounded panicky.

Herb took a step toward me, but it was too late. The dog came back through the doorway.

And so did a man, with a gun in his hand.

CHAPTER TWENTY-NINE

"Mr. Jacobs," I said, in a too-loud voice, "what are you doing here? And why do you have a gun?"

The stocky developer answered with a string of expletives. "Get in here!" He waved the gun to indicate we should enter the dining room.

Heart racing and stomach roiling, I obeyed.

Buddy stuck close, his hackles up, a low rumble in his throat. He knew what guns were and had reason not to like them.

I held my hand out, palm facing him—the *wait* signal. I moved toward where Merrilee sat at the dining table, close enough that I could dive behind her if need be. Better her than Bumpkin should this guy start shooting.

Merrilee's eyes were wide, her hands clenched together on the table in front of her.

No wonder her message had sounded off, if she'd been forced at gunpoint to lure us here.

But *why* had Jacobs lured us here, and why had he involved her?

Herb had nervously edged around the doorframe and now

stood with his back against the wall. Dolly sat at his feet.

I prayed that Clint could hear what was going on and that he wouldn't make any noise.

Not that he can do anything. He doesn't know where we are. My heart sank at that realization.

Jacobs took up a position where he had all of us in his line of vision. But he kept the gun pointed at me, maybe because I was in the middle.

I swallowed hard. Buddy knew how to grab a gun hand. He'd done it before. But my fear was that Jacobs would reflexively pull the trigger. My hands went to my baby bump, as if they could stop a bullet.

"Did you know she was coming?" Jacobs demanded of Merrilee.

"No! Why would I know that?" Her tone was a bit peevish.

Great, Merrilee, make the guy with the gun even angrier.

Jacobs ran a hand through his hair, grabbed a hunk of it and pulled. He let out another string of expletives, then glared at Merrilee. "I'm a Christian. I don't kill innocent babies."

What? Ms. Snark exclaimed internally. *He's a pro-life murderer?*

Merrilee stared at me. "She's pregnant? I thought she was just fat."

Grr, please let me slap her! Ms. Snark begged.

I understood the desire, but the very large handgun in Jacobs's hand was a deterrent against any sudden movements.

We all froze for a beat, except for Herb, whose head swiveled back and forth among the three of us. He looked pretty calm, under the circumstances.

"So," I said to Jacobs, struggling to keep the panic out of my voice, "what was the plan if Herb had shown up by himself?"

I needed to keep him talking, until I thought of my own plan. And at the very least, I wanted Clint to hear the evidence that this guy intended to kill us. Something a little more straight-forward than his comment about not killing babies.

"The plan," Merrilee said, "was that he would ram his car

into a tree."

Wait, why was *she* answering me?

She pulled a folded piece of paper out of her pocket. "With a suicide note on the seat next to him, confessing to Char's murder."

Crapola, she's in on this!

"The murder case would be closed once and for all," Jacobs said. "You and your husband would stop nosing around, and we could get on with things."

"What things?" I asked.

"Getting the land I need."

"Why do–"

Merrilee jumped up. "Enough chit-chat. The question is what are we going to do now?" She turned slightly to glare at me. "I vote we keep the plan for Herbie here, but we need to make her disappear too."

I raised my hand partway, as if to get a teacher's attention in class. "Um, there's a tiny flaw in your plan. Herb doesn't have a car. That's *why* I came, as his ride."

Yet more cursing from Jacobs. "How could you *not* know that he doesn't drive?" he yelled at Merrilee.

"Why wouldn't I assume he drives? He's moving to a house out in the middle of nowhere."

"Uh," Herb spoke up, "I was gonna shop for a car while waiting for the loan to go through. I have a driver's license."

While all this was happening, I watched the gun intently, waiting for Jacobs to get distracted enough that he moved it away from my belly.

Unfortunately, his aim was rock steady.

My arm down at my side, I surreptitiously gave Buddy the on-duty reminder signal. *Be ready, boy!* His nose touched my palm.

"Okay," Merrilee said, "we stage an accident with both of them in her car. No suicide note, just a plain old car accident." She snapped her fingers. "At the curve on County Road 348."

I felt the blood drain from my face. I knew that curve. It was deceptively sharp and banked slightly the wrong way. The two wooden crosses in the grass beside it, surrounded by plastic flowers, testified to lives lost there in recent times.

Jacobs was shaking his head. "I told you, I don't kill babies."

"Well, what else do we do? Lock her up for how many months until the kid pops out and then kill her?"

Jacobs looked as if he were considering that plan. His gun remained steady, but he was distracted enough he failed to notice that a door behind him was slowly opening.

I'd forgotten all about Dolly sniffing at it earlier. The thought flicked across my mind that it was probably Frank, their accomplice. But why was he hiding?

I held my breath as the door swung farther open.

It wasn't Frank.

Sheriff Rick stepped into the room, a gun in *his* hand. "Enough!"

I blew out pent-up air. My muscles relaxed so fast that my legs turned to jelly.

But why was the sheriff glaring at *me*?

"You still here?" Jacobs said, his tone casual. "I thought you left."

Sheriff Rick turned his glare on the stockier man. "You might have qualms about unborn babies, Jacobs, but I don't."

CHAPTER THIRTY

I almost fainted.

Herb rushed forward and grabbed my arm to steady me.

"Hold still, you two!" Sheriff Rick barked. To Merrilee, he said, "That curve won't do. There are lots of people who've gone off there and lived to tell about it."

He glanced at Jacobs, who glared back. "I knew I couldn't trust you to get this right," Rick said. "Here's *my* plan."

The power struggle might have been interesting to watch, if they weren't both holding guns, pointed at us.

"We drain most of the gas out of her car," the sheriff continued. "Wait until dusk, then leave it on the side of the road. A little farther along, we stand them beside the road, like they're walking to a gas station, and I run them down with my truck."

Now my legs were threatening to give out for a whole different reason. I kinda preferred the getting-shot idea over being hit by a pickup.

But the waiting until dusk sounded promising…gave me time to think of something. Maybe I could somehow convey to Clint where we were.

"Control your dog!" Rick had lowered his gun down toward Buddy.

It registered that my boy was growling. "Sit." His butt hit the ground. Again, I gave him the *wait* signal.

He quieted but was watching me intently.

The situation had changed, though. He could only grab one bad guy's arm at a time, and the other one would have plenty of time to shoot him.

"You two, get in there," Rick gestured past the small breakfast bar that separated the kitchen from the rest of the room. "Sit down on the stools. Hands on the counter."

What stools? I stepped up beside the end of the breakfast bar and saw them behind it, backless wooden stools. Sitting on one of those until dusk was going to kill my back.

If we make it to dusk, Ms. Snark pointed out, *Sheriff Rick's gonna kill* all *of us.*

"Go on," Rick ordered, but Herb hesitated.

"Dolly needs to clear the room for him," I said.

"What room?" Rick's voice rose. "It's a five-by-eight space. Nobody's hiding there."

"Our rational minds know that." Actually, Herb probably could push past his anxiety at this point, but I was stalling, looking for an opportunity to disarm these men. "Even Herb's mind knows that, but–"

"Shut up, woman!" Rick yelled. He grabbed Herb by the upper arm and started shoving him forward. "Get in there."

"Drop the guns. Don't move!" Clint's voice, roaring from the other doorway.

"Sheriff's Department," a deputy shouted from beside him.

Jacobs immediately dropped his gun and raised his hands.

Rick whirled around, gun still in hand, but no longer pointed at us. "Good, you're here. I caught Jacobs trying–"

My heart stuttered from terror that he'd raise his gun and shoot Clint.

Then somehow Herb was on Rick's back, grabbing his gun

arm from behind and twisting it around at a very unnatural angle.

Rick yowled and his pistol fell to the floor.

"Buddy, get gun!"

Herb flipped Rick onto his back and sat on him, pinning his arms to his sides.

Meanwhile, Buddy had pounced on the gun. He lifted it, the barrel in his teeth, and brought it to me.

Merrilee squeaked and ran for the doorway.

"Stop her," I yelled. "She's part of it all."

"Don't worry," the deputy said. *Sergeant*, I corrected myself as I recognized him from the day Herb had been arrested.

"We heard the whole thing. One of my men is outside. He'll grab her."

He'd no sooner said it than a very young deputy hauled Merrilee back into the room.

Jacobs looked at her, tears running down his broad, tanned cheeks. "I'm sorry, honey."

"Shut up, you twit," she snarled.

Honey? So *Jacobs* was her secret fiancé, not Frank.

⊷──⊷

Clint, Herb, and I stood by my car, the dogs at our feet, while the deputies loaded their prisoners into the cruiser. I watched Herb out of the corner of my eye. I was more shaken by the whole thing than he appeared to be.

He caught me looking his way and smiled. "Marcia, I keep telling you, I'm a Marine. *Real* threats don't scare me."

I gave him a shaky smile back. "And even the ones in your head don't seem to be bothering you as much."

He paused, his expression thoughtful. "Yeah, it's becoming routine to let Dolly clear a space and then enter. Only a few twinges of anxiety now."

Herb offered to drive my car back to town, and Clint immediately seconded the idea. "Can you pick up her mother?" He rattled off their new address. "Meet us at the sheriff's department."

I was thinking it was time to graduate Herb from training, when Clint turned to me. "Ride with me, Marcia." It was not a request. He was in sheriff mode.

Once we were in his car, Buddy secured in the backseat, Clint started the engine. But instead of pulling out after the sergeant's cruiser, he spent a couple of minutes setting up a conference call through his Bluetooth with the members of the county council.

Then he put the car in gear. As he drove, he succinctly spelled out what had happened.

After a stunned silence, they appointed him interim sheriff. "Make that *temporary* interim sheriff, folks," Clint said. "I like retirement."

He disconnected and said to me, "Give me the background."

He knew some of it. I filled in the gaps. When I got to today's events, I started shaking.

What's the matter with me?

You're preggers, you idiot, Ms. Snark pointed out.

My hand went to my baby bump, and I admitted reluctantly that she was right. Facing danger was a whole new ball game with Bumpkin onboard. Especially when I hadn't been expecting that danger. I thought I'd held it together pretty well while things were happening, but now...

"How'd you know where we were?" I asked Clint.

"Your mom has a good memory. She recalled you sayin' that Herb was buyin' the first house the two of you had looked at. Fortunately, I wasn't far away. We were at our new place, takin' measurements for furniture. And the sarge was nearby as well, on another call, with a rookie he's training."

I fell quiet, thinking about what might have happened if we hadn't been so lucky, if Clint and the sergeant hadn't been nearby.

It still would've been okay. They weren't going to do anything to us until dusk. We would've figured out something.

Was that Ms. Snark, actually trying to comfort me?

Yeah, don't get used to it, she said in her more normal snide voice.

The reunion with Mom at the sheriff's office was short and

breathtaking, literally. She grabbed me and hugged me so hard I thought my lungs would collapse.

"Mom," I gasped out, "the baby."

She quickly let go. "Sorry." She held me slightly away from her, running her hands up and down my arms, as if checking for injuries.

"I'm fine, Mom."

She gave me a weak smile. "I had a nice chat with Herb on the way here. He was singing your praises and Dolly's. You do important work with the dogs and the veterans…" She trailed off, implying that she wished I'd stick with that vocation.

"Thanks. I'm going to keep training dogs, just not as many per year." I opted to leave it at that.

After Herb had given his statement, I suggested he and Dolly take Mom back to the motel. "Will's on his way. Buddy and I'll wait for him."

I was tired, but I wanted to stick around and see if I could find out more about who had done what, and especially how Sheriff Rick was involved.

Clint walked up to me. "Marcia, I'd like you to observe an interview."

My mouth fell open.

There is a God! Ms. Snark declared.

CHAPTER THIRTY-ONE

I closed my gaping mouth. "Of Rick Young?"

Clint shook his head. "I had a deputy bring in Ms. Mathers's fiancé. I need to know more about what was going on, before I talk to the main suspects."

Isn't having civilians observe against some rule? Ms. Snark asked internally.

Clint winked at me.

I think that's a yes, I told Ms. Snark, *but what are they gonna do, fire him?* She snickered.

Clint led the way to the observation room. "You know this guy. I don't," he said over his shoulder. "You may be able to give me a reading on whether or not he's lying." He pointed to a small microphone next to the one-way mirror. "I've got an ear bud. If you speak into that, I can hear you, but he can't."

Okay, he was indulging my curiosity, no doubt so I wouldn't pepper him with questions later, but he did want my input. My chest warmed.

In the interview room, Clint sat with his back to me, Frank

Hawkins across the wooden table from him. Clint pointed out that he was recording the interview. "You're not under arrest and I'm not going to read you your rights. But I will tell you that anything you say may end up being used against you if you are later arrested. You can have your lawyer present, if you want." He paused. "You certainly shouldn't incriminate yourself, but if you withhold any information that isn't self-incriminatin', or lie about somethin', that won't look good."

Frank was vehemently shaking his head. "I had nothing to do with what happened today."

"So what *did* you have a part in?" Clint leaned back in his wooden chair as if they were having a casual conversation. The chair groaned softly in protest.

Frank looked down at the table. "I'd brokered the deal for Fred Jacobs to purchase the land he built the industrial park on. A few months after the buildings were up, he came to me and said he wanted more land, to expand it. I didn't quite get why, since not all of the buildings were rented yet. But I helped him draft a letter to the residents of Palmetto Springs, offering them generous buy-outs for their homes. About two-thirds of them took the offers."

Probably glad to get away from the ugly, noisy industrial park.

Frank had paused. He cleared his throat. Clint pointed to the plastic glass at his elbow.

Grabbing it, Frank gulped some water. "Unfortunately, most of the holdouts were on Herb's block, the area closest to the industrial park. Jacobs claimed he needed those properties in particular to connect the two areas. Otherwise, he'd have to spend more on infrastructure. New roadways, water and electric lines. He wanted me to figure out a way to pressure those property owners to sell."

That seemed kind of lame to me. Paying top dollar for those houses was cheaper than some extra infrastructure?

"About then, Char got wind of what he was doing. She was adamant that she wasn't selling Herb's house, but Jacobs kept pushing me to do something."

"Marcia tells me," Clint drawled, "that you admitted to her and Will about fakin' a ghost in his house."

Frank took another sip of water and carefully put the glass down on the table. "I'm not proud of what I did, but I'm not sure it's illegal. I rigged the house to seem like it was haunted, and I made up a story about a woman committing suicide there. I thought that would do the trick, that Herb would want to move out."

"That's fraud, you jerk," I muttered.

Clint reached up and tapped his ear, then pretended to scratch it. Oops, I hadn't realized the mic was that sensitive.

"But it wasn't working," Frank said. "Herb's fear of whatever ghosts are inside his head was stronger than his fear of some girl ghost." He dropped his gaze to the table. "Then Char died…"

"You have any part in that?" Clint asked, again in a casual tone. I'd been on the receiving end of a couple of his interrogations, back when my client was a suspect in the flea market murder. I knew Clint was not being the least bit casual about all this.

But still his tone rankled. I wanted him to grab Frank by the front of his shirt and shake him good. I took a deep breath to calm myself.

Again, Frank was vigorously shaking his head. "No, I swear I didn't…I loved her." His voice was almost a wail.

"Who do you think did kill her?"

Frank shrugged, the nonchalance of the gesture belying the anguish in his voice a few seconds ago. "At first, I wasn't sure what to think. It could've been suicide. Char was a lot more insecure than she let on. But it crossed my mind that Merrilee might've drugged her. She hated Char's guts, even though Char naïvely believed they were still friends. Now I'm thinking it was Jacobs. She was an obstacle to him getting the land he wanted."

Why that particular land, though? That question kept niggling at my brain. There was undeveloped farmland on two sides of the park.

"Why was Jacobs really after those properties?" Clint asked, and I almost laughed out loud. I must be getting pretty good at this investigating thing if my line of thought matched that of a pro like Clint.

Frank's eyes darted around the room. Then he heaved a sigh and his shoulders sagged. "Jacobs found phosphorus rock deposits when they excavated for the buildings. He got them assessed and it's a particularly rich vein."

"What's phosphorus rock?" Clint asked.

I'd never heard of it either.

"The element phosphorus is extracted from it," Frank said. "Very important ingredient in fertilizer, and used in some other things, too."

"In other words," Clint said, "it's valuable."

"Very. Much more lucrative than renting out warehouse space. He's been mining it, as best he could, mostly at night. The entrance to the mine is inside one of the warehouses."

The warehouse Will and I had been standing near last night.

"He discreetly took some soil samples in the surrounding area," Frank was saying. "Phosphorus only showed up in quantity in Palmetto Springs."

Clint nodded. "So those other undeveloped lands nearby weren't any good to him. Why not put up a big ole fence around the industrial park, so he could mine it more openly?"

"He was going to do that, once he had the rest of the land. He was afraid if he got more blatant about the mining operation before then, somebody would catch on and there'd be a bidding war over Palmetto Springs." He paused, sipped more water.

"He needed all the phosphorus he could get. Merrilee is not an easy keeper." The last part was said almost gleefully.

"Is that why she broke up with you, because Jacobs had more money?" Again, the casual tone, even though the question had some bite to it.

But Frank shrugged again. "And because I wouldn't do more to pressure Char and Herb. Merrilee was already involved in Jacobs's dealings, had invested some of her own funds in his company."

J and B! Jacobs and Brooks? And MNF, the fake company… When we'd realized our mystery client's connection to all this, I'd wondered if those initials might have stood for Frank and somebody. But it was Fred—Merrilee and Fred.

"I didn't like the idea that she was mixed up with that sleaze ball financially," Frank was saying. "So we fought some more, and we finally broke up."

But what about... I leaned forward. "Ask him why he co-signed a $700,000 mortgage for her, *after* they'd broken up."

Clint nodded slightly and asked the question.

Frank's eyes went wide. "How'd you know about that?"

Clint let out a humorless chuckle. "You think I don't check people out before I come into this room?"

Again, I almost laughed out loud. He hadn't had time to check anything out. My chest warmed. Our research was helping him here.

Frank dropped his gaze. "She forced me to do it, threatened to tell Char how I'd faked the ghost in Herb's house."

And guess what, Ms. Snark commented, *you're stuck with that mortgage now, 'cause Merrilee's going to prison.*

I'm actually feeling kind of sorry for him again, I told her.

You're such a softie.

Probably true, but I was hoping that part of my personality would keep me from becoming jaded and cynical in my new line of work.

"Let's talk about Char's suicide note for a minute," Clint said.

Frank looked off to the side and sighed. "I found something in Char's papers yesterday. I was debating what to do, whether to turn it over. It was a pros and cons list. She did that sometimes when she was trying to make a decision. It was titled *Fire Merrilee*."

He glanced sideways at Clint, then away again. "Like I said, Char wasn't as sure of herself as everyone thought she was."

Yup, an insecure narcissist. Mom and I had nailed that diagnosis.

"She was often at odds with herself. On the one hand, she wanted to be the hard-nosed businesswoman that her mentor had taught her to be. It was like she was still trying to please him, even though he's dead. She didn't care all that much about the money she made, but she knew that would've impressed him."

Frank paused, staring off into space. "But she also wanted people to like her. I think she was pretty starved for love as a kid. Her parents worked all the time. The only love she got was from nannies, but when she got too close to them, her mother would fire them and hire someone else."

"So," Clint said, his voice downright gentle, "you think the suicide note had been addressed to Merrilee?"

Frank nodded and finally looked at Clint. "Yeah, it's exactly the way Char would have phrased things, if she had to fire someone she cared about."

"Why did she care about Merrilee?"

"When Merrilee started with the agency, Char took her under her wing, taught her how to be a good agent—like John Reynolds had done with her. I think she saw it as paying it forward." Frank's face sagged with sadness. "It must have been a hard choice for Char to make."

Now Char's reaction to me made more sense. Had she been projecting some of her anger at her protégé onto me, another woman about Merrilee's age, who was potentially disrupting her relationship with Herb?

"On that pros and cons list you found," Clint was asking, "what were Char's reasons for firing Merrilee?"

"Somehow Char had found out about the eminent domain seizure letters, and she figured Jacobs and Merrilee were behind them. She'd confronted Merrilee, who told her it was too late. The letters were already in the mail. From Char's notes, it sounded like Merrilee had given her some song and dance about the county taking the land and leasing it to J and B."

"Did Char know about the phosphorus?" Clint asked.

Frank shook his head. "That wasn't clear from her notes, but I don't think so. Char could negotiate a shrewd deal, but she was an ethical person. She would've blown the whistle if she'd known about an illegal mining operation."

"So you think Merrilee was in on Char's murder?"

"Probably," Frank said. "I'd wondered if it was her, but I couldn't figure out how she got Char's body into that room. Then

when Will and Marcia found that the tunnel had been expanded…
I thought, well, Merrilee certainly wouldn't be strong enough to
haul Char's body through there."

"Frank built that tunnel originally," I said. "He admitted that
to us yesterday."

Another slight nod of acknowledgment from Clint. "Jacobs
could've carried her, though."

"Yes, but Merrilee would've had a better shot at slipping
something into her coffee or a drink."

"What about the sheriff? What was his involvement?"

Frank looked startled again. Apparently, Clint hadn't given
him all the details about this afternoon's events.

"I'd only just begun to suspect he might be taking payoffs
to stay out of things," Frank said. "That's why I was hesitating
about taking Char's notes to him. I tried to talk to him once about
the eminent domain notices, but he ducked my questions. And
Herb's neighbors have filed noise complaints about the industrial
park. The sheriff's department never did anything. I think Rick
was walking a fine line between wanting to keep the bribe money
coming and wanting to keep his job as well."

Well that ain't happening now, Ms. Snark commented.

I smirked. I never had liked the guy.

Clint had stilled in his chair.

It dawned on me that he was waiting to see if I had anything
else to offer. "Ask him again about the eminent domain notices.
I think he knows more than he's saying."

"The eminent domain notices, whose idea were they?" Clint
asked, again in the casual tone.

Frank stiffened. "First I heard of them was when Herb got
his letter."

I snorted.

Clint hitched one shoulder slightly in the air. "That's not
exactly what I asked," he said, a touch of steel in his voice now.

Frank sighed, sank back in his chair. "I've been in real estate
for fourteen years, and I'll tell you, there's nobody worse to deal
with than a stupid rich man."

"You mean Jacobs?"

Frank gave a slight nod. "If he'd consulted me beforehand, I would've told him it was too risky. It was too easy for people to find out they were bogus. Honest, I didn't know about them in advance."

A likely story.

"I asked Merrilee about them," Frank said. "Jacobs told her that Holly at the planning office suddenly going on early maternity leave was too good an opportunity to pass up."

Why did she have to suddenly go on early maternity leave? Did she have complications? A fist squeezed my heart. I rubbed my baby bump. *Please God, keep Bumpkin safe and healthy.*

"Jacobs was offering big payouts," Frank was saying, "with bonuses if people moved out quickly. Might have pulled it off, especially since they'd killed–" He broke off, his face crumpling for a second.

Then he sucked in air and sat up straighter. "I suspect he thought that by eliminating Char, he could get Herb to sell."

Clint nodded. "And Jacobs couldn't afford to let Char reveal what she'd found out about the letters and that he was behind them."

"He didn't figure on Marcia and her detective husband being on the scene." There was an undercurrent of glee in Frank's voice again.

His expression turned sly. "I guess I am in a bit of trouble here, aren't I? Could I get some kind of a deal if I had useful information? Something that might help you…" He trailed off.

Clint was quiet for a beat. "I'll speak to the District Attorney. *If* the information is indeed useful."

"I think some people farther up in the county government are involved, maybe were paid to look the other way about the eminent domain seizures."

"How far up?" Clint asked.

"The chair of the county council."

Dang! Call-me-Bobby is a crook? Ms. Snark's tone was half surprised, half gleeful.

"And guess who's sleeping with Rick Young?" Frank said.

"Barbara Hersh," I yelped.

Clint flinched.

"Sorry," I said softly.

"So Jacobs isn't totally stupid," he said to Frank. "He had the good sense to grease some palms?"

A slight shrug from Frank. "Jacobs's biggest flaw is that he thinks people are sheep, and he can bully them into doing what he wants."

Ah, thus the weird paragraph in the eminent domain letter. He figured the residents of Palmetto Springs would quietly roll over if they thought a judge would come down on them for even talking about it.

"Anything else?" Clint asked in the interview room.

I suspected the question was aimed at me as well as Frank.

"I got nothing," I said into the mic.

Frank shook his head and stood. "Don't worry, Sheriff. I won't leave the area." He twisted a ring on his left hand. It looked like a wedding band. "Not with Char buried here. We were going to be married next month, on a trip…to the Bahamas." He choked a little on the last few words.

Clint rose from his chair. "Well, it'll be up to a judge to decide if he believes you won't leave town. Turn around, please. You're under arrest."

"For what?" Frank said over his shoulder, but with no surprise in his voice.

"We'll start with fraud." Clint snapped handcuffs on him. "It's not okay to rig a fake ghost in someone's house for financial gain, even if you do have the homeowner's permission to be there."

Clint handed Frank off to a deputy, then met me at the door of the observation room. "What do you think?"

Mentally muzzling Ms. Snark, I said, "I think he's telling the truth basically. Oh, he's shading some stuff to make himself look better. But mainly he's an easy-going schmuck who tends to fall in love with bossy women."

Clint chuckled. "That's my take, too." He made an after-you

gesture.

I eased past him, but suddenly he twisted around in front of me and grabbed my hand to shake it. "Thank you for your cooperation, Ms. Banks-Haines."

A jerky movement behind him caught my eye. I leaned slightly to the left to see past Clint's bulk.

Sergeant Adams was ushering Frederick Jacobs into the interview room.

Clint doesn't want the sarge to know he bent the rules, Ms. Snark surmised, *by letting us observe.*

Meanwhile, Jacobs had stopped moving, his face pale under his tan. "Banks-Haines?"

Will chose that moment to arrive. He stepped up and wrapped an arm around my shoulders. "Yeah, I'm Will Haines, and she's my wife, Marcia Banks. We own *Baines* PI Agency."

Jacobs paled even more, as the sarge shoved him into the interview room, none too gently.

Hmm, he's definitely not as dumb as Frank thinks he is.

Clint was looking confused.

I tilted my head toward my husband. "He has a couple more pieces of the puzzle to tell you about."

"Why did he hire *us* to do his background checks?" Will lamented.

I smiled up at him. "Sometimes coincidences do happen."

"Or," Will said, "he saw that we were recently incorporated and figured we'd be hungry enough to not ask too many questions."

Which sadly, was exactly what happened.

Then I thought of something else. "Dang, I should've suggested you ask Frank about that insurance policy. Herb didn't know anything about it."

Clint shook his head slightly. "I want to talk to the insurance company first, get more details."

Will grinned. "Already done."

"What?" Clint arched a shaggy eyebrow at him.

"I had asked Elise to see what she could find out about it,"

Will said. "First she researched how hard it would be to take out a policy on someone else without their knowledge. The answer is very hard. For one thing, the insured would have to have a medical exam, especially for a policy that big. Then she pulled photos of Char and Merrilee off of the real estate agency's website and sent them to the insurance rep who wrote the policy. He identified Merrilee's picture as the Charlene Mathers who took out the policy. She had a fake ID and even went through the medical exam pretending to be Char."

"That was very industrious of Elise," I said.

Will grinned again. "She said it was a lot more fun than searching databases."

"Thanks." Clint clapped him on the shoulder. "That tells me what to charge Merrilee Brooks with."

My husband met his gaze, his face sobering. "First-degree murder."

"Yup," Clint said. "She planned to kill Ms. Mathers all along, and frame Herb for it."

A couple more pieces of the puzzle fell into place in my brain. "No wonder she had no qualms about admitting to me that she hated Char. I doubt she was ever inside Herb's house, so there would be no fingerprints or trace evidence to link her to the crime. She got Jacobs to literally do the heavy lifting. Sheriff Rick had been paid off to look the other way, to not do a very thorough investigation. And if it ever came out that it wasn't a suicide, the insurance policy would cinch the frame-up."

"She probably intentionally told you about her hatred of Char," Will said, "figuring her honesty would throw you off. And she knew you'd find out about it anyway, eventually."

Clint was glancing back and forth between us. Then he chuckled. "Y'all are gonna do just fine as private eyes."

EPILOGUE

On a pleasantly cool November day in Belleview, twenty minutes north of Mayfair, I stepped up onto the wooden deck in front of the double-wide that Rusty, Buddy, and I had visited many times over the last couple of weeks.

I had to stand sideways to get my big belly out of the way, so I could ring the doorbell.

The door flew open. Elise had no qualms about doorways. She just couldn't make herself leave her house.

Her plump bulk twisted and turned, trying to see past me. "Where is he?"

"Um, he and Buddy are behind me. I'm afraid I'm a walking, talking barricade these days."

"Hey," Elise said with a chuckle, "don't be telling fat jokes to the fat lady."

I snickered.

She stepped back and I maneuvered myself through the doorway, the dogs on my heels.

Elise dropped to her knees. "Hey, boy. Come here."

The mutt joyfully obliged, licking her face as she hugged him. His rusty red coat was close to the same color as her hair.

Elise rose. "Come have a cup of tea, before we get started."

I wrinkled my nose. "Is it herbal?"

"No, black tea, but decaf. My nervous system does *not* need additional stimulation."

I let out a grateful sigh.

We settled at her kitchen table. Rusty crawled under it, resting his chin on Elise's foot.

I smiled. I would be leaving the dog with her today. Their training was almost complete.

Buddy had opted to lay down by the door. He'd developed that habit after I'd left him with Becky for that one day. I guess he figured I couldn't leave without him if he was blocking the exit.

"So, how's business?" Elise asked.

"Pretty good. We're getting a couple of new cases a month now. A lot of them from this one disability insurance company." Will had been right. Disability insurance fraud and adulterous spouses were our bread and butter.

Of course, Elise already had some inkling of this, since we'd been sending more business her way lately.

"Assuming all goes well with Bumpkin here, Will may no longer be a member of the Marion County Sheriff's Department in about six weeks." One month after my due date.

We now knew the baby was a girl, thanks to a recent sonogram. But we hadn't agreed on a name yet, so she was still Bumpkin.

Elise winced. "That would make me nervous. What if something happened to him before then?"

I tensed.

"I'm sorry," she quickly said. "I guess my social skills need work after all these years cooped up in this place."

She's an anxious person, Ms. Snark commented internally. *Of course, her mind would go there.*

I resisted the urge to chuckle since that would confuse Elise. More and more, Ms. Snark seemed to be with me instead of against me lately.

I took a sip of tea, trying to decide if I should blurt out what I had to say or attempt to lead up to it somehow.

"So, what happened with that case in Crystal County?" Elise asked. "Can you tell me now?"

Actually I could, since the trial of Merrilee Brooks had ended last week.

I filled Elise in. Frederick Jacobs had crumbled, turning on his fiancée after she'd scorned him. He'd confessed that they had gone to the airport the evening Char was going out of town to meet with a client. Merrilee "accidentally" ran into Char and insisted on buying her a drink while she was waiting for her plane to board, to show there were no hard feelings. When Char started feeling the effects of the drug Merrilee had slipped in her drink, the younger woman offered to help her to the ladies' room. Instead she'd led her woozy ex-boss out to Jacobs's car, waiting in the airport parking lot.

"But Merrilee remained adamant that she was an innocent pawn," I said. "Thank heavens, the jury saw through her. There was so much evidence."

Frank also had testified against her, in exchange for a lighter sentence on the fraud charge. And he'd been charged with accessory after the fact regarding Char's death, because he hadn't revealed his knowledge of the hidden passages in Herb's house.

Turns out the things you withhold during a police investigation can get you in trouble, even if you didn't commit the crime. Which made me a little nervous regarding old Milt's secrets—but then, no one was investigating him nor had anyone asked me questions.

"Rick Young originally tried to spin it that he was working undercover," I told Elise. "But he eventually confessed, after Jacobs admitted to bribing him to help cover up Char's murder. Rick said that once he'd done that, he was in too far and had to make sure the frame against my client held up."

He'd tried to make it sound like he just got caught up in things, that he wasn't really a bad guy. But I knew better. I shivered now, at the memory of his comment about being willing to kill babies.

We suspected that either Rick or Jacobs had orchestrated the attack on Clint and the torching of the house, but Clint hadn't been able to find any hard evidence.

"I hope they're all going to jail for many years," Elise said.

"They are." I took a deep breath. Time to blurt. "Elise, we want you to work for us."

She blinked several times.

"We're trying to set up a group health insurance plan, before Will leaves the sheriff's department. But we need at least one other employee to make that happen."

Elise blinked again. Now her mouth was hanging open.

"We thought about signing Buddy up, but figured they'd catch on to that." I'd rehearsed the joke, but it fell flat.

"Health insurance?" Elise said, blinking yet again.

"Yeah, and the other advantage is that, as an employee, we can tell you the details of the cases, which will make it easier for all of us to do our jobs. You'd fall under our confidentiality agreement with clients." That speech Will had suggested.

"That way, you can do more research besides background checks, like you did on the insurance policy in the Crystal County case. The testimony of the insurance agent was what convinced the jury the crime was premeditated."

Elise was nodding, the ends of her mouth quirking up in a tentative smile, but her eyes looked worried.

"We can still do our communicating online and by phone," I reassured her. "And you can do freelance stuff on the side, if we're not keeping you busy enough."

Elise blew out air, then grinned. "Yes, yes, yes." She jumped up, startling Rusty, and danced around her living room. "Yes, yes, yes."

Rusty stood by the table, let out a soft woof. He'd been trained to respond to anxiety. He wasn't sure what to do with joy.

I smiled at both of them.

Finally, Elise settled again at the table. "So how is your client doing, the one with agoraphobia?"

"A lot better. He loves his new house."

Herb had followed through with the purchase, despite what

had gone down there. "No more running from demons," he'd said.

It had turned out that the sellers were not moving to Argentina, and they were willing to wait until he could get his financing lined up. Merrilee had overplayed her hand with all that stuff about them being anxious to settle fast. If she'd just said they wanted to have the walk-through sooner instead of later, I might not have become suspicious.

He hadn't gotten much for his own house—what with the ugly buildings next door and dead bodies and all—but Char had indeed left him a substantial sum in her will.

"Do you think…" Elise trailed off. With eyes now shiny, she was watching her new dog drop down beside Buddy by the door. "Could Rusty do that for me?"

I reminded myself to tread lightly. Elise's situation was different. True panic disorder, which she had, was biologically based, unlike Herb's anxiety, which was learned.

"What does your psychiatrist say about your meds?" I asked.

She sighed. "That the anxiety is about as controlled as we can get it. My therapist thinks it's mostly conditioned associations that keep me confined in here." She waved a hand in the air, indicating her house.

"Then yes, Rusty can help you break those associations, but it may take some time."

A tear breaking loose, Elise reached out and grabbed my hand. "Thank you, Marcia. I have some hope now. Haven't had that in quite a while."

I felt something wet trickling down my cheeks.

Crapola, these dang pregnancy hormones!

Ms. Snark snickered. *You're such a softie.*

AUTHOR'S NOTES

If you enjoyed this book, please take a moment to leave a short review on the ebook retailer of your choice. Reviews help with sales and sales keep the stories coming. You can readily find the links to these retailers at https://misteriopress.com/authors2/kassandralamb/.

The next book in this series is *Auld Lang Mayfair,* and the one prior to it is *One Flew Over the Chow-Chow's Nest.* (You can find all the books, in order, on my website at https://kassandralamb.com/all-the-books/.)

This book was proofread by multiple sets of eyes, but proofreaders are human. If you noticed any errors, please email me at lambkassandra3@gmail.com so I can have them corrected.

Heck, email me anyway. I love hearing from readers!

And you may want to sign up for my newsletter at https://kassandralamb.com to get a heads up about new releases, plus special offers and bonuses for subscribers. You will receive a free novelette, *The Tell-Tale Bark*, the prequel to the Marcia Banks and Buddy Mysteries, AND a free novella, *Sweet Sanctuary*, the prequel to my traditional mystery series, the Kate Huntington Mysteries.

Also, misterio press now has a readers' group on Facebook (https://www.facebook.com/groups/misteriopressmysteries/) where we chat with readers and also offer giveaways and other goodies. Please stop by and check it out!

It takes a village to create a book, and the main residents of my village include my sister authors at *misterio press*, especially Candace J. Carter, Kirsten Weiss, Liz Boeger and Sasscer Hill who all helped tremendously by critiquing and/or proofreading this story. Thank you so much, ladies! Also much gratitude to my beta readers, Ann and Gina, and to my wonderful husband who always does the "final" proofread. I put final in quotes because I have a tendency to mess with things right up until the story goes into final production, and sometimes I inadvertently introduce new errors. So any boo-boos you found are my fault, not his.

And a special thank you to the three people who have had the biggest impact on my writing journey—my friend and the cofounder of *misterio press*, Shannon Esposito, my wonderful editor, Marcy Kennedy, and my good friend and alpha reader, Angi Semegon. If the fates had not put each of you in my path, I seriously doubt this book or even this series would have ever happened.

Marion County, Ocala, Williston and Belleview are all real places in central Florida, but the town of Mayfair and Crystal County are made-up locations. Book 9 in the series, *Lord of the Fleas*, was set in Crystal County and Sheriff Clint Burns was an important secondary character in that book. And at the very end of that story, he meets Marcia's mom who is down from Maryland, visiting for Thanksgiving.

When I set out to write this book, I intended to develop Mom's character a bit more, but I was surprised to find Clint's character and his relationship with Marcia evolving as well. I love it when characters take over and write their own stories!

I also developed Elise's character a bit more in order to illustrate a more classic case of agoraphobia. This "fear of the marketplace" (i.e., fear of crowds that can culminate in the inability to leave one's house) is sometimes caused by other things, such as in Herb's case. But most often it is a by-product of panic disorder, a biologically based anxiety disorder.

Folks with this disorder have random panic attacks that become associated in their psyches with wherever they happen to be at the time. So they have an attack in the grocery store, and then they avoid grocery shopping; they have an attack at the post office, and they won't go there anymore either. Slowly their world shrinks as these learned associations between the anxiety and the places they go multiply.

The other disorder highlighted in this story is narcissism. People with this personality disorder most often have a history of emotional neglect and abuse. While they appear to be confident, often to the point of arrogance, on the surface, they are actually full of self doubt. The narcissistic bluster is overcompensating for their internal insecurity.

The two treatment approaches mentioned in this story are most definitely real. Systematic desensitization is a well-established strategy for treating phobias. Using relaxation techniques to help the client remain calm, s/he experiences bite-sized exposures to the object or situation they are afraid of, until the association between their anxiety and that object/situation is replaced with a calmer reaction. In Herb's case, the addition of a service dog who can reassure him the space he is entering is not inhabited by hidden enemies makes the process even more powerful.

Deep pressure therapy was originally used for autism. It was discovered by a woman named Temple Grandin. Like many folks on the autism spectrum, she has an overactive nervous system that causes her to be easily overwhelmed by stimulation. As a teen visiting her grandparents' dairy farm, she noticed how the cows calmed down when they were in the squeeze machines used to keep them still while they were being milked. She tried out the squeeze machine herself and felt an immediate calming effect. She then developed a squeeze machine for humans, controlled by the person in it.

Since then, deep pressure therapy has been applied to other disorders, especially those involving anxiety, such as PTSD.

I'm glad that I have been able to illustrate, in this series, the various psychological issues that veterans of combat may experience, and it's been particularly delightful to highlight all the tasks service dogs can do for them to make their lives better and help them heal.

Sadly, this series is winding down. I have one more novella planned, set a little over a year after the events in this story, so that we can check in on Marcia and Will and see how things are going.

I know I'm going to get emails from readers asking why. There are two main reasons. One, I've run out of new and unique story ideas that would work well for these characters and the series' premise. And two, Marcia has completed her "character arc" for the series.

She started out a somewhat neurotic young woman, with a severe case of commitment phobia. She was a bit immature, impulsive and snarky—all traits she knew she should work on improving. Sometimes she was able to, and other times they got the better of her. But over the course of the series, she has matured, become more self-controlled (most of the time), and she has overcome her fears of commitment and parenthood. In this story, I show her beginning to make peace with her snarky alter ego, which will become more thoroughly reintegrated with her personality in the final novella.

After that, it will be time for me to leave her alone and let her get on with her life, enjoying her new vocation and her little family.

In the meantime, I've started a new series of police procedurals, and I'm having a lot of fun with that new challenge. Check out Chief of Police Judith Anderson's debut as a main character in *Lethal Assumptions, A C.o.P. on the Scene Mystery.* I hope to have Book 2 in that series out in the next few months, and hopefully *Auld Lang Mayfair* by the end of 2022 (or early 2023).

Here's a short synopsis of *Auld Lang Mayfair*:

Should auld acquaintance be forgot…
The last year has been quite eventful for Marcia Banks-Haines and husband Will. They've successfully launched their private investigations agency and they've completed their family with an adorable baby girl.

After celebrating their little one's first birthday, they're about to ring in the New Year with friends and neighbors. But there's something more than champagne bubbling in Mayfair, Florida.

The local matriarch, Edna Mayfair, is always looking for ways to boost the community's economy. Her latest scheme is the addition of a row of shops along Main Street. A couple of her new tenants, though, have something other than fair commerce in mind.

When old hostilities set off New Year's fireworks, one of the shopkeepers ends up dead, and a friend of Marcia's is the prime suspect. Determined to clear her, Marcia and Will set out to uncover the real Grim Reaper.

ABOUT THE AUTHOR

Kassandra Lamb has never been able to decide which she loves more, psychology or writing. In college, she realized that writers need a day job in order to eat, so she studied psychology. After a career as a psychotherapist and college professor, she is now retired and can pursue her passion for writing.

She spends most of her time in an alternate universe with her characters. The portal to that universe, aka her computer, is located in Florida, where her husband and dog catch occasional glimpses of her.

Kass has completed ten full-length novels in the Kate Huntington Mystery series (set in her native Maryland, about a psychotherapist/amateur sleuth), plus four Kate on Vacation novellas (with the same characters). She is also the author of the Marcia Banks and Buddy cozy mystery series, about a service dog trainer and her sidekick and mentor dog, Buddy. There are six novels and four holiday novellas out in that series, which is set in north central Florida. A seventh novel is planned for late 2020/early 2021.

To read and see more about Kassandra and her books, please go to https://kassandralamb.com. Be sure to sign up for the newsletter there to get a heads up about new releases, plus special offers and bonuses for subscribers.

Kass's e-mail is lambkassandra3@gmail.com and she loves hearing from readers! She's also on Facebook, Goodreads, and Bookbub, and she hangs out some on Twitter @KassandraLamb. She blogs about psychological topics and other random things at https://misteriopress.com.

Kassandra also writes romantic suspense under the pen name of Jessica Dale (https://darkardorpublications.com/).

PLEASE CHECK OUT THESE OTHER GREAT *MISTERIO PRESS* SERIES:

Karma's A Bitch: Pet Psychic Mysteries
by Shannon Esposito

Multiple Motives: Kate Huntington Mysteries
by Kassandra Lamb

The Metaphysical Detective: Riga Hayworth Paranormal Mysteries
by Kirsten Weiss

Dangerous and Unseemly: Concordia Wells Historical Mysteries
by K.B. Owen

Murder, Honey: Carol Sabala Mysteries
by Vinnie Hansen

Full Mortality: Nikki Latrelle Mysteries
by Sasscer Hill

ChainLinked: Moccasin Cove Mysteries
by Liz Boeger

Steam and Sensibility: Sensibility Grey Steampunk Mysteries
by Kirsten Weiss

Never Sleep: Chronicles of a Lady Detective Historical Mysteries
by K.B. Owen

Bound: Witches of Doyle Cozy Mysteries
by Kirsten Weiss

At Wits' End Cozy Mysteries
by Kirsten Weiss

Payback: Unintended Consequences Romantic Suspense
by Jessica Dale

Steeped In Murder: Tea and Tarot Mysteries
by Kirsten Weiss

Travels of Quinn
by Sasscer Hill

**Plus even more great mysteries/thrillers at
https://misteriopress.com/bookstore/**

www.ingramcontent.com/pod-product-compliance
Lightning Source LLC
Chambersburg PA
CBHW070909180626
46817CB00003B/985